NECROMANCING
THE STONE

NECROMANCING THE STONE

Lish McBride

HENRY HOLT AND COMPANY

NEW YORK

Henry Holt and Company, LLC
Publishers since 1866
175 Fifth Avenue
New York, New York 10010
macteenbooks.com

Library of Congress Cataloging-in-Publication Data
McBride, Lish.
Necromancing the stone / Lish McBride.—1st ed.
p.   cm.
Sequel to: Hold me closer.
Summary: Six weeks after escaping from the necromancer Douglas,
Sam LaCroix is under the protection of the Blackthorn pack of
werewolves and fey hounds and unsure if his necromancer rival is dead.
ISBN 978-0-8050-9099-4 (hc)
[1. Supernatural—Fiction. 2. Magic—Fiction. 3. Dead—
Fiction. 4. Werewolves—Fiction. 5. Seattle
(Wash.)—Fiction.] I. Title.
PZ7.M478267Nec 2012   [Fic]—dc23   2011043448

First Edition—2012

Printed in the United States of America

1 3 5 7 9 10 8 6 4 2

To Fatty. Ha ha—sucker!

NECROMANCING THE STONE

WELCOME TO MY WORLD

𝔍 tasted blood as I went down. I lay there for a moment, crumpled at the base of an old pine tree, and relearned how to breathe. I wondered when I had gotten used to falling on my ass. Or more specifically, being thrown on it. A squirrel flitted onto a tree branch, stopping to throw me a look that said, "Oh, it's just you again."

"Everyone's a critic," I mumbled.

Sean's head bobbed into my vision, blocking my view of the squirrel. "You're talking to yourself," he said. "Did you hit your head too hard? I'm trying to be gentle, but you humans are so damn fragile." He scratched his nose. "Amazing that any of you survive, actually."

"I was talking to a squirrel," I said.

"Oh, well, that's okay then."

Not much fazed Sean. He offered me a hand and pulled me slowly to my feet. His brother Bran came up from behind him and grabbed my chin, checking my pupils, then my ribs, and any other spot he thought I might have injured. I was getting used to this, too.

I'd had to adjust to a lot recently. About a month and a half ago, a man named Douglas Montgomery had walked into

Plumpy's—where I used to be a much-esteemed ninja fry cook—and informed me that I was a necromancer like him. This didn't mean much at the time, because I didn't know what a necromancer *was*. I'd had to look it up in a dictionary.

It had been a strange six weeks since then. Douglas had murdered my friend Brooke and delivered her severed head to me as a warning. Apparently he missed the memo that you can send a message pretty easily with a piece of paper and a pen. He'd also threatened, beaten, and kidnapped me. My best friend, Ramon, had come to my rescue, only to get infected in the process by a rare strain of were blood, this particular sample in the flavor of the Ursidae family. He was currently recuperating, and if he was ever released from the private hospital facility he was in, he'd have to adjust to the fact that he could now turn into a damn *bear*. It had been a pretty hectic time, but hey, you know, it's good to keep busy.

There were upsides to the whole mess. While Douglas was holding me hostage, I'd met a girl—I mean, screw dating websites and house parties; apparently all the really eligible ladies are being held in cages these days. I would have liked to see Brid fill out a dating questionnaire, though. What would she put? "Hi, my name is Bridin Blackthorn. I'm next in line to rule the local werewolf pack. I like long walks on the beach and destroying my enemies. I have four older brothers, so watch your step. We'll be forming a queue to the left for potential suitors."

And, trust me, there would be a queue.

Anyway, while hanging out in the aforementioned cage,

we'd hit it off, and we'd been dating ever since we escaped with the help of Bridin's family.

In the struggle surrounding our jailbreak, I'd killed Douglas. Not really sure if that's a win. I mean, I'm not dead, so yay, but in general I'm not too hip on the whole killing-people-to-survive thing, either. Even if Douglas was trying to sacrifice me and harvest my creepy powers at the time, I feel like killing people for doing awful things is probably setting a bad precedent for dealing with negative behavior. But I wasn't really thinking of moral implications at the time. When I stabbed Douglas in the throat, I was only thinking that I didn't want to die. On top of that, it never occurred to me that the spell Douglas had been conducting would backfire and I would steal all *his* creepy powers instead. Like I said, I'd been busy.

Since then, I'd entered into an odd sort of status with the Blackthorn pack. Because of my services (a fancy way of saying "saving a pack member's life and ridding Seattle of a supernatural menace"), I was under their protection. Sort of. Brannoc, their leader and Brid's dad, could have left me for dead if he'd felt like it. I'd asked him why he hadn't. His response had been that I seemed okay, and if they let someone waltz in and kill me, there was no telling who would take my place on the Council, which governed the local supernatural set—another thing I was trying to adjust to. Lots of dominos had toppled after Douglas's death. One of them was his seat on the Council, since dead men can't govern. They'd needed a live body to take his place. Guess who'd been nominated? Personally, I thought I was a terrible choice, but no one really asked me. Politics had never been my forte. As a kid, even class clown seemed like too much responsibility.

The funny part was, most of the Council seemed scared of me. Necromancers tended to make people twitchy. I was certainly better than Douglas, though. I'd been on the Council for a few weeks, and I hadn't killed anyone or masterminded any maniacal plots yet. So they were pretty sure I wasn't in the same weight class of evil as Douglas. Compared to him, I wouldn't even register as a featherweight. I'd never been considered evil before I found out I was a necromancer. The reputation would be kind of cool, if it weren't such a pain in my ass.

Anyway, it was all very pragmatic of Brannoc to let me live, though his reasons weren't terribly reassuring.

Because Brannoc wanted to *keep* me alive, I was getting self-defense lessons from Brid's siblings. She has four brothers, though I didn't meet Sayer and Roarke until a few weeks after my abduction and escape. They were currently off running errands, so Sean and Bran were picking on me today—under the watchful eye of Brannoc, of course. Usually the whole clan of brothers joined in the fun. I believe this was to remind me what would happen if I wasn't nice to their baby sister. If I ever displeased her, these boys would be the ones shredding my remains.

Because after Brid got done with me, remains were all I would be.

My self-defense lessons wouldn't actually help me if I came up against anyone in the pack. Brid and her brothers are hybrids—part werewolf (on their mother's side) and part fey hound (on their father's). The rest of the pack was either straight werewolf or fey hound, either of which was enough to take one scrawny necromancer. I glanced over at Brannoc, who was sitting under a tree, keeping an eye on things. Even though he was relaxed, his back against the bark, a piece of grass between his teeth, I knew if I snuck up and jumped him, I wouldn't land punch number one. I'm only human, and I can't compete with someone who could easily arm wrestle a bear. Or is a bear. But not every creature I might come up against would have super strength, and I was tired of getting wiped with the floor. I was still getting wiped with the floor now, but at least I was learning. Not fast enough, though. Brannoc had assigned Sean as my bodyguard until further notice. Good to know everyone had faith in my ninja skills.

After a thorough examination of my injuries, Bran declared me alive and told me to get back into the clearing. Sean was doing the sort of warm-up jog I'd seen boxers do before a match. I didn't think he needed the warm-up. I considered mimicking him, but figured I'd just look stupid. He rolled his neck quickly to each side, a small crack coming from his adjusted vertebrae. I got into position across from him.

He pulled at a chunk of his auburn hair, which made me think of his sister. Of the siblings, Sean resembled Brid the most. He shook his head as if he'd followed my train of thought.

"You got a twig in your hair there, lover boy."

I shrugged, settling into a crouch. "Just going to get more, I'm sure."

Sean grinned. "That's the spirit." He stopped his warm-ups and mirrored me.

Bran stood in the center, a somber referee. "Sam, this time I'd like you to concentrate on how you fall."

"I've had plenty of practice on that."

"Apparently not," Bran said. "You're still not rolling into it. Learning to fall is every bit as important as learning to fight. A seasoned fighter knows how to take a tumble, lessen the possibility of injury, and turn it to his or her advantage. The way you're doing it, you're going to get hurt."

I was already hurting, so I didn't feel I could argue with him. Instead I listened as he glossed over the technique again, telling me how to go with the impact.

Good thing, too, since twenty seconds later, I was tumbling back toward the base of that same tree. This time I tried to roll with it. I was so shocked when I rolled back up on my feet that I almost lost any advantage I'd gained. Sean came barreling toward me. I twisted to the side and sprinted along the tree line. Brannoc's whooping laughter followed me as I ran, but it didn't sound mocking. Not that I cared if it was. There's a time for pride and then there's a time for self-preservation.

The evening sun was slicing through the trees, leaving patches of shadow on the ground. I knew the only reason I'd managed to dodge Sean was because he was moving slowly for me. At his normal speed, I didn't stand a chance. Running wouldn't solve anything, but I kept doing it anyway. I was tired of ending up on the ground.

I ran until I got a stitch in my side. It took longer than

you might think. I may not be able to fight, but I've been skateboarding for a long time, and it's very aerobic. The first thing you learn is how to run. Cops and security guards don't appreciate skaters.

Brannoc's voice filtered through the trees. "Stay along the tree line. You'll get lost if you cut into the woods."

"Or eaten by something," Sean shouted helpfully.

Holding my side, I cut back toward the clearing. I walked slowly and tried to even out my breath. Sean and Bran were waiting patiently for me when I arrived. When I got close, I stopped and sat down, waving my hand in a circular motion to let Brannoc know I was ready for my lecture. Instead, his mouth twitched in what was almost a smile.

"That's actually the smartest fighting you've done so far."

"I ran," I said, panting.

He shook his head. "You were facing an opponent who outclassed you. You were thrown and got back up. Instead of being proud and stupid, you were smart. In a real fight, you only win if you live. Running was your best option."

"Sean would have caught me if he'd tried."

It was Bran who answered me this time. "Yes, he would have. But you won't always be up against Sean."

I picked a blade of grass and twisted it between my finger and thumb. "Running isn't going to work forever."

Bran sighed, rubbing a hand through his brutally cropped hair. Bran's looks were as somber as the rest of him, but I think most girls would still refer to him as "dreamy."

"No, it isn't. I know you're frustrated, Sam, but the reality is you're in a world now where the majority of the people you run into will be able to snap you like a twig."

"My world was like that before."

Sean coughed, but it sounded suspiciously like a laugh. I threw a pinecone at him. He caught it without looking and stuck it down his pants. Why? Because it would make me laugh, and while Bran was great at teaching, Sean was the master at keeping morale up.

Bran crossed his arms. "Bottom line? You've got to play to your strengths, and right now your strength is running like hell." He motioned for me to get up. "You don't have to like it. Just do it."

Brannoc stayed close to watch this time, his arms crossed and an amused look on his face. Bran stood to his left, a solemn reflection of his father.

Sean pointed to his head again.

"What," I said, "another twig?"

"You're bleeding a little."

I swiped at my forehead; my hand came back with a slight smear of red. Bleeding seemed to be my biggest strength. I certainly did a lot of it. I wiped my blood on the grass—and felt them as soon as my hand met the tickle of the grass blades.

When people think about necromancy, if they ever think about it at all, they envision dark rites, dead goats, guys in robes making spirits do their bidding. And this very well might be true. I was still pretty new to this sort of thing. The only other necromancer I'd ever met, Douglas, was one robe short of that stereotype. But I knew that wasn't the way it had to be. I couldn't even kill a goat to eat it (I'm vegetarian), and I absolutely never made ghosts do my bidding. The spirit I saw the most, Brooke, tended to order me around, if anything. And I didn't even own a bathrobe, let alone a cloak or whatever. I generally spent my time in jeans and T-shirts, today's example sporting a very excited-looking Yoshi dinosaur. A far cry from the dark and brooding image of the typical necromancer.

My point being, there are a lot of stereotypes floating about when it comes to my kind. There are even more when it comes to what we do. As far as the undead go, people tend to visualize Hollywood-style zombies running amok and gnawing on brains. Or crawling out of graves and eating brains. Or, I don't know, dehydrating brains so they can snack on them during their next camping trip. Either way, brains are involved. But most of those movies feature the biological undead, where some sort of virus or toxic waste takes perfectly normal people and turns them into unstoppable killing machines. I've never actually seen that. The few times I've raised the dead, I don't remember anyone asking for brains at all. Like I said, I'm still new, but a zombie under control isn't going to bite anyone, and even if it did, the only infection you'd probably get is from the normal freakish bacteria found in the human mouth.

I guess I'm getting a little sensitive about the whole thing.

They always show zombies rising from a grave, too. I mean, that kind of makes sense, but what people don't seem to understand is that death is around us all the time. When you drive down to the market, you pass squashed animals. In the store, you roll your cart by aisles and aisles of flesh. In fact, you're probably wearing bits of creatures right now. People are, and have always been, surrounded by death. We've learned, as a species, over the years, to ignore it.

The problem with me is that the part that sees death, the part that's supposed to be ignored and dormant, is—if you'll excuse the terminology—alive and thriving. And since I'd just spread my blood thinly on the grass, it was whispering to me exactly where each little piece of death was. I stared at the thin crimson smear and remembered that getting injured, while it seemed to be a hobby of mine, really wasn't my skill set.

Death was.

Maybe I couldn't toss Sean around, but that didn't mean I couldn't one-up him. Brannoc was right—I had to start fighting smart. I concentrated on each of those little islands of death, the tiny daily tragedies of smaller creatures that the human race was blind to. I gently woke them, pulled them above-ground. And it felt natural, good, like taking a deep breath of fresh air after hiding from monsters under your covers for an hour. By the time I got up, I was smiling. Relaxed. And surrounded by death.

Sean had started walking toward me but slowed when he saw what I'd done. He came to a stop and stared. I followed his eyes as he looked. Raccoons, squirrels, blue jays, and owls, all part of the normal collection of Pacific Northwest wildlife. But all very, very dead. I counted them in my head. About twenty all together. I think there was even a mole in there somewhere.

"You, uh." Sean paused and scratched his cheek. "You know I'm top of the food chain, right?"

I shrugged. Sean laughed, but I could see Bran staring at the creatures like I'd finally done something interesting.

Sean returned my shrug and came at me.

I didn't move—I didn't need to. Sean may be strong and fast, but the thing about the undead is that they can just keep coming. An owl swooped down at his eyes, making him swerve away from me. The raccoon jumped onto his back while the smaller birds began to dive-bomb. Sean stopped his forward assault, attempting to swat while he turned around and tried to get the raccoon. But for every bird or mole he swatted, another took its place. Pretty soon he was just spinning, a ball of flailing arms and feet.

And the squirrel? I watched as it slid up Sean's pant leg. Sean didn't seem to notice until the furry little guy hit about mid-thigh. Then he stopped flailing and screeched, directing all his attention to swatting at his leg. I watched as the squirrel popped out of the hole in the knee of Sean's jeans. Sean swatted it off, and then, apparently having had enough, he ran off toward the house with tiny scratches dripping blood, the owl still dive-bombing his head and a constant torrent of curses flowing behind him. I think I heard him yell that he'd see us at dinner, but I'm not sure—Bran was laughing too hard for me to make it out. Most of us wouldn't laugh at seeing our sibling assaulted, but I'd learned that weres, and Bran especially, had very different senses of humor.

"I suppose you can call them off now," Brannoc said with a smirk.

I summoned them back, the squirrel getting to me first. It ran up my leg and sat on my shoulder. I reached over and scratched its head in thanks. "You think he learned his lesson?" I asked.

Brannoc came up and reached toward the squirrel, looking at me for permission before he gently patted its head.

"That depends," he said, his lip twitching in amusement. "What lesson were you trying to teach him?"

"Top of the food chain is nice, but there are a lot more things on the bottom."

Bran had regained control of himself and was nodding solemnly. "If he didn't, then it might be something we'll have to go over. There are others besides Sean who could use that lesson desperately."

I didn't say anything, but I agreed. I'd only known the pack a short time, but I'd started to notice that some of them acted like they were invincible. Powerful, yes. Strong? Most certainly. But invincible? That was a dangerous notion to cling to.

I gave the squirrel one last scratch on the head and then returned all the animals to the ground, my heartfelt thanks sending them into the abyss. Though I knew it was right, it always made me a little sad to send things back. I'd never been great with good-byes.

Brannoc slung his arms around Bran and me, pulling us into a loose hug. "You staying for dinner?"

He phrased it like a question, even though we both knew it was more of a statement. Even if I didn't want to, I'd be talked into staying. The pack seemed to take my scrawniness personally, taking any chance to fatten—or toughen—me up. I didn't mind. The pack had a damn good cook.

Although technically owned and maintained by the *taoiseach*, or clan chief, the Den is a large open-beamed lodge enjoyed by all of the Blackthorn pack. And when I say large, I mean it—I've seen smaller apartment buildings. The list of permanent residents is fairly small, namely Brannoc, his family, and a handful of staff. There are always extra people there, though. Families that need a place to stay, weres visiting from neighboring packs, people petitioning to get into this pack, or the random people like myself. Pack members, if they can afford it, tithe a certain percentage of their income to the Den. That money makes sure everyone is taken care of. It's homey and loud and would probably remind me of summer camp, had I ever gone to summer camp.

It took a few minutes to clean the dirt, blood, and grass off me before dinner. Not surprisingly, the downstairs bathroom in the Den was well equipped with first-aid supplies for those of us who couldn't speed-heal.

Once I was presentable, or as close as I was going to get without a full shower and a wardrobe change, I went off looking for Brid.

2

COME ON-A MY HOUSE, MY HOUSE, I'M GONNA GIVE YOU CANDY

Some guys like leggy blondes. Some like them bookish or brunette or petite, and apparently some like them plastic, or plastic surgeons wouldn't have such big houses. And I'm not against any of those traits, except for the plastic, because that gives me the creeps. But for my money, you couldn't get any more perfect than Bridin Blackthorn.

She was short, but not overly so. A few inches over five feet, maybe. The red of her tank top accented her skin, which was turning dusky from the summer sun, or as dusky as an ivory-skinned girl could get. Her feet were bare, which is what she preferred, and I could make out the muscular curve of her calf through the slit in her sarong. No matter how many times I saw her, my mouth tended to go dry and my heart always sped up. It made me feel like a brain-dead schoolboy.

"Are you going to keep skulking in my doorway like a common pervert, or are you going to remember your manners?"

I rapped my knuckles on the doorjamb. "Friendly neighborhood perv. May I come in, dear lady?"

She scoffed and waved me in, keeping her back to me. I

kicked the door shut with my heel and slid up behind her. Her coppery hair had purple and green streaks in the front and was getting a little longer in the back, just starting to curl up a bit at the ends. If I'd told her it looked cute, she probably would've socked me. I kissed her neck, letting my fingers trace down her shoulders, past her elbows, coming to rest lightly on her hips. I waited for her to make the next move, if any. Brid was Alpha and didn't take pushy behavior lightly.

She leaned into me, pulling my hands farther around her. "You done taking your beating yet?"

I nodded. Her hair smelled like shampoo. Sandalwood and orange spice. I smiled. I recognized a LaCroix product when I smelled one. "Yes, thoroughly thrashed. You're using the shampoo I gave you. You like it?"

Brid patted my hands and pulled away, going back to her task of straightening her room. She spent most of her time in the city by the university where she went to school, so there wasn't much to clean up. "I do like it. It doesn't stink."

Though that sounded like an insult, she meant it to be complimentary. Weres have an excellent sense of smell, much better than a human's. That meant most bath products literally stank to them. Brid was only half were, but that didn't weaken her nose. And since the fey half of her leaned toward natural things, well, it made it hard to shop for her. I'd brought it up to my mom since she makes a lot of products for her business.

My mom is an earth witch, which means she's a whiz with plants. She uses them to make ointments, medicines, and lately, bath products. Realizing the problems the weres and hybrids were having, my mom had begun experimenting with softer natural scents and even some unscented products. A few people in the pack had tried them out, and they'd gone over like gangbusters. My mom could barely make them fast enough. The orange and sandalwood was new, and one I'd specifically requested for Brid. I'd given it to her on our last date—we'd gone to see one of the outdoor movies they show in Fremont, and though we'd both seen the feature about a thousand times, we had a blast. It was impossible for me not to have a good time with Brid. She could take me to a seminar on time-shares and I'd leave with a smile on my face. A smile probably similar to the one I had now, caused by a memory of Brid's candy-sticky fingers on mine.

I flopped onto her bed. Closing my eyes, I settled in, resting my head in my palms. "So, what's up, buttercup? We still on for tonight?"

"You've been spending too much time with Ashley." Ashley was a harbinger—a guide from this world to . . . wherever dead people went. She wouldn't fill me in on where that was, exactly. Part of her job was working with necromancers. I think she was supposed to be a guide for me, but really she just tried to boss me around.

"I don't know what you're talking about." There was a lump underneath me. I shifted and pulled out a set of child-sized markers. I pulled a blue one out of the pack. "You got an art project, Brid?"

She walked over and snatched them out of my hand. "For your information, they aren't mine. Some of the kids were up here earlier."

I waved the blue at her. "Sure, kids. Is that the story we're going with? If I dig around, am I going to find glitter and pipe cleaners? Your old My Little Ponies? Dare I say a naked Barbie or two?"

She grimaced. "Maybe your sister had Barbies, but I sure didn't."

"Haley? Please. She fed her Barbie to the cat."

She grabbed at the marker, and I didn't bother trying to play keep-away. Brid was faster on the draw. She tackled me, using her body weight to pin me down. I weighed more, but she knew what she was doing. You don't grow up with four brothers and not learn how to wrestle people bigger than you. Besides, it wasn't like I minded being pinned down. Torture, I know, but I was just going to have to suck it up and take it like a man.

Brid propped herself up on her elbows. "Nothing wrong with My Little Ponies, though." With great care, she uncapped the lid. She studied the marker carefully before leaning down and drawing on my upper lip. I couldn't see it, but I figured it out pretty quick. I was reasonably sure that I was now sporting a blue curlicue mustache and a tiny goatee. I reached up, pretending to feel the tip of my new mustache.

"Does it make me look debonair?"

With a mock-serious look, she said, "Very macho."

I sighed. "Will this come off before dinner?" I had a sudden image of myself sitting down at the big table with blue facial hair. With the pack. And Brid's whole family. No, thank you.

"Relax," she said, licking her thumb, "it's washable." She wiped at it with her thumb and I dodged.

"Are you about to clean me with your spit?"

She cocked her head. "What? You squeamish? It's not like you haven't had my spit on you before."

I frowned. "That's different."

"How?"

My frown became a scowl. She had a point. Not that I was going to tell her that. "It just is."

Her face became thoughtful. She leaned forward, coming in for a kiss. Her lips were soft. She pulled back a fraction and gently bit my lip. A soft brush of lips and nose against my cheek, then a slow, long lick on my new blue goatee.

"Any issue with that?" she said quietly.

I had to clear my throat to get the words out. "Hell, no."

Both of her eyebrows went up as she grinned. "So I win?"

I held up my hands. "You win. I crumble beneath your argumentative powers."

"I was captain of my debate team."

"I just bet you were. As long as you make sure you get it all off before dinner. Some of the pack appears to be immune to my considerable charms." This was somewhat of an understatement. Most seemed to like me, but there was definitely a camp of holdouts in the Blackthorn pack. I couldn't tell if it was because I was dating Brid and they were protective or if they simply didn't like me. I wasn't used to being instantly disliked. Until the whole necromancy thing, people either liked me or ignored me, with the occasional instant hater, but reactions were generally mild upon meeting me. That changes when you come out as a necromancer. People are immediately suspicious of you. I find it funny, usually, because I am not an imposing guy, but it was less funny now that it was interfering with my love life. I hadn't had a love life in a while, and I wanted to keep it.

Brid reached down, her hand popping back into sight holding the rest of the markers. She pulled a different one out of the pack and waggled it in front of me. Red.

She popped the cap off with her thumb. The plastic clacked as it hit the floor.

"Wanna keep debating?" I could hear the cap as it rolled under something, probably never to be seen again. "Or would you rather have a long discussion about my family, which probably won't be nearly as entertaining and definitely won't entail as much making out?"

I rested my hands on her waist. That lump was back in my throat and took a minute to clear. "O Captain, my Captain."

She drew a little heart on my neck, right over the pulse, and grinned.

3

HELLO DARKNESS, MY OLD FRIEND

Douglas woke up in between. He didn't know what else to call it. Not limbo. Limbo implied true death or another plane. It also implied a religious bent that he just couldn't quite put stock into. Religion had never done much for Douglas Montgomery.

No, he was still on the same plane, or at least close to it. Not quite dead enough to be a true ghost.

Which meant his fail-safe had worked.

There were two parts to death. The obvious one was the physical—the heart slowed and stopped. Synapses quit firing, blood came to a halt, and in general the body went through the complicated process of shutting down. But the physical shutdown wasn't enough. You could keep someone physically alive with machines, but that didn't qualify as fully *alive*. If they were missing that spark, that intangible thing that made people who they were, then they weren't really with this world anymore. They had moved on, despite the desperate pumping and whirring of modern medicine's machinery.

Alternatively, if you kept the spark going while the corporeal withered and fell away, then you weren't completely dead either, which was precisely what he'd done. The idea had come to him from an old folktale his mother used to tell him about a giant who'd hid his heart away and so couldn't be killed. Of course, hiding his heart wouldn't work—that was pure nonsense—but the theory was sound. It had taken him a long time and a lot of work to do it, but he'd managed, and it had obviously been worth it.

Douglas wasn't whole. He'd hidden his spark, a metaphysical version of life support, and all he had to do was get it back. Which meant he had to get his act together and sneak into his house to get it. Having the beginnings of a plan made him feel better. A mental list began to form. He loved lists. There was something so inexplicably *tidy* about them, even the intangible ones. His top desires, in a very particular order, were:

- Kill Brannoc, the interfering bastard, before he figured out what was going on. If anyone on the Council might get wind of Douglas's partial resurrection, it was the ever-vigilant *taoiseach*. Brannoc's death, in his opinion, was long overdue. Once he was out of the way, the pack and Council would flounder, so encompassed in their grief and the resulting chaos that he wouldn't even hit their radar screens until too late.
- Get his spark back.
- Get his house back, his things, his *life* back.
- Then slaughter the miserable shit who had killed him and taken it all away. This he would do last, and he would enjoy every second in a way that he hadn't enjoyed anything in decades. Pure pleasure.

Ruminating on this last idea, he began to wonder if physical torture was enough. Sam wasn't a threat like Brannoc, despite the fact that he'd managed to come out the winner in their last altercation. As far as Douglas was concerned, Sam was the very definition of a fluke. He wouldn't be so lucky next time. Perhaps he didn't deserve a quick demise—surely a game of cat and mouse wasn't uncalled for? Sam had seemed particularly put out that Douglas had killed his friend. Were his friends his weak point? Or perhaps people he held even more dear? He'd have to ask James how Sam felt about his family. Douglas smiled.

That settled, he came back to his more immediate state. He sat on a marble outcropping and examined his body. This bored him quickly. The vessel of his flesh wasn't important, necessarily, and he couldn't glean much from looking at it, aside from mundane facts like how he died and how long it had been rotting in this place. He already knew how he'd died, though he was loath to remember it. Stabbed in the throat by an ignorant pipsqueak. As for how long . . . six weeks, maybe longer? He supposed it made little difference.

He was much more interested in the sitting itself. Did he actually have enough presence to "sit" on this ledge, or was it just a construct of his mind? Did it matter? Yes, he decided, it did, but only in the sense of its implications. If he was in fact sitting, that suggested a certain amount of corporeal form. It meant that he could still have an effect on the world, body or no, if only in a minor way. After much consideration, he decided that he was, indeed, sitting, but not as fully as something completely alive. His action was a shadow of reality, but if he concentrated, the shadow filled and became almost full. It wasn't the casual action of a living creature, but it was still an *action*.

To Douglas, this was very good news. A ghost he might have been, but an ineffectual spirit he was not.

He studied the slab underneath his feet. James had exquisite taste. He knew this, but sometimes it was good to give credit where it was due. He'd chosen well when he purchased the boy. Quite well indeed.

Douglas was currently in a mausoleum in a private cemetery, that much he knew. The rest he'd left up to James. Mausoleums weren't common in this part of the country, but he'd felt that, should something happen, it would be easier to get out of one than if he'd been buried in the ground.

Douglas was nothing if not practical.

After a few false starts, he was able to put one foot in front of the other and walk, which was harder than it sounded. He couldn't really feel anything, so it was like trying to walk with a fully numbed body. Difficult, but possible. He was able to leave the mausoleum, but he couldn't go far. Walking that much made him tired. There was a lot of concentration involved, and he was still trying to get used to moving his spectral body around. So a few feet at first, then a bit farther afield once he got used to things. He was patient. Like all things, Douglas would master this new state. Then he would go down his little checklist. So much to do.

A new body would be nice, as well. Something less bloated and rank, a fresh new model. He rather liked the old one, but he couldn't return to it as it was, since it was currently rotting a mere few feet from him. Without the benefits of the modern preservatives commonly used in burials, his shell was turning into a putrid mess. Perhaps he could rebuild it later—he was a necromancer, after all. If he did have to go through the hassle of getting a new body, he'd try to get one roughly the same size. He didn't want to have his suits re-tailored. He was very picky about the cut.

But first he must contact James. Have him go through the books, find out what to do about the incorporeal situation, or at the very least discover how he could leave the cemetery. It would be quite difficult to extract a fiery vengeance from here. Perhaps he should have finished researching this project before. Moved it up the priority ladder. He of all people should have remembered that death often came unexpectedly. Douglas sighed and rested himself on a stone bench. He'd cheated death so long, he'd begun to think he was invincible. Hubris, thy name is Douglas.

Well, lesson learned. No point dwelling on it. Best to look to the future. He leaned back, resting some of his weight on his palms. Not so bad being half dead. The sun shone brightly down on his face as he closed his eyes. A breeze drifted in from the side, bringing the smell of trees and flowers. It was a fine day to be mostly alive. To be contemplating the future.

Douglas wondered how he should kill Brannoc and Sam—so many wonderful choices. Birds twittered around him, several different chattering voices claiming what was theirs. Birdcalls, a warm sun, and plans to be made. A fine day to be mostly alive, indeed.

4

OUR HOUSE,
WAS OUR CASTLE AND OUR KEEP

After a dinner engineered to necessitate rolling instead of walking as a primary means of transport, I made my good-byes and headed for the door. I had one arm in my hoodie and was this close to freedom when I was stopped by a rather gruff voice. You know the voice—it's the one men try to use in action movies. That gravelly, testosterone-laden whisper.

"You haven't seen Brid around, have you?"

I turned around, still trying to put my other arm in my sleeve. The were wasn't immediately familiar—I had to think for his name. Eric? He swaggered over, all sneer and machismo. I found myself backing up to give him room, and before I knew it, I was pushed against a wall of coats, their hanging pegs poking into me.

"She went that way," I said, pointing and trying not to sound as uncomfortable as I felt. I don't like people in my personal space, unfriendly male werewolves even less so. Though not as big, he reminded me a little of Michael, an emotionally rabid were who'd helped Douglas kidnap me.

"Is there something else I can help you with?" I asked, keeping a jovial tone.

He didn't seem to hear my question. His nostrils flared and he leaned in, his chest only millimeters from mine. "You may have fooled the *taoiseach*, but you haven't fooled me, and I'm not alone."

"Huh?" I'm extremely witty when I'm confused.

"You smell like death and blood, and I don't like it. You can keep up your friendly act now, but we all know that won't last. It never does. In the end, what you are will win out."

"What I am?" The problem with conversations like these is, when you don't know what the person is talking about, it's a little hard to argue against them.

"Necromancer," he snarled.

"Werewolf," I threw back. See? Rapier wit.

"Eric?" Bran must have come into the entryway, though I knew better than to take my eyes off Eric to see.

The young were leaned back, his threatening face changing into one of calm and good nature. "Yes, sir?"

"Why don't you go see if the cook needs any help with the dishes?" Bran phrased it like a question, but we all knew it wasn't.

"Of course, sir," Eric said, all polite submissive tones, but his eyes weren't so pleasant. He didn't want to take that order— whether it was because he wasn't done with me or because he didn't like Bran, I wasn't sure. Interesting. He stared at me for one long second, then turned and left.

"What was that about?" Bran asked.

"Just a friendly chat. You know me, always making friends."

"Yes, I see. Are you aware that you have marker on your neck? Are you also aware that you have a similar hue to your tongue?" I don't know why he whispered. When everyone in the immediate area has supersonic hearing, every whisper is a stage whisper. "And I couldn't help but notice some similar colors on my baby sister."

I closed my eyes with a wince, my skin turning a charming crimson, I'm sure.

"You earned a lot of glares at the dinner table, Sam. Generally from unattached males like Eric, all of them making the connection between your colored tongue and the ink smears on their *tánaiste*. Their *future leader*—and all of them strapping young bucks who probably don't appreciate you poaching on their turf." He stared at me to see if I understood, and I silently made a note to not walk down any dead-end corridors or dark alleys by myself.

"I groaned. Did Brannoc see?" The pack leader is not stupid; he knew I was dating Brid and most likely assumed we didn't spend our time holding hands and drinking milkshakes (which we should totally do sometime), but that didn't mean he wanted the realities of our relationship shoved in his face. Sure, he was the pack leader, but first and foremost, he was still a dad, and Brid was his baby girl. His *only* baby girl. If I pissed him off, he wouldn't even need a shotgun and a shovel like most fathers. He could tear me to pieces bare-handed and then choose from miles of forest where to hide the body.

"Who do you think sent me out to have a little chat with you?"

"Thanks for not talking with your fists," I said. I have a little sister, and I'm not sure I'd be as understanding with any of her boyfriends.

"I've seen you fight," he said, turning. "It would've been a terribly short conversation."

Brid and I were in my car before I realized that Bran had actually made a joke. I'd only heard the threat at first.

Brid and I caught a movie after dinner, so it was late when I pulled up to the house. I was still trying to get comfortable calling it my house. I could say it in my head all I wanted, but in my heart, it still felt like Douglas's house. I hadn't lived there very long, so perhaps I would settle in with a little time? I wondered if repainting it would help. Either that or I could start peeing on all the outside corners. That seemed to work well for dogs.

I got out of my car, making sure to avoid the hedges. They tended to take the occasional swipe. And I don't mean that I accidentally caught my pants leg on them once in a while— they would actually reach out and grab me. I took a minute to survey the grounds; my car settling was the only sound I could hear at first. I patted the hood of my Subaru. Douglas had unintentionally left me a much fancier car—cars, really— when he died, but I didn't want to drive them. I didn't even want to go into the garage and look at his other cars. James liked to go in there and wax them, though. He enjoyed shiny things. To me it was just more stuff that didn't feel like mine. Of course, I let Frank drive them, which seemed to irritate James, for some reason. I'd been working with Frank at Plumpy's when all the madness happened, and I'd grown to like the little guy, so I'd hired him on to help me settle in and to save him from a fate worse than death—the dreaded fast food career. So now he ran errands, and I'd made him sell his death trap of a car and drive Douglas's. Frank looked nervous behind the wheel, probably out of fear of wrapping a classic car around a pole somewhere.

Or perhaps the fear was based on the way James glared every time anyone went near the garage. And speaking of the devil, I heard the soft paws as my four-footed associate approached. Small, liquid silver eyes stared up at me, reflecting the stars above my head. I could sense his tail switching back and forth more than I could see it, his black patches blending in while the white bits reflected the moonlight.

I leaned against my car and sighed, rubbing a hand over my eyes. "It's been a long day, James. A long, somewhat odd day. Let's not cap it off with me sitting in the yard talking to a cat, okay?"

James gave a derisive snort—strangely suiting his feline persona—and shifted into his dragon form, which is about the size of a schnauzer. He flapped his wings once and settled in, puffing a ring of smoke at me while he did.

I tried not to sigh in exasperation. "Yes, that's much better. Talking to a cat was weird, but speaking to a miniature dragon completely fulfills my desire for normalcy." He blew a thin jet of fire at my shoes. I jumped up with a yelp, and he snickered.

"Cute," I said. "You're like a reptilian version of Muttley. Can you do what I asked now, please?"

A swirling mass spiraled upward, like smoke reaching for the heavens, and then he stood before me. Not for the first time, I wondered where his clothes came from and how he managed to wear them without looking ridiculous. James wore an old duster jacket, the kind you might see on a gunslinger or in PI movies. It was something I was used to seeing on John Wayne and Humphrey Bogart, and a look I knew I couldn't pull off, but it fit James somehow.

He was never naked when he shifted to human in front of me. I preferred it that way, but it still made me wonder.

Through a fluke of circumstance, I'd inherited James. And by that I mean that after I killed Douglas, his former owner, I got everything in the Montgomery estate, including James. My silver-eyed friend was a *pukis*, or a house spirit. That didn't necessarily mean that he literally went with a certain home—more like a lineage of people. Douglas had no relatives when he died, and so I got James, my manservant for life. I tried to free him, I really did, but he found the very thought to be insulting. He was what he was, and I had to get used to it.

Like it or not, because of Douglas's death, I got a lot of things I could've done without: more creepy powers, a house I was afraid of and all of his weirdo stuff, along with his *pukis*. I hadn't wanted any of it, but the supernatural community wouldn't let me sell it. Something about Douglas's evil knickknacks killing unsuspecting humans. So I had to move in, because nothing is worse than death by tchotchke.

James had three forms: cat, small schnauzer-sized dragon, and human. The third had been a surprise until I moved in and asked him how he'd managed to do all of Douglas's errands with no opposable thumbs. He'd morphed, poked me on the head with one of said opposable thumbs, and finished by stealing my yogurt. I still hadn't quite figured James out.

He was taller than I was, and thin. Though I'd never seen him swim, he had the body of a swimmer. When he was a cat, he was white with black spots, and as a dragon, he was a blur of black scales with the occasional shine of silver underbelly. When he was human, he was that same ghostly shade, and his hair was the same inky black, but a bit curly. I didn't ask him what happened to the other spots. Knowing James, he'd strip down and show me. No matter what form he was in, his eyes stayed the same.

And his attitude. Mustn't forget that.

"You're still mad about the collar thing, aren't you?"

James crossed his arms and sniffed, looking out onto the lawn.

"It was just a suggestion. We didn't mean to offend you." Frank, worried that someone might mistake James for a stray and pick him up, had brought up getting James a collar. Well, more than brought it up. He'd bought one. Black suede, with little silver studs. He thought James would like it. It had been a massive miscalculation. James threw an amazing screaming fit, which ended with him giving Frank the cold shoulder for days. He wouldn't say a word to Frank during that time—just threatening glares. More than once I'd walked into the kitchen to catch James menacing Frank, and managing to do so while quietly stirring a cup of tea.

It made a rough situation worse. James had been Douglas's assistant. Not knowing this, I had hired Frank as mine. Before

I even set foot on the grounds as the official owner, I'd managed to offend the one person who could have helped me easily transition into the house.

After the collar incident, a cold war had developed between James and me; he was less subtle about his issues with Frank. I had to watch James carefully because, let's face it, Frank was pretty easy to pick on. Watching James harass Frank was like watching a python take on a sick, three-legged mole.

And I'd quickly learned that James was the key to managing my new homestead. He knew every corner, every secret, every creepy or crawly that called it home. The creepy crawlies were definitely becoming a problem. The attack hedge was the least of it. The garden gnomes were stealing my clothes, toilet papering me in my sleep, and hiding booby traps wherever they could. They were like tiny little Wile E. Coyotes. On top of that, the Minotaur kept popping my tires, and I'm pretty sure the gladiators etched into the pediment were rifling through my things while I was out. Sneaky little Roman bastards. Or were they Greek? It hadn't come up in conversation.

The whole thing was driving me buggy, but I was trying to ignore it, assume it was hazing. Eventually they'd stop and we'd all be friends, right? Right. And then we'd all hold hands and skip around the yard singing "Kumbaya."

James continued to pout.

"Seriously, he was acting out of kindness. He really was."

"Uh-huh, sure." He turned and waved me in. "Let's get you out of the night air at least."

Once inside, I went straight to the kitchen and grabbed a soda. James refused to buy me any beer. For a master thief and shady character, he certainly seemed to stick to the letter of the law if it inconvenienced me. I had no idea how old James was, but I was sure his license put him safely over the drinking age.

I set a soda in front of Frank, who had taken over the kitchen table with books. He appeared to be jumping between several large and dusty tomes. I didn't think he'd noticed the soda or me. I snapped fingers in front of his face and whistled.

"Earth to Frank."

He jumped visibly and reddened. "Sorry." I shook my head and pushed the soda into his line of sight. He accepted it gratefully. Frank had graduated from high school this year. I'd gone to his graduation. With Ramon safely in the were-hospital, trying to get used to his sudden were-bear status, and Brooke in her new ghostly form, I had to represent the team. Brooke had gone, of course, but no one could see her. Someone had to scream for Frank when he walked across the stage. His parents weren't really the screaming type.

Despite his recent freedom, Frank had been hitting the books pretty hard. Like me, he was trying to catch up on understanding our new world. In fact, Frank seemed to take it even more seriously than I did, since he was my helper monkey. Sometimes when I got up in the morning, I found typed notes waiting for me on the fridge. And sometimes, out of pure know-it-all-ism, James corrected those notes, covering them with red ink. When James wasn't being aggressive-aggressive, he was being passive-aggressive.

"Learn anything cool?"

Frank shrugged. He looked tired. And older. The last six weeks had put a few years on him.

"Who knows?" He took a sip of his soda. "It's hard to tell what's truth and what's recorded rumor."

"If we're talking about me," Brooke said, materializing next to me, "then I can honestly say it's all rumor. Unless you were discussing how awesome I am. Then it's all true." She leaned in and gave me a kiss on the cheek before doing the same to Frank, who blushed, and James, which I think she did out of stubbornness more than actual affection. She very much wanted everybody to just get along. Brooke had been the only girl in a house full of brothers, so she was used to bullying guys around.

Even though Brooke had been killed as a warning to me, which sucked, there were at least some perks to being the mayor of Zombieville. She was one of my guides now, sort of a ghostly girl Friday. The trade-off was, since I was a necromancer, being around me made her visible. We still had to hide her when she was somewhere she might get recognized, though, like Frank's graduation.

I pulled up a chair and sat down. James gave our sodas a dark look before handing us coasters, managing to rap Frank on the knuckles as he reached for his, and getting a glass of water for himself. He didn't like soda. Something about rotting teeth and blah blah blah. We slipped coasters under our sodas in a synchronized motion, Frank surreptitiously sticking his bruised knuckles in his mouth as he did so. James had been training us like seals.

Frank slouched back in his chair and closed his eyes. I don't think any of us had been sleeping well since Brooke's death. I know I wasn't. I kept dreaming of Ling Tsu, the zombie panda I'd put back to rest after the Douglas debacle. The image of him sitting there, avoided by his fellow pandas, holding a sheaf of bamboo that he didn't really need to eat anymore, confused, sad, and alone . . . it had kind of stuck with me. If Brooke was the upside of my gift, then Ling Tsu definitely represented the dark side of it. I never wanted to use my powers to inflict misery on anything or anyone, even if the job paid well. Knowing that didn't stop the nightmares, though.

"Ramon coming home tomorrow?" Frank asked.

"Yeah. He's been cleared for a trial run." I hadn't seen Ramon in weeks. While he acclimated to his new therian-thropic lifestyle, which Frank informs me is a generic term for someone who changes shape, the pack had kept him under wraps. Something about staving off accidents. I hated to admit it, but a part of me was relieved. Guilt does funny things to a person. I'd never imagined I'd be happy to avoid my best friend.

Brooke clapped her hands in glee, obviously not harboring any sort of guilt or fear like the rest of us.

James made a face. "Yes, well, as per your orders, his room is now ready, and that abomination outside the house should be finished."

The "abomination" being the half-pipe I'd asked for. James seemed to have a thing against skateboards and had referred to my project as an "eyesore of gargantuan proportions." Like the statues dotting the lawn weren't already eyesores? His response had been that "at least the statues serve a purpose." I couldn't argue that point—the statues were a defense system. When someone attacked, they came to life and ripped the intruder into confetti. Not nice, but certainly useful.

I'd given up arguing and ignored him after that, and just to further wreck his Martha Stewart fantasies, I'd insisted that it needed to be out front.

"It wasn't an order, James, I asked you to do it. Nicely. With a *please*."

"Either way, I feel like I'm running a home for wayward boys."

He wasn't far off on that point. Frank had moved in when I did. I'm not sure if Frank's parents had even noticed he was gone yet. Sean, who was probably on his way over, had been staying there as well. He didn't watch me as closely at home. The house had some pretty good security, even apart from the killer statues: gladiators, attack hedges, and of course, the gnomes. I wasn't 100 percent sure they'd protect me, but I was still probably safer here than anywhere else.

And now Ramon would be joining us. Home for wayward boys, indeed.

Brooke perked up even more, her blond ponytail swinging as she bounced excitedly in her seat. "Like in *Annie*! Can I be Miss Hannigan? I love orphans! And Carol Burnett! My mom and I used to watch that movie all the time." Her face took on a wistful cast.

"We're more like *Oliver!*" Frank said. "Minus the orphan thing, accents, and soul-crushing poverty."

"Besides," I said, leaning toward Brooke, "we all know James would be Miss Hannigan."

James flicked my ear, hard, then took a sip of his water like he hadn't done a thing. "They are delivering the new fridge tomorrow and will have it installed before your friend arrives." He made a face. "I guess I'll need to go to the grocery store again." He glared at Frank. "And if you aren't too terribly busy, I could use a hand wiping down the new fridge as well as shopping." He surveyed us all and sighed. James's sighs always had a vaguely regal quality to them, like he was sighing at peasants. "I guess I'll have to start shopping in bulk." He made the word *bulk* sound dirty.

"Why?"

"Because all of you eat like half-starved wolves."

"That's because some of us are half-starved wolves." Sean entered the kitchen and went straight for the fridge. "Or is that starved half-wolves?" He pulled out a soda, grabbed an apple, and hopped up on the counter, ignoring James, who had pointedly pulled out a chair.

I shook my head. "No, I meant why the new fridge? What's wrong with the one we have?" Douglas's fridge was a stainless-steel masterpiece. I'm not that into appliances or anything, but this one was nice and probably cost more than my last apartment. I had the strange desire to hug it every time I came into the kitchen.

James pushed in the extra chair with a look of resignation and turned back toward me. "I'm not replacing the one we have. I'm getting a spare." He pointed at Frank and me. "Besides you two growing boys, you have a were hybrid—"

"Fey wolf, were-hound . . . you know, I'm not sure we've settled on a proper appellation," Sean corrected him through a mouthful of apple. He ran a hand down his chest. "Whatever we are, though, we're damn sexy." He stretched and flexed his biceps for us while making some very dubious "sexy" faces.

"Whatever, and now a were-bear. Do you have any idea how much he'll need to eat?" James asked.

"Not really," I said.

"Of course not," James said, sounding put-upon. "That's why I have to think of these things. Hence the new fridge, a possible Costco card, and will you *please* tell him to get off the counter!" James was pissed off. Usually, he had a pretty good poker face, but we'd finally, apparently, pushed him over the edge. Little specks of spit had flown out of his mouth, and his face was an angry red.

I put down my soda gently. "Why don't you just ask him to get down?"

"Because," James said through gritted teeth, "this isn't my house, it's yours."

Ah. Sometimes I was a little slow. "James, I'm sorry." His head snapped around toward me. "We've invaded your space and made you feel, well . . . look, and this applies to all of you." I waited to make sure I had everyone's attention. "Technically, I own this house. I'm still trying to adjust to that. That being said, James, this is your home. You've been here the longest. . . ." I trailed off. "How long *have* you been here?"

James gave a one-shoulder shrug. "I'm not sure. Those sorts of things blur after a while. I remember it was right before the video for *Thriller* came out, because we watched it on the new television we'd bought upon our arrival. Douglas thought it was highly amusing."

Frank scrunched up his nose in thought. "That was before I was born. How old are you?"

Again, an indifferent shrug. "Old enough to know better."

"Okay, let's not get distracted," I said. "What I was saying is that, James, well, you know how everything works around here. If there is a rule you'd like us to follow, let us know. We're all trying to live here together. Peacefully." I waved a hand at Sean. "If Sean is annoying you by sitting on the countertops, ask him to get off. If you need any of us to help you do something, let us know. You get paid to run this place; it's your job. If we're standing in the way of that, tell us to move."

"We're a team," Brooke chimed in, "so let's freaking act like it."

James schooled his face back into a polite mask. I didn't like that mask. It reminded me of his former master. Former friend? I wasn't sure how to qualify the relationship he'd had with Douglas. I rested my chin in my hand and stared at him. "But don't get pissed off at our ignorance if you're not sharing what you know. Got it?"

He thought about it, then nodded. "Got it."

"Now, how about you share some of your knowledge?"

James stared at his water for a moment. "Perhaps you should follow me to the basement."

5

LET'S GET TOGETHER AND
FEEL ALL RIGHT

I hadn't been in the basement since I'd escaped from it. As far as I was concerned, the house had no basement. And now I was following James down into it. Joy.

The steps had a little creak to them. That was still the same. As I reached the bottom and looked around, I could tell James had been down here to clean. It wasn't dusty, and there weren't blood splatters everywhere. Also, Michael's corpse was gone. And Douglas's. I shivered.

The bookshelves were still lined with musty, ancient books, notebooks, bits of chalk. The manacles were still on the walls. The table where I'd almost died rested in the same spot. My eyes went to the cage. That, too, remained.

"We're going to need to do a massive redecoration down here. Some color swatches, window treatments, maybe some Pottery Barn catalogs or something, the whole shebang."

James examined the room. "Before you go throwing all of this in the trash heap, you might want to consider its value."

I kicked the cage with my shoe. "What value? I won't sell this." The cage was really only good for one thing—restraining

Brid and Sean's particular type of hybrid. There weren't any of those that I wanted to cage up. "What would I use it for?"

Sean sidled up to the cage. He examined it. "You could ask Dad," he said. "He might want it destroyed." He ran a hand over the runes at the top. "But it might come in handy."

I blinked at him. "You're the last person I'd expect to argue for keeping this cage."

Sean tapped it thoughtfully with one finger. "I don't like it, Sam. I'm not saying we should all throw our sleeping bags in there and have a slumber party. But it might be useful if one of us goes rogue someday."

I considered the idea. He was right. Still. "James, this is necromancer powered, right?"

"Yes, Master."

"Stop it," I said absently. So unless I revved the cage up or it fell into the hands of another necromancer, which was unlikely, we were fine. "Okay," I said. "We'll keep it for now." I looked around the room. "But some of the rest of this stuff is going. I will not now, or ever, need a table with leather cuffs."

"More's the pity," Sean said. He looked around. "What?" he said. "Am I the only one thinking the table might be fun? With a little cleaning, a nice-looking girl, six-pack of beer . . ."

James didn't react, but Frank and I gave Sean looks of disgust. "You guys have no imagination," he said with a shake of his head.

I rubbed a hand over my face. Long-ass day. "You know what? We'll discuss this later. Now, James, what do you have to show the class?" James gave me his best game-show-host grin and swiveled toward the bookcase.

What James had to show us were dozens of old college-ruled-paper notebooks. Most were filled with Douglas's precise writing. Michael had probably scrawled the few that weren't. The handwriting was far too messy to be James's. Each notebook painstakingly explained every one of Douglas's experiments, and each one made me want to raise the fucker from the dead just so I could kill him a few more times.

They were spread out on the dining room table. We each had a notebook in front of us, grabbed at random from the pile. Frank's face was decidedly pale. Brooke's held a stern look of disapproval. Sean wasn't pale, but he didn't look happy. After the first few pages, he'd grabbed some beer he'd hidden from out of the fridge. James wouldn't buy any beer for the house, but Sean sure would. It was nice having room-mates.

Sean had plunked one of the sweating brown bottles in front of me, but I'd barely touched it. Nothing really seemed appetizing when you were reading about the systematic torture of . . . I looked at the front page of the book. A fifteen-year-old homeless boy. Apparently, Douglas had been curious to see what would happen if he injected several different blood samples from various kinds of shape-shifters into a single human being. He started with teens and moved up. Children, he decided, weren't worth the risk, since most shape-shifters don't shift until puberty.

Bloody freaking hell.

I shut the book and took a swig.

Sean was partial to ales, and he had good taste, but the flavor fell flat in my mouth. Gee, I wonder why. As I drank, I noticed that everyone else was having about as much fun as I was. Frank seemed close to crying, Brooke was muttering to herself, and I thought Sean might rip his book in half at any moment.

James didn't have one in front of him. He wouldn't even glance at the stack.

Sean closed his slowly. He looked at the pile. "Every single one of these is a person."

James, still not looking, said, "Sometimes more than one."

Sean tossed his book back in with the rest. "How could you do this? Why? For fucking knowledge? Kicks? What?" I thought Sean might leap across the table and strangle James on the spot. He managed to keep himself in his chair, but he gripped the table until his knuckles turned white and I heard the wood creak.

James faced him, his mouth set in a firm line, and his eyes flashed silver in the dining room light. He appeared to consider several responses as he looked at Sean. Finally, he shook his head. "I serve, Sean, that is all. What the master does with my service is up to him."

Sean growled. "So you really are a tool."

Before I could even consider blinking, James was across

the table. He had Sean by the throat and pinned to the wall. Hot damn, he was fast. If it wouldn't have gotten my face torn off, I might have clapped.

Seriously, it was impressive.

Sean's eyes were a touch wide as James got in his face. "You listen here, you spoiled, arrogant brat," James spat. "Not all of us have Daddy to run to. We don't all have silver spoons jammed into our gullets." He leaned in closer, until his nose was almost touching Sean's. "Some of us live slightly more complicated lives." With that, he dropped Sean to the floor. He turned to me. "If there isn't anything else, Master, I'd like to retire for the night."

I held up my hands in surrender. "Go for it." Before I finished speaking, James had stalked out of the room, leaving it very, very quiet.

Sean sat down and took a sip of his beer. "Wow."

No one responded. Wow, indeed. I got up slowly, gathered all the notebooks, and set them back into the box we'd used to bring them upstairs. We hadn't even managed to bring up half of them. Now I was glad we hadn't. I snatched one out of Frank's hand.

"Hey!"

I glared at him.

Frank stood his ground. "We need to read those. They're important."

"Maybe," I said, "but do we have to do it all tonight?" Frank opened his mouth, shut it, then opened it again. While he impersonated a guppy, I rummaged in a hutch in the corner. I pulled out Trivial Pursuit and dropped it onto the table where the notebooks had been. "Right. Let's talk about something else."

Nobody argued.

𝕴t was hard to sleep after the day I'd had. I mean, I'd had worse. And someone, somewhere, was having an even worse time of it than me. I tried to keep that in mind. No matter how crappy your life, someone will probably beat you in the my-life-is-crap category. Not that I don't let myself whine a little now and then, but sometimes it's good to keep your misery in perspective.

I threw back the covers and snuck into the hallway. A few doors down was my own private little heaven. When I'd first moved in, I'd been surprised to find out that Douglas and I actually had something in common. You know, besides our ability to wrangle the dead. In addition to being a raving psychopath, Douglas had been a music nut.

The music library had plush carpet and wall-to-wall bookcases built to hold hundreds of records. Only a few CDs were present, and then only albums that couldn't be purchased in vinyl. The rest of the room was sparsely furnished. An overstuffed leather couch and chair, a coffee table, and a tiny accent table with, of all things, an even tinier china duck. Above Señor Quackenstein, as I had named him, was one of the few shelves that wasn't tightly packed with music. Instead Douglas had a framed first edition of Bowie's *Hunky Dory* on display there.

I guess even pure evil likes David Bowie.

I shuffled past to grab something quieter to listen to. The album I wanted was up a little high, and I had to get on my tiptoes to reach it. I finally grabbed it, but the effort set me off balance, and I stumbled right into the end table. Poor Señor Quackenstein tumbled to the floor and . . . broke? On carpet? Frowning, I picked him up. No, not broken. He'd popped open, which was super weird. I'd never even noticed a seam on him before. Inside, hiding in the back near the tail, was an egg-shaped stone about the size of a chestnut. It looked like jade. The sides were intricately carved, tiny cherry blossoms on a branch winding up from the bottom.

I rolled it over in my hand. Odd that anyone would hide something so pretty. Odder still that the egg felt cold to the touch, almost magically so. Marble was sometimes like that. Was jade? I examined it carefully, because that's how you should treat a new thing in Douglas's house: carefully and like it could kill you at any moment. There was something different about the egg, but I was too tired to really think it through.

My pajama pants didn't have pockets, and I was reluctant to leave the egg lying around. I opened up my pouch—my mom had told me never to open it, but that was before I'd known what it really was—and tucked the egg inside. Mom had made the pouch to hide me from the things that go bump in the night. You know, the kinds of things that might want to talk to someone like me. It was also supposed to hide me from, well, someone like me. I figured it could hold on to the egg for a little while. Record in hand, I turned off the light and headed back to my room.

Haley woke me with a phone call, which was a little unusual. My sister is a texter, especially if she thinks I might be asleep.

I mumbled something—it might have been "hello," or it might have been "piss off." It's hard to be sure of these things sometimes.

"Be nice," she said. Which meant I'd probably told her to piss off.

"Sorry," I grumbled, but I only half meant it. "What's up?"

"Are you free tomorrow? I wanted to see if maybe you'd pick me up from the library."

"Of course. Yeah. Wait." Something was wrong with the conversation, and I was having a difficult time brushing away the cobwebs and figuring out what it was. Finally, my brain caught up with an almost audible ding. "Why aren't you catching the bus?" Haley was an independent kind of girl and liked to function without the help of, say, me. So generally she only pestered me for rides if she couldn't catch a bus or she needed some other favor.

"Can't a girl just want to see her big brother?"

Alarm bells now. Flashing red lights. Danger, Danger, Will Robinson. "What happened, Haley? And skip the bullshit, please. I haven't had any coffee yet."

"It's nothing. Really. Sort of. It was probably just a prank. Mom's overreacting, and now she doesn't want me catching the bus home by myself."

A flicker of the last violently delivered message—namely Brooke's head in a box—surfaced before I could suppress it. Now that I was paying attention, I could hear the tiny vibration of fear in Haley's voice. I should have noticed it instantly. "What kind of prank?"

"Don't freak out, Sam. Mom's bad enough."

"I will freak out less when you tell me."

"Someone left a knife in the door." Her voice was nonchalant, trying to mask her fear, trying to make it sound as if someone had simply left flowers.

"A . . . knife? No note? Nothing else?"

"That's it. Knife. Door. It's not a big deal." Before I could argue or lecture she said, "Please don't worry. We're fine."

I rubbed a hand over my face. Of course I was going to worry. But I could do that on my own time and not lay it all on Haley. "Okay. I'll pick you up tomorrow. Just be careful. And, Haley—carry some Mace or something, will you?"

She forced a laugh, and we went over the details before she hung up. Haley might be shrugging it off or downplaying it so I wouldn't worry, but I knew better than to ignore threats. Just like I knew better than to think this didn't involve me in some way. Who on earth would threaten my baby sister and a witch who makes shampoo? No one, unless they were actually aiming at me. A chill eased up my spine, and I shivered.

I couldn't go back to sleep after that.

Grass tickled my hands as the sunlight created a warm red glow on my eyelids. It made it hard to keep them closed. I was practicing my newfound skills with a game of hide-and-seek with Ashley and Brooke. A game, I might add, where I was always It.

Though I was never very good at it, I was worse that day—it was hard to concentrate on practice when I kept replaying my conversation with Haley in my head. I squeezed my eyes shut and searched. I could sense Ashley off to my left, the crackling presence of a Harbinger. I could feel the shadows of plants, trees, and animals. The outlines came together in my head. But I couldn't see Brooke. I tried harder. Nothing. Which wasn't possible, since I knew she was hiding out there somewhere. I just didn't know where. I turned around. Still nothing. I steadied my breathing and thought. Where else could she be? I turned back around and tilted my head up slightly. In my mental sketch of the forest, I could clearly see Brooke's long legs dangling over a tree branch. They were swinging back and forth nonchalantly, because apparently to Brooke being that far up in a tree was no big thing. I guess once you're dead, falling from great heights loses some of its scariness. I smiled and opened my eyes. "Olly, olly, oxen free."

James walked out onto the lawn, his tail twitching. "What's next, kick the can?" He sat next to me, his head high as he told Frank where to set the picnic basket. "He's a member of the Council, and you have him playing children's games."

Ashley shot him a withering look. "He needs to learn precision, and his grasp of the basics is fuzzy at best."

"Why are you back in that form again?" I asked. "You could have carried the basket yourself if you'd switched."

James turned his cool feline gaze on me. "What, Frank is too good to carry food, but it's okay for me to do it?"

"No," I said, exasperated. "That's not what I meant. I . . . you know what? Never mind. If you want to be a kitty, be a kitty."

"I don't mind," Frank said as he set down the basket. He opened it and took out a blanket, followed by an assorted picnic lunch. I had no idea what I was paying James, but based on his picnic-assembling skills alone, he needed a raise. I moved over to the blanket and snagged a piece of cheese.

Ashley flopped onto her side, her pigtails swinging. She arranged her skirt. I'm not sure why, but she generally dressed like a Catholic schoolgirl. "Hand over the goods, Frank."

Frank reached back into the basket and pulled out a plastic container. I didn't have to look into it to know that it held Belgian waffles with fresh strawberries. The smaller container probably held syrup. I'm sure James even had whipped cream somewhere. As part of a bargain, I owed Ashley a steady supply of waffles. After I moved in, James took over on the days I was home. At first Ashley argued and said this was against the spirit of the agreement. But after one spectacularly awful batch of waffles by me, Ashley conceded. The kitchen is just not my domain. Not sure I have a domain. I should get one.

Brooke settled down next to Ashley and pulled out her spectral clipboard. She'd become very fond of it. "Speaking of Council," she said, "don't forget the meeting is at four."

"How could I forget? No one here would let me if I tried."

"Well, someone has to keep your shit together in my absence." The voice came from behind me. A little lower than I remembered, like someone had taken a slight bass growl and added it over his regular voice. Changed or not, I knew that voice. I hopped to my feet in an instant.

Ramon stood a few paces back, a black duffel bag slung over his shoulder. Dessa, the daughter of a local seer named Maya who'd helped us out during the Douglas thing, stood a few paces back, waving. She was also related to June, the only other necromancer I knew personally. I should also add that Dessa is a stone-cold fox—Ramon's words, not mine.

I felt most of my guilt and worry vanish when I saw Ramon grinning fit to explode. The guilt would return, probably in spades, but I'd worry about that later. I hugged the bastard. He hugged me back without hesitation. I could feel some of his new strength, though it was obvious he was trying to be careful. He squeezed me again.

"Man, it's good to see you."

Aaaaaaaaaand the guilt was back. The pack had told me not to visit, but I hadn't tried very hard. "They told me—"

"I know," he said. "No worries. Now, let's break it up before people start to question our sexuality again." I laughed and let him go.

"They told me the same thing," Dessa said. "So I just texted him instead." Why hadn't I thought of that? Because I'd been afraid of what his return texts would say, probably. Or worse—that I'd get no reply at all.

Brooke squealed and clapped, jumping up to give Ramon a quick ghostly kiss on the cheek. "I would've visited, but you wouldn't have been able to see me. Besides, someone needs to keep an eye on these two." She kissed his other cheek, just for good measure.

"Good to see you too, *chica*," he said.

I introduced him to the rest of the group. James, doing his best to look abused even in feline form, ordered Frank to make up a large plate of food and pass it to Ramon. He took it with a thanks and dug in. It was good to see him up and healthy again. The last time I'd seen him, he'd been unconscious in a hospital bed, strapped down with wires and cuffs. He'd been fighting the infection then, all because he'd barged in, white-knight style, to save me. It had been touch-and-go for a bit. Now he looked back to normal, with the exception of a few pounds of muscle added on. Ramon used to be as slender and scrawny as me. Not anymore. Just one more new thing to get used to. I pointed out the new skate ramp—as if he could miss it—and called it a welcome-home present. James made sure to refer to it as an eyesore that was ruining the lawn, and I made sure to ignore him.

"Let's go check out your new digs so you can put your crap away," I said, punching Ramon in the arm.

I wasn't sure what to expect from Ramon's new room. James could be a bit unpredictable at times. I think after all his complaining, I expected something Spartan, cold, maybe just enough effort to get by, like a prison cell or a college dorm. Instead, I was greeted by a massive four-poster bed complete with curtains and dark cotton sheets. The frame looked like oak. There was a matching desk and nightstand. James had even unpacked Ramon's stuff left over from the move out of our old apartment.

"Wow." Ramon flopped onto the bed as I continued to gape.

"Yes, well, it was the best I could do on short notice." James hopped up onto an armchair. "I put what few things you had from Sam's place away. I hope you don't mind, but I thought it might help you settle. Feel free to move anything you like."

I ran and threw myself on the bed too. It poofed. A feather mattress. Hot damn. "How come you didn't do this with my room? I still have milk crates holding up a plywood shelf for my books."

"If you remember, you insisted on bringing your own stuff, including that moth-eaten thing you call a mattress. You wouldn't even put your music in the library, or your books. Ridiculous."

I hadn't wanted to mix up my stuff with Douglas's. I know it sounds weird, but I felt like, once that happened, this new house situation was permanent, and I wasn't sure I was ready for that. Besides, evil bastards shouldn't like good music. It just doesn't go with torture and dark machinations. Which reminded me, I should show someone that egg I found. But I was really comfortable. . . . I sank deeper into the bed.

"I don't remember that," I lied.

"You referred to it as a 'slippery slope,' saying you didn't want to get used to Douglas's wealth and lifestyle. Why you think luxury leads to the dark side is beyond me. Having nice things doesn't necessitate evil. You work hard. Why can't you sleep on something that isn't a home for millions of dust mites?"

He had a point. I didn't want to get any closer to being like Douglas, but did that mean I needed to keep my room in a squalid condition because that was familiar? Was I just being stubborn?

Ramon got up and started exploring his room. "You kept all your crap furniture?"

"Most of it," I said. "The stuff that would fit in my room. James wouldn't allow some of my stuff in the common areas."

"I was afraid it might give the other furniture ideas. Pretty soon the whole house might start slumming it."

"Be nice," I said. James's only response was a slow feline blink.

"You're like one of those monks who beats himself with a cat-o'-nine-tails in order to stay penitent." Ramon opened one of the desk drawers and turned to James. "You even put office supplies in here. Thanks, man. I owe you one." He peered more closely at it. "Is this engraved?"

"What does it say?" I rolled a little closer on Ramon's heaven mattress.

"It has my name," Ramon said, slowly. "And what appears to be a bear paw print."

I watched his face to see his reaction as he stared at the paper, looking for any hint of anger or self-pity. I wasn't really sure yet how Ramon was taking his . . . condition. A wave of relief went through me as the corner of his mouth twitched in amusement. He laughed, a deep, belly-wrenching laugh, and thanked James again.

James stiffened a little, his ears twitching forward in attention, like he hadn't expected the gratitude. "You're welcome. I also took the liberty of purchasing some basic bathroom items for you. They are in the washroom across the hall. You'll have to share with Sean, I'm afraid."

Ramon shrugged. "That's cool. I'm just glad to have an actual bed. No more couch living for Ramon."

"Don't talk about yourself in the third person," I said. "It's creepy."

Ramon pulled out his desk chair and sat. "Sam, I know why you held on to your stuff, but seriously, you're not going to go all evil just because you get a new bed and a shelf. I don't think you're bought off that easy. But if you're worried, I can keep an eye on you."

"Yes," James said drily, "we can always keep your stuff in the basement with the rest of the torture devices should the need to self-flagellate arise at any point."

"All right, all right," I said. "I give. James, you win. May I please have new furniture?"

He gave me a slow, regal blink. "As Master wishes."

"Cut it out."

Then he stared at the clock and left, soft paws padding down the hall. I got the message. It was time to go greet the other Council members.

6

EVERY TIME IT RAINS, IT RAINS PENNIES FROM HEAVEN

Douglas examined the coin lying in James's hand. Flat and silver, the writing or the symbols had been worn smooth long ago. He couldn't even hazard a guess as to its country of origin. It was attached to a heavy, braided cord that was stained with age. Supposedly, it was a piece of hangman's rope, which Douglas found a touch excessive.

"The previous owner must have had a flair for the dramatic."

James made a noncommittal noise. "If I'm ever in the underworld, I will ask him." He pulled a long silver chain out of his pocket. "I figured you'd want this." He took his knife out, cutting the cord quickly. Once the coin was on the chain, he slipped it over Douglas's head. Douglas felt an icy resonance when it hit his chest. A hypothermic blast, then feeling, real feeling, and not some ghostly approximation, returned. He stretched his arms out and looked at his hands. Solid. Real. At least as long as the coin was around his neck. No need for the rotting shell of a body in the mausoleum. He was tempted to kick up his heels in triumph. Well, almost.

"Where on earth did you obtain a Stygian coin?"

James shrugged. "Does it matter?"

"Not really. Impressive, though." Douglas stretched, enjoying the feeling of having substance again. The coin was like a tiny silver miracle.

"You're welcome." James sat down on the marble bench of the mausoleum, adjusting his duster as he did so. "My place is here—I should be here with you," he said forcefully. To Douglas it seemed that James said this more to himself than anything.

"Nothing would draw suspicion faster than if you left. Everyone knows a *pukis* only changes hands if the owner dies. Your disappearance would cause problems." Douglas examined James's face. He supposed most would look at it and see only faint boredom, nothing more. But Douglas had owned James for a long time. He could see concern in the tilt of James's head, fear in the slightly pinched brow, and an overall confusion in the set of James's body. For a brief second, Douglas wondered if it might be too much, asking him to serve two masters.

Then James changed the subject, and Douglas let him. "That coin should enable you to move more freely, anyway. Though my earlier suggestion still stands."

"Starting over seems a lot like quitting to me, James."

The *pukis* shifted, looking uncomfortable. "You have a chance at a clean slate. Go anywhere. Be anyone. I implore you, let it go."

"Let my murderer go free? No consequences? Let bygones be bygones, and such rubbish?" Douglas snorted. "I think not. Besides, I'm not willing to throw away all the work I've put into this area. It will take some adjustments, I know, but the removal of a few key obstacles should do the trick." The key obstacles being Brannoc and Sam, of course. It would feel good to get those two off the Council, then once they were safely taken care of, Douglas would emerge and disband what was left. No more governing by democratic discussion. He would rule. And after that, he could start expanding his realm, one piece at a time. The possibilities were endless.

James looked down, and his hair slid over his eyes. He had to twitch it away with a shake of his head. Douglas had never seen it so long and noticed for the first time that there was some curl to it. Then he realized that this was because he hadn't been there to tell James to get a haircut. It wasn't exactly a game they played, but it was close. James would get a bit shaggy. Douglas would threaten him with some scissors and a bowl. Then, feigning submission, James would make an appointment at the barber's. That exchange was no longer taking place, and even though it was but a small moment in their otherwise lengthy lives, Douglas grieved for it. Briefly. Then the grief turned to anger, as it always did with him.

"You were overconfident last time," James said softly.

"He was lucky."

"He might be lucky again."

"I highly doubt that. Did you fulfill your other task? It's about time we started our campaign against one Samhain LaCroix."

James hesitated before answering.

"James."

"I purchased the athame—plain and common, just like you asked, but . . ."

Douglas tapped his fingers impatiently on the wall of the mausoleum. His delight in the ease it took to tap his fingers overwhelmed his frustration with James, but only momentarily. "Should I be sending my condolences to the LaCroix family or not, James?"

The lock of hair slipped back onto his forehead as James shook his head. "It's just . . . I thought . . ." His jaw clenched as he looked away. "I thought I would draw it out more. Build the situation up. Spread him—and his resources—even more thin than they are." He looked back at Douglas pleadingly. "Do you see?"

"If you didn't stick her with the knife, then where did you stick it?"

James looked at his feet. "In her door."

"Her bedroom door? Not the front door?"

James nodded.

Douglas continued his *tap-tap-tap* on the wall and considered this. Sam was such a sensitive boy, disgustingly sentimental by nature. With people like that the best way to hurt them was through the people they held dear. Killing the blond girl had proved that.

He'd cycled through several targets and had landed on one: Sam's sister. With that in mind, he'd sent James over to slice her up like a Christmas ham. A nice visual and a very clear point, but then again, over very quickly. Perhaps James's version would be ultimately more pleasing.

"Dramatic," he said. James performed best when he wasn't micromanaged. Sometimes he forgot that. "I like it." Yes, this way was infinitely better. James had violated the inner sanctum.

He'd breezed past defenses and doors and sidled right up to his quarry—mere feet away. No one in the LaCroix family would be sleeping easy now. Which would mean that when he actually killed the girl, it would be that much more effective. Oh, the guilt Sam would feel—the powerlessness! Douglas wanted to do a jig at the idea, but settled for a smile. It seemed more dignified.

In contrast, James was so still that he almost appeared to be meditating. Finally, he asked, "Why her?"

Douglas paused before answering, but only because he was surprised that James had asked the question in the first place. "Anyone in my house posed some risk—too easy to be seen there, and I'd rather avoid it. Brid was also hazardous—besides, I'd like her to be alive so that she can receive the full impact of future events. That left Sam's mother and sister. Out of the two, I thought Haley would be the easiest target. Why do you ask?"

"Just wondering if there was a better choice, tactically speaking," James muttered. "But you seem to have come to the best conclusion."

"Naturally."

He stretched then, just because he could. With the coin on, Douglas felt as good as new. Solid. Like nothing had happened to him. If they hadn't been hanging out in a mausoleum next to his rotting shell, he'd say he wasn't dead at all. As long as he kept the coin on, of course. That might become a nuisance eventually, but he could deal with it later. For now, he'd handle the problems directly in his path, like Sam. Of course it was only natural for James to fret, but really, what could

Sam possibly do? Kill him twice? "You seem troubled by my orders. Should I be concerned about your loyalty, James?"

James stared at his shoes, taking his time to respond. "I'm worried about you." He'd never been particularly demonstrative, even in his youth. Douglas had owned him since James was but a boy, and even then he'd been quiet, scrawny and pale, but with an air of gravity rare in someone so young. The way he was acting now was tantamount to an emotional breakdown in everyone else.

Douglas placed a hand on James's shoulder. "I know."

An unspoken phrase hung between them both: *You are all I have.* Neither of them had ever said it, not once in all their time together. But they both knew it was true. People had floated in and out of Douglas's life, but James was the only one who'd stuck.

Though it was warm and pleasant outside, the air inside the mausoleum was chill and quiet. James cleared his throat. "The coin should help you find what you're looking for, at any rate."

Douglas held the Stygian coin up for a better look. Remarkable. "Are you sure it wasn't where I'd left it? In the china figurine in the music room?"

James shook his head, his silver eyes cloudy. "Empty. It's somewhere in the house, I assume. Perhaps you moved it at some point and forgot?"

"Not likely. That's not the sort of thing one misplaces."

"I can't see it the way you can. It would be best for you to look—more efficient that way." James pursed his lips. "Are you absolutely positive that you need it?"

"Yes. The coin is nice, but it's more of a temporary measure.

I need the egg to be completely restored. Besides, it wouldn't do for anyone else to get ahold of it. Consequences of a dire nature and all that." Douglas let the Stygian coin drop against his shirtfront. "Ask around—carefully. Maybe the gnomes found it and did something with it. Don't let on what it's for. I don't want them thinking they have something to barter with."

"Lovely. If those little barbarians got it, then it could be anywhere."

"Just don't let *him* find it," Douglas said, his hand resting on James's shoulder.

James made a noise. "Even if he did, he wouldn't know what to do with it."

7

SMOKE ON THE WATER

I unbuttoned the top of my shirt as I looked at the Tongue & Buckle. I wasn't used to button-up shirts. I only owned two. The one I had on was new, a gift from my sister. Just thinking about her made my fingers worry nervously at the next button. The shirt was black, short-sleeved with tiny little skulls on the pocket. On the back, a Day of the Dead style Virgin Mary. Haley has a wicked sense of humor.

James didn't insist on much, but he did insist on dressing up for meetings. Ridiculous, since one of the members had a hard time wearing pants. Wait, what was I thinking? James insisted on tons of things. I undid another button.

"You're one away from a nice seventies look." Sean put his feet up on the dash.

"I'd need chest hair for that. And gold chains."

"True." He leaned farther back into the passenger seat, if that was even possible. Sean, at least, never bitched about my Subaru. "You know, you're going to have to go in eventually. And the longer you wait, the longer you're in those clothes."

I flicked a piece of lint off the black slacks James had dug up for me. He'd grunted at inspection. That grunt probably meant he'd be taking me shopping soon. Or it might have been directed at my Cons. You never knew. He needed to cut me some slack. My last job had been flipping burgers. You didn't buy dress shoes for a job like that. With a job like that, you couldn't even afford dress shoes. Or clothes. You couldn't afford anything, really.

Sean looked over at the pub. "What did Groucho Marx say about being aware of any job that requires new clothes?"

"The quote is that we should 'beware of all enterprises that require new clothes,' and it's Thoreau, not Groucho Marx."

"Oooh, listen to you. 'It's Thoreau.' Well, we didn't all go to college for a quarter."

"I went for a year, not a quarter, and shut up." I stared at the door with him. I wished Sean could go in with me. Backup might be nice, but it had been explained to me that taking in a bodyguard was a sign of weakness. It meant that I didn't trust the group. It also meant that I didn't think I was as strong as they were. Of course, I did feel that way, but the important thing was not to show it.

"Groucho, Thoreau, whatever."

"Don't you have tutors at the Den?"

"Yup. That doesn't mean I pay attention to them."

"Fair enough." I opened the door. "Don't wait up."

"My entire job right now is to wait up."

I shut the door and headed for the bar.

Zeke looks like a bodyguard. He's huge—a mass of muscle and sinew. He'd break my neck if I tried, but I'm pretty sure you could actually grate cheese off his abs. Not that I wanted to know about his abs, but his shirt was so tight I could make them out, and he's a lot taller than me, which makes them hard to miss. I had a sudden image of him using his abs to grate my face. Unpleasant.

And yet, for some reason, Zeke seemed afraid of me. I couldn't figure it out. I had slipped on the light suit jacket that went with the pants, and it flared out as I spread my arms for my pat down. Then I shucked off my Cons so he could inspect those, too. Zeke was thorough. He waved me on, then reluctantly pulled out one of the old wooden chairs for me to sit in so I could put my shoes back on. I nodded thanks as I tied my laces. Everything, with the exceptions of the staff and patrons, looked stained with age and use, giving the pub a strangely cozy feeling. If I ever got over my nervousness about coming to meetings, I might really like the Tongue & Buckle.

My shoes were tied, and I couldn't delay anymore. It was time to join the rest of the Council.

The meetings took place in the back room of the bar at a giant curved table. I grabbed an empty seat next to Brannoc, which is where I usually sat, because he was the one person I knew. He smiled at me—more welcoming than the greeting I got from Kell. The vampire didn't like me much. From what I gathered, it had something to do with Kell being dead and me being the mayor of Zombieville. I didn't know too much about it. As soon as I could think of a polite way to bring up Kell's potential enslavement via necromancy, I'd ask. Until then, I just tried to be nice.

The Council is a motley crew. It's composed of me, Brannoc, Kell, a satyr named Pello, a witch named Ione, a fury named

Ariana, and Aengus, the bartender. I wasn't entirely sure yet what category Aengus fell into, or what a fury was exactly, besides what I'd read in Greek mythology. Overall, a very intimidating group. I guess that's kind of the point.

We didn't have a whole lot of stuff to deal with this time. Petitions to move into or out of the area, mostly. I got roped into accompanying Pello and Kell to a meeting with a representative of the local sea folk. I wasn't really sure what that entailed. I hadn't even known we had an underwater contingent.

I ordered a soda from the bar during the break. While I waited for it, I sat on the stool and stared down at my coaster. What the hell was I doing? I had no idea what the other members of the Council were even talking about half the time, and I couldn't ask them any questions because, once again, it was another thing that would make me look weak. How the hell was I supposed to help anyone, when I didn't even know what was going on? I spun the coaster in a circle. I was so screwed.

Brannoc slid into the seat next to me and ordered a beer. "How you holding up?"

I let the coaster go, watching it fall and settle onto the bar. "I shouldn't be here."

"And why is that?"

"Because I have no idea what I'm doing." I rested my chin in my hand. "I'm still trying to figure out how this whole thing works."

Brannoc handed Aengus money in exchange for the beer. "And you're afraid you might screw it up."

I nodded and put a straw in my soda. "There has got to be someone better qualified for this position."

Brannoc took a sip of his beer. "Are you sure about that?"

"I'm going to get someone hurt."

"Maybe," he said, "but when you're in a position of power, that's always a possibility. People rely on your choices, and sometimes the outcome of those choices isn't favorable and someone suffers because of it. That's life." He put his beer down. "A good leader learns from those mistakes. He doesn't quit out of fear of them."

"I didn't mean it like that."

"Yes, you did, but that's okay—your fear is natural. What you have to remember, Sam, is that there is always someone who knows more than you, or is stronger than you, but that doesn't always mean that they are better qualified."

"That actually sounds like the definition of better qualified."

Aengus came up to us and wiped the bar with a rag. "Whining, though more acceptable from youth, is no less unbecoming."

I frowned at him. "I wasn't trying to whine."

"Then you were accomplishing it quite well without even making an attempt." He left to pull a beer for somebody else.

Sometimes I hate it when people are right. "Sorry," I said.

Brannoc shrugged. "The person you were describing— more power, more knowledge—could be Douglas."

I grimaced.

"I know," Brannoc said, "but it makes my point. I encourage you to continue to learn and push yourself, but knowledge and power don't make you good at this, not on their own."

I had a hard time picturing myself as the best suited for anything at all. What did I know about being a member of the Council? The last job I had involved a spatula and a name tag. "Then what does?"

"Caring about the people asking you for help, trying to do your best by them, and putting them before your own wants and needs. That is the kind of person who should be on the Council."

I glowered at him. "Now you're just trying to make me feel better."

Brannoc laughed and clapped me on the back. For a brief second, he reminded me of Sean. "If I was just trying to make you feel better, I'd have encouraged you to run while you still could."

"Great," I said, "now I feel worse."

8

SLOW RIDE

James avoided looking at Douglas while unpacking the supplies he'd brought. The cabin he was in, though cleaned by a service on a fairly regular basis, had very little actually in it and so had to be stocked with all manner of things that Douglas would need.

"Usually you discuss changing tactics before you implement new plans," Douglas said idly, seemingly unconcerned. Something about the way James was handling things was different, and it was niggling at him. Douglas abhorred niggling. A niggle meant he had missed something small, which meant it was easily overlooked and hard to correct. Details can make or break any plan, regardless of size. So he kept picking at the niggle, hoping to find where it led.

"You left it to my discretion." James's gaze never wavered from the cabinet as he organized salt, chalk, and any other thing that needed to be handy. "I understand that you're anxious to get things moving at a quicker pace, but please remember that you do prize me for my ability to anticipate your wishes." James threw an icy gaze at the third member of their party—just a quick flicker—before returning to his chore. "It's an ability I have proved time and time again to be an asset your other assistants *lack*. Need I remind you of Michael?"

"You're right. It's just that I can't remember the last time you disobeyed an order," Douglas said as he watched James shift the items yet again. "I think that cabinet is as orderly as it's going to get."

"You can always kill her later." When Douglas didn't immediately nod his head in approval, James shrugged, his face set in a distinct pout.

"What is the saying? If you keep making that face, it might freeze that way?" James's sulking always amused Douglas.

"Fine, you didn't like how I carried out your errand. But it certainly didn't warrant your bringing in a replacement." He waved his hand at their company, currently slouched next to Douglas.

Douglas patted the head of his new underling sitting at the table. Not his best work, but reliable, and that went a long way. "Oh, come now. We both know he won't replace you, and you're being silly to even look at it like that. Remember, right now you technically belong to Sam, and so your ability to answer my beck and call is a bit hampered. After I resurface and claim what is rightfully mine, then of course there will be no need. But until then . . ." Douglas didn't expect James to clap or cheer or anything ridiculous like that, but he had expected a small smile, perhaps, or some hint at expectation. Instead he saw only that same frustration and concern.

James set some more chalk and yet another container of salt on the counter before turning his attention to the new subordinate. "Are you sure Minion won't draw undue attention?"

Minion looked at James, a wooden expression on his face as he contemplated what James had just called him. "My name is—"

"Your name is Minion while you're here, and you'll bloody well like it," James spat.

Minion nodded. "I understand." He turned, his expression still that unreadable blankness. "Master, he makes a good point. People like to take my picture. And won't I be missed?"

Douglas rolled his eyes. "Have a little faith. I'm not going to take Minion anywhere he's going to be seen. As for being missed, I told his people that he was going on some mystical retreat to get in touch with himself or some such nonsense."

Minion nodded. "That was wise, Master," he said slowly. Of course, he said everything slowly, so it was hard for Douglas to tell if this particular utterance was any slower than usual.

James continued to storm about the kitchen, closing doors a little harder than he needed to, slamming a box of new trash bags and dish soap down on the counter. "Seriously, what did you do wrong with him? It's like the muscles in his face are frozen. How does he even get work like that?"

"That's not fair," Minion said. "I do plenty of good work."

"Please," James said, "the last good thing you did was *My Own Private Idaho*. You're just a guilty pleasure now. An institution of ridiculousness."

Minion sulked, or at least Douglas thought he might be sulking. His expression hadn't changed, but his shoulders appeared to slump a little.

"Now, now, children, let's not fight." He glanced at James. "And don't mention that movie. That's when the . . . accident . . .

happened, and it upsets him. While I don't really care for his feelings, I'd like him to be functional and useful. Otherwise what's the point?"

James crossed his arms. "What kind of moron tries to do that with a bottle of Jäger and a stuffed deer head, anyway?"

Douglas gave a slight shrug. "I was told it was a cast game of truth or dare that got out of hand. Besides, it was the toaster that really overdid things."

Minion nodded somewhat sullenly. "We are but dust in the wind, dudes." He brightened. "But the Master brought me back so that no one would be deprived of my work. Right, Master?"

James sneered. "Is that what they told you?" He looked Minion up and down. "And you believed it. Of course you would." He leaned in, sticking his face up close to his object of ridicule. "I caught a matinee of that movie, and you know what? I couldn't tell the difference between the scenes when you're alive and the scenes filmed after the incident." He gave the last two words air quotes.

"That's because Master does such good work," the zombie returned, a note of blind devotion in his voice.

James harrumphed and went back to straightening things and preparing the cabin. "Despite having to divide my time, I still think I'm more useful than he is."

"Really, James, this behavior is quite unlike you."

James didn't answer. Instead he kept putting away groceries and slamming doors, but his expression lost some of its angry sneer.

Douglas rested against the counter. "This has nothing to do with Sam's sister—I simply wanted to have someone around to do legwork for me. I don't know if he'll be recognized, but it would be far worse if I was, and it's easier to explain away a celebrity sighting than if I was seen. I'm supposed to be dead, remember?"

James slowed down. "Yes, I can see how that might be a touch awkward."

"Exactly. And might I also remind you that you can't always run off and do things for me, either? Sam might start asking questions."

James didn't meet his eye, but Douglas could see brief flickers of indecipherable emotion on the boy's face as he thought it through. But he wasn't a boy anymore, was he? With a shock, Douglas realized that James was acting like a hurt teenager. His kind aged slower than humans, making it possible for them to stay with a family line for generations. Douglas watched as James pushed his hair out of his eyes. Late teens, but *pukis* or not, the angst and mood swings were certainly there. He felt something in him relax. Of course, that was why James was acting so odd. Stupid of him not to figure it out sooner.

"What's your next move, then?"

Douglas grabbed a fake apple out of Minion's hand and put it back in the bowl, twisting it so the bite mark was hidden. "Those are wax, Minion."

The creature looked confused. "It's not an apple?"

"No." He watched in disgust as Minion spit the wax out onto the floor. "How exactly do you function in Hollywood?"

James calmly advanced on Minion before he could answer and smacked him on the nose with a rolled-up newspaper. "Bad Minion! We don't spit on the floor. Now clean it up."

The creature hung its head. "Yes, sir. Sorry," he added shamefully.

"I'm beginning to understand why you always say it," James said with a scowl as he oversaw Minion's work.

"Say what?"

"That good help is hard to find."

Douglas nodded. "It is a rather limited commodity, isn't it?"

ANOTHER ONE BITES THE DUST

When I got home from the Council meeting—and after I had accompanied Kell and Pello to a disastrous meeting with our underwater contingent—Ramon and I finally got to break in the new half-pipe. He also got to break in a new skateboard, a welcome-home gift from me. The last one had met an unfortunate end while trying to save my hide. I didn't do anything fancy—I'm not the best on a board. Ramon is, though. When I needed a break, I sat in the grass and watched him go, twisting and turning in the floodlights we had up, and I realized how lucky I was to see that again. As guilty as I felt for complicating Ramon's life, it could have been worse, and it could have been just me on that half-pipe.

I climbed into bed after that and settled down into my blankets, thinking the whole time how great it was going to be to do this in a new bed. With a new mattress. Maybe with Brid in it. Heaven.

My phone went off at some point. I didn't know what time it was, only that it was still dark and I was exceptionally groggy. I answered with a curse.

"Sam?" My name came out as more of a sob than a question.

It took me a second to recognize the voice as Brid's. I wasn't used to hearing her cry.

"Brid? What's going on? What's wrong?" Late-night phone calls are never good, especially if someone is crying on the other end of the line. Panic chased away the last remnants of sleep, and I sat up and got out of bed, trying to talk to Brid while I searched for my pants. I knew there was no way this conversation was going to end with me going quietly back to bed.

"My dad." I couldn't understand anything after that. Just sobs and mumbled words. I heard howling in the background. The sad, mournful sound of it crawled up my spine.

"I'll be there as soon as I can," I said. And then she hung up. I was left in the darkness alone, except for the growing pain in my chest. I felt a little like howling myself.

My Subaru station wagon, though a fine and practical vehicle, was not built for speed. Douglas's old Mercedes-Benz Coupe, however, was. With James at the wheel, his driving gloves on and his manner relaxed in a way that told me he was indifferent to the speedometer, I was starting to understand how this car had once been envisioned as a racecar. Even though we were traveling mind-screamingly fast, I was willing the car to move faster. The downside to the Coupe is that it seats only two people. Ramon was trailing behind us, clinging to the back of Sean's motorcycle. I couldn't imagine going that fast on a bike. Of course, if the boys crashed, they would probably get up and walk away. I would have to be scraped off the asphalt with a spatula.

We had left Frank at home. I didn't think it was a good idea to bring a fragile human amongst upset werewolves. The fact that I was just as fragile didn't give me any comfort.

It usually takes about thirty minutes to reach the Den. James made it in fifteen. He slowed the car as we pulled into the parking area of the large cabin. I looked up at the house that was usually so welcoming. I felt none of that warmth now. The motorcycle slid in noisily behind us. Sean didn't even come to a full stop before he jumped off the bike and ran to the house. Ramon caught it, barely, and set the kickstand. Then, with him and James by my side, I walked up to the Den.

The front door hung open, and the entryway was quiet. I shouted hello, but no one answered. I'd never seen the Den quiet or empty. It was both now. Ramon placed a hand on my shoulder.

"They're in the woods," he said. Before the words were even out of his mouth, Sean was sprinting toward the edge of the forest.

I glanced at him.

"It's a were thing. Trust me."

I felt James move to my side, turning with all of us to look at the trees. "We better get there fast," he said. "I don't think they're going to hold together long."

"I don't blame them." I squinted at the tree line. It was still dark and clear, but I couldn't see much past the lights left on in the Den. The night was silent too—no bugs, no birds, even the wind was nonexistent. The quiet was cut by a chorus of mournful howls. "Any idea how far off they are?"

Ramon was listening and looking just like I had been, but with different results. "A few miles, give or take."

"Okay." Now that I was here I wasn't entirely sure how I could help. The only thing I did know was that I needed to be a few miles away, in thick, dense forest, and I needed to be there ten minutes ago. "Ramon, you go ahead."

He didn't argue. Instead he took off like Sean had and was at the tree line before I could count to five.

"You have a plan, Master?"

"Don't call me that."

James gave me a look that clearly said now was not the time.

"No, I don't have a plan. You got one?" He didn't respond. "Pretty please, with sugar on top?" It was the *please* that did it. Manners appeared to have that effect on James.

He turned to me and gripped my shoulders. His silver eyes flashed in the moonlight as he looked down at me. "Close your eyes and look."

To anyone else, that command might sound contradictory. But I knew what he was talking about. I closed my eyes and opened myself up to the night around me. When I felt centered, I asked, "What am I looking for exactly?"

"Anything big enough to carry your weight."

The Blackthorn land is mostly woods, which makes sense for a people who either turn into wolves or something very close to wolves. With the exception of the Den and a sizable lawn, they keep the area as close to natural as they can. Which means lots of wildlife, which means lots of dead things, whether you like it or not. Needless to say, I wasn't going to run out of things to raise anytime soon, but as for something big enough to carry my slow human self, well, that was another story.

I was about to shake my head when I found what I was looking for. I must have relaxed or made some sort of sound, because James said, "You found something."

Instead of answering, I jumped down the steps and onto the grass. I started searching the ground for a stick, a big rock, anything I could use to draw a circle into the thick turf. What I was raising probably wouldn't hurt me, but with raising the dead, the rule "better safe than sorry" wasn't one you wanted to ignore. James stopped me, thrusting a long silver knife into my view. For a second, in the light of the moon, it looked like Douglas's knife, and I flinched. The blade that almost took my life. The one I used to take Douglas's. I hesitated. James made an agitated sound and shoved it into my hands. I relaxed immediately. It wasn't Douglas's. And since there was a *J* carved into the handle, I guessed it was James's.

"A gift," he said. "Part of a matching set. And I want it back."

"Thanks." The blade cut into the earth easily. James took care of his possessions, and besides I wasn't digging deep. I just needed a circle. As soon as it was done, I stood up and James snatched the knife back. He sliced a small gash into his own arm.

"You're going to need your strength," he said before I could get a word of protest out. He held his arm over the circle and squeezed, forcing his blood to drip down into the earth. There was no more talking after that.

For a necromancer, blood is like money. In any other situation, I might see the humor in that. But what I mean is, it's currency. We use it to get Death to lend us an ear. Or in this case, a ride.

With the blood, I closed my circle and gave a call. Farther off in the field, about three feet underground, I got an answer. And with James's blood paving the way, I let loose my gift. My power reached out, pulling aside dirt and stone, parting it like the Red Sea. Up came the bones, white bleached things that had been there awhile. They didn't stay white long. Flesh slid over them, muscles, sinew, skin. Hair grew, and in less time than it takes to order pizza, I had a full-grown bull elk galloping my way.

If I hadn't known that the elk was my friend, I would have wet my pants. Between Frank's love of *Animal Planet*—or as Brooke likes to call it, the channel where cute things eat other cute things—and my mom's love of nature, I knew a lot about local wildlife. A male Roosevelt elk stands about five feet at the shoulder and about nine feet when you factor in the giant antlers of death attached to its head. On average they weigh around nine hundred pounds, and you don't, under any circumstances, stand quietly as one comes charging at you.

He stopped in front of me and stood, a wall of muscle and elegance. I'd never been this close to one. I touched his nose. If I hadn't just witnessed his resurrection, I would have sworn he was alive. But he wasn't. I kept my hand on his nose and scratched under his chin.

"Hey, Stanley."

James came up behind me, wrapping a strip of gauze around his arm. He'd probably had it in his pocket. He was like one merit badge short of being an Eagle Scout, that's how prepared he always was.

"You named it?"

"Not an it. A he." I gave him another pat. "It's human nature to name things." James glanced at me then, an odd look on his face. "What?"

"Nothing," he said. "You better get going." I nodded assent and had James hoist me up. I'd never been within ten feet of an elk until today, and now I was going to ride one. Sometimes my new life is kind of awesome.

Elk run really fast. That's the only thought I managed while I clung to the huge creature as it whipped through the trees. The fur felt coarse and dirty in my hands as I gripped tightly, branches doing their best to unseat me. I pushed Stanley in the direction of the pack. He didn't want to go, a remnant of his life telling him that he was racing toward not one but many predators. It took lots of soothing words and a bit of a mental push to convince him that the predators would leave him alone. Wolves don't eat dead things.

James flew behind us, now in his dragon form, little more than a shiny blur in the corner of my eye. I didn't dare turn and look at him.

I didn't know what was going on, but just based on Brid's call, I expected the pack to be a mess when I got there. I expected to see them boiling about, a chaos of weltering emotion. And some of them were. Many were openly crying. A few were howling. But all were doing it while they worked.

The pack was building a pyre.

I watched for a moment as Bran, his brutally short hair dripping, his muscles covered in more sweat and dirt, yanked a dead log the size of a pony onto the pyre. He didn't howl. He didn't make a sound, not even a grunt, as he threw the log. But I could see the tears streaming down his face as he worked—as they all worked. I slid down off Stanley's back and walked over to Bran.

He stopped throwing logs as I came closer. One by one, his siblings detached themselves from the mob. Sean had his arm around Brid, offering a comfort and support that was strangely offset by the open fury in his eyes. I don't think I'd ever seen Sean so serious. Sayer and Roarke stood silently behind them all. Sayer, I'm told, takes after their mother. Darker-haired and gray-eyed, he was quiet, despite his name. His twin, Roarke, favored Brannoc. Brown eyes, brown hair, and at first I made the mistake I think most make—I thought the twins were more like Bran than Sean and Brid. Serious. But then they'd hung out with Sean and me one night, and I realized quickly that I was wrong. They may not say much, and they may not be loud, but I think the twins are the ones responsible for their younger siblings' sense of humor and genial disposition.

Oddly enough, it was Bran who hugged me first. He wasn't a demonstrative man to people who weren't family. But he squeezed and said, "Thank you for coming," before setting me back on my feet.

I gave him the awkward man-pat and said, "Of course."

I tried to shake the twins' hands but they pulled me in for rough hugs too. Sean didn't even let me make the gesture of a handshake. He was also uncharacteristically silent. Brid tried to speak. She really tried. But she ended up having to shake her head as tears filled her eyes. Then she threw her arms around my neck, crushing me. I held her—I'm not sure how long. She buried her face in my neck and breathed. I felt the wetness of her tears, but she gave no other sign that she was crying. I'd never seen Brid try to restrain emotion before.

She pulled away and sniffed. "Sam." She choked on my name and had to start over. Pulling herself up straight, she looked me in the eye. Any trace of her crying was gone. "Samhain Corvus LaCroix: Brannoc, my father and former *taoiseach* of the Blackthorn pack, has granted you the status of friend. You have performed bravely for us and eaten many times at our table. We hope that this status will continue and only grow in strength."

I wasn't sure what I'd expected Brid to say, but the sudden formality was shocking. And one word stuck out. *Former.* As in no more. The phone call, the pyre, everything suddenly clicked into place. Brannoc was gone. My gut lurched, and I wished more than anything that I could leave. My heart hurt. And I thought about how I kept losing the people who were important to me and how much that sucked. But all these thoughts were selfish, and that was not the kind of person I wanted to be. That was not the kind of person the pack needed.

As for Brid's speech, I wasn't sure the entire pack would agree with her sentiment. Many of them did not want to see our friendship grow in strength, and they'd pay cash money to never see me eat at their table again. In fact, a good portion would have liked to see me facedown in a ditch. I glanced at James. He nodded slowly. Okay. Apparently that was all I was getting information-wise for the moment.

"Of course," I said. "Whatever you need."

Brid leaned in and kissed me solemnly on the cheek. When

she leaned back, her face was a mask. "What we need is answers, and we'd like you to help us get them. The pack and I would be eternally grateful." I nodded, and she took my hand, leading me past the pyre and into the trees. Stanley, James, and Brid's siblings followed. It made for a very strange procession.

We came to a smaller clearing lit by a few hastily made torches. As I got closer, I saw why. They didn't want to leave the body of their father, their leader, in the darkness. I let go of Brid's hand and walked forward. Brannoc did not look peaceful. His body lay sprawled on the grass. I could tell from the blood and the way he was lying that he'd died facedown. He'd crawled a few feet on his belly and then the life left him. Someone had turned him over after that. James came up behind me. Stanley tried to follow, but I sent him to the outer circle to wait.

"He was a good leader," James said.

"He was a good man," I said. The torchlight flickered over the body. That's how I had to think about it—the body. If it wasn't a person, maybe it wouldn't hurt as much. Yeah, right. I dropped my voice, though Brid's family was distracted enough that they probably weren't listening. "What's going on, James?"

"How do you mean?" he whispered.

"The sudden formality back there, the stuff Brid said. I feel like I'm missing something."

James knelt closer to the body, and I followed suit. "When aren't you missing something?"

"Not the time, James."

"Sorry, Master."

He sounded almost contrite, so I let it go. "I know you understand things better than me. Please."

He looked out past the tree line. "They didn't just lose their father, they lost their leader."

"I got that."

"Don't interrupt."

"Sorry."

He kept going. "Like so many things, you get the immediate problem, but not its implications. Brannoc is dead. The pack has a new leader. Your lady friend is the new *taoiseach*. That means any diplomatic tie, any pledge to the former clan chief, has to be renewed. She's the new head honcho, and things are going to change. Lots of things." He rocked back on his heels. "I imagine the werewolves will be a bit distracted for a while." He said the last almost to himself.

"Oh." I got the feeling I still wasn't fully getting it. But whatever it was would have to wait. "What exactly do they want me to do?"

James stood up. "What do you think?" He handed me his knife again, handle first. "At least try and act like you know what you're doing. You're making me look bad. If you insist on tarnishing my reputation like this, no one will want me after the pack turns you into bloody confetti."

I took the knife.

I drew a circle around Brannoc's body, trying not to look too closely at it. I didn't want to see. But of course, when you don't want to look at something, that's exactly when your eyes betray you. He had dirt in his hair. I don't know why I noticed that, but for some reason, it deeply offended me. I brushed it away. It was wrong for him to be like this. This wasn't the way people like Brannoc should die. I closed my eyes for a moment, choking on the anger and the sorrow. I wouldn't be able to work like this, and the pack desperately needed me to. So I did what I learned to do when my stepfather, Haden, died. I shoved it away into a dark corner of myself. Not gone—it would never be gone—but out of the way so I could function. So I could do what I needed to do. I didn't have the luxury of mourning right now.

There was still plenty of blood in the circle. It was damn near a fresh death, but I still added a little of my own to re-activate it. Blood dripped down my arm and splashed onto the ground, covering the dark stain of Brannoc's own. I felt the result immediately. I didn't even have a chance to close my eyes. I was just suddenly . . . somewhere else.

No, that wasn't right. I was in the same clearing, but now it was empty. The torches, Brid and her family, James, all of them had vanished. Even Stanley was gone. I was in an empty dark forest alone. I looked up. The moon was in a different position. Huh.

"Ash?" I called out for her, my voice floating out over the clearing. No response. I tried again, this time putting some will into it. "Ashley!" Usually she pops right into existence, but this felt a lot like the time Haley and I had made taffy at home and we'd had to keep pulling it. Sticky and tough, yet I couldn't quite get a handle. Finally Ashley shimmered in, like a slow dissolve.

She blinked a few times, surprise fluttering across her

features while she looked around. "Where the hell did you bring me, Sam?"

"Funny, I was going to ask you the same thing."

"Honestly, I have no idea, but wherever we are, it practically reeks of magic." She wrinkled her nose.

"Pretty, isn't it?"

I jumped up about ten feet.

We both turned, and that was when I saw that we weren't alone in the clearing, after all. There was a woman in a long dress about ten feet away from me. Her red hair trickled loose past her waist, white flowers and vines weaving in and out of it. The flowers opened, wilted, crumpled, and then bloomed again, the cycle repeating as I watched. It was dizzying. I shivered.

She walked toward me, and try as I might, I couldn't move a muscle. I had the strangest urge to drop to my knees. Not a compulsion, really, but something told me it would be a good idea. So I did it. The soil under my knees felt cold, and a pebble was digging into my shin, but I stayed with my head down until I could see her feet. She was barefoot.

"That is very sweet, but somewhat unnecessary." Her rich voice held a note of laughter in it.

Still, she sounded pleased. The gesture was worth it, then.

"Stand, Samhain Corvus LaCroix, stand before you catch your death. Besides, I refuse to spend the evening addressing the crown of your head."

When I got up, she was seated on a log by a crackling fire and Ashley was looking at me rather strangely, but she had curtsied when she'd seen me drop to my knees.

There were a lot of things I was still adjusting to, and sudden magic was one of them. "Neat trick," I said, nodding at the fire.

"Thank you." She patted part of the log next to her. I sat down, tilted slightly in her direction. She took my chin in her hands and examined my face for a few long moments, lingering mostly on my eyes. I'd gotten used to this kind of thing. I relaxed and let her do whatever she had to do, enjoying the fire in the meantime. Finally, she patted my cheek. "You'll do fine."

"Thanks?"

She pulled off her mantle and settled it about my shoulders. It felt like velvet, thick and soft, warm as if it had been sitting in the sun. I pulled it around me and felt not just warmth, but comfort. While that mantle was wrapped around me, I felt my chest loosen. Everything tight and terrible left my heart and took a breather.

The flower lady turned a smile on Ashley, who had taken a seat across from us and was currently scowling in our direction.

"Your loyalty does you credit, little Harbinger, but rest assured that I mean your ward no harm."

"Uh-huh. Well, I'll remain skeptical if it's all the same to you."

"As you wish," the woman replied, her smile gaining an amused twist.

I hadn't felt this good in a long time. Settling in, I stared at the fire and my surroundings, waiting for her to ask for what she wanted. There was always something.

The flowers in her hair bloomed, died, and bloomed again before she spoke. It was kind of cool.

"You are wondering, perhaps, why I am here instead of Brannoc?"

"The thought had crossed my mind." More precisely, I had been wondering what had gone wrong. I didn't have the best control, and sometimes my magic did odd things.

"His death," she said, "was traumatic. And I would prefer he rested. I have a certain interest in this particular family line. How would you put it? We go way back?"

"All death is traumatic." I'd seen a few deaths in my life, and I'd yet to see anyone go smiling.

"I can see how you might believe that, but it's not true."

I pulled the mantle tighter. Seattle nights can be chilly, even in the summer, but wherever we were, it was much colder. "Traumatic or not, his family deserves to know what happened. They're counting on me for information. Some help."

"I know."

"You're going to send me back with nothing, aren't you?"

She blew on the fire, and the flames climbed, grew, and crackled, responding to her whim in an unnatural way, like they wanted to please her. "Nothing, no. Just not what you came here for. I'm sure his family would love to see him, just as I'm sure they'd love answers, but I must consider what is best for all my children, so I'm stepping in, whether the pack wishes it or not. Brannoc is one of mine, and I *will* protect him from further hurt. That is all you need to know for now."

"Even if your interference keeps us from finding the killer?"

"Even then. I am not saying that I am beyond vengeance, Samhain. But I am patient, and that can wait. The victim comes first, not the killer."

I wanted to argue, but I caught a look from Ashley just then. She was shaking her head ever so slightly, her eyes now more speculative than skeptical. I got the message. No talking back to the flower lady.

She was going to take back her mantle soon too, I just knew it. I sighed, pulling the fabric up over my cold nose. "What am I supposed to tell them?"

"Tell them his soul is resting, that you cannot help them in this way."

"So, what you're saying is that I'm useless." I should have felt angry or upset, but nothing seemed to shake the peace I was feeling. Creepy, yes. But I knew my zenlike feeling would end soon and I would be right back in the muck of things.

"That depends. Is this all you have to offer?"

"I don't think my ability to burp the alphabet would be helpful right now."

She blinked at me and tilted her head. "Can you really do that?"

"Just to *R*."

She laughed then, an endless, sunny peal. At least, I wished it had been endless. True beauty always seems short-lived. Ugliness just keeps on going. She leaned forward and kissed me on the forehead. "Yes, you'll do fine."

"I'm glad you think so."

"Faith is important, Samhain, and I have an abundance of

it. You will find a way to help them, I am sure of it." She leaned back, pulling the mantle with her. "In fact, I am counting on it. And you're going to need that faith. There is a darkness out there, a sickness. I don't know what it is, but it's reaching out to you." She patted my cheek, looking worried. "Be careful." Then I was cold again, standing heartbroken in a field, a concerned Ashley by my side. We were surrounded by the pack. They looked pissed. I could still feel the warm press of the woman's lips on my forehead.

Have you ever looked up and realized an entire crowd has gone quiet and everyone is staring right at you? I felt like I'd walked into a church naked—it was that awkward. Brid stepped away from her brothers. She reached out and gave me a little shove. "You're back." She didn't wait for me to answer. "And you smell weird."

"So you keep telling me." I hiccuped.

"No, you smell like . . . flowers."

I sniffed my jacket. I did smell like flowers.

James slid up behind me. "Where on earth did you go?" He ripped my jacket out of my hands. "And stop sniffing your jacket. It's unseemly."

"Who are you—Miss Manners?" I was going to say something more, something amazingly witty, but instead I had to run to the bushes and be noisily sick. As I retched, I could see Ashley anxiously talking to James, her hands fluttering around her. Being that he was James, he patiently listened to her while leading her closer to where I was doing my best to relive every meal I'd ever had.

As they got closer, I could hear James cursing under his

breath. He only used bad words when he was really pissed. Once I was done communing with nature, he grabbed my chin and tipped my head toward the torchlight. He peeled back my eyelids and examined my pupils. I don't think he liked what he saw, because he kept his frowny face on.

"What in Hecate's name happened to you?"

I tried to answer him, I really did, but Ashley glared and shook her head, making a zip-lips motion at the both of us. James grabbed me by my collar and slapped me. Not a light tap, either. My cheek stung in the cold.

"Ow."

"Master, this is important. What happened to you?"

Ashley pinched him. "Now isn't the time for that conversation." I think James was too surprised to actually react.

I stared back at him. I couldn't even shake my head in frustration—there was nothing there. It was like a part of me was drunk or dipped in Novocain. I was having a hard time understanding and reacting to things. A different part of me was noting it and trying to fix the problem, but it wasn't getting anywhere.

Brid came up behind James, who looked like he was about to shake me.

"My father?"

Her eyes were hurt and raw—I so badly wanted to help her. Even if I couldn't really feel it right now, I knew it. "I can't . . . his soul needs rest." What an amazingly shitty and lame thing to say to her.

She closed her eyes in defeat, a tear escaping and cutting down her cheek. "I see." Brid turned and walked away.

The pack followed her, either shooting me nasty, accusing glares, or not looking at me at all. Some of them were arguing and not doing anything to hide the fact. I heard words like *trust* and *incompetent* being thrown about pretty liberally, and none of what they were saying sounded complimentary. New leader, new slate, all I'd done seemingly gone in their minds. I watched them go.

The brothers were last. Bran picked up his father's body and carried it back to the pyre, Sayer and Roarke flanking him. Sean stopped to place a gentle hand on my shoulder. He shook his head at me. "Maybe now isn't the best time for you to be here. The pack . . ." He didn't finish the sentence, just shook his head again and turned away from me, following the path his siblings had set.

James didn't want to stay for the whole funeral, and not just because of Sean's warning. Something was wrong with me, and he didn't like it. Ashley was hovering like an agitated mother hen, complete with hand-wringing.

"I didn't know you cared." I hiccuped again, my stomach churning.

"I don't," James said. "But it would reflect poorly on me if you died while in my charge. Besides, I don't want you to vomit on my shoes."

I slapped him on the back. "There's the James I've come to know and love."

Despite James's well-stated reasoning, I ignored his demands. Whether I was in the pack's favor right now or not, I was staying. Brannoc had been a good friend to me, a mentor since I became, well, me. The least I could do was watch. The body burned, and the pack howled. I was still strangely numb. At some point, I reached into my jacket and found a flower. A morning glory, its twisted vine holding on to the inside of the jacket's lining, the white flower open and full. I slowly walked up to the fire and tossed it in. I said good-bye to Brannoc Blackthorn. After that, I finally let Ramon and James escort me back to the car, a worried Ashley bringing up the rear. I didn't even know I was crying until James wiped my face with a handkerchief.

Then I threw up on his shoes.

10

SOUL DOUBT

James had to drive, since I was having a hard time doing complex things like walking and not vomiting. Ramon wasn't in great shape, either—as we passed under streetlights, I could see the muscles in his face twitching. Judging by the looks James kept throwing him, I think Ramon was struggling to keep from changing.

I closed my eyes to try and block out the spinning that had started once I got in the car, and I must have fallen asleep at some point, because the next thing I knew, Ramon was carrying me. I was surprised to see we were at my mom's house.

"This is so romantic, Ramon. You're like my Latino Romeo."

"Keep it up, and I'll give you something to vomit about."

James was in such a rush, he almost disregarded the path and tried to walk right through my mom's garden.

Ashley grabbed the back of his coat, yanking him to a stop. "You better not, unless you want a less-than-helpful reception."

James replied with a nod of his head and followed the twisting path to the front door. He knocked once sharply, then held his arms behind his back, looking for all the world like he'd just stopped by for a polite chat.

Haley cracked the door open as far as the chain would let her. That was new—we'd never had a chain before. She cocked an eyebrow about my in-Ramon's-arms status but said nothing as she slid the chain and opened the door, revealing her pajamas. Skimpy pajamas.

"You should get a robe," I said. "Don't you think so, James?" He stood there, hands now clenched, his posture stiff. "James?"

He straightened suddenly, coming back to himself.

"Yes," he said. "And a better lock." Then he pushed Ramon and me through the door. In one motion, he slipped off his own jacket and slid it over Haley's shoulders. "I'm sorry to intrude this late, but we need your mother's services quite badly." As if summoned, my mom came out of the kitchen. She was also in her pajamas, her strawberry-blond braid swinging. She paused a moment, taking us all in. Frowning, she ushered us to the kitchen table.

Ramon dumped me at the table while James and Ashley had a whispered conference with my mother. My sister plopped down across from me. Amusement shone in her gray eyes as she pulled her black hair back into a ponytail. Physically speaking, Haley and I look a little like night and day. She takes after her dad, Haden. So while she's a bit taller than my mom, and we all share the same pale skin and freckles, Haley is definitely a LaCroix, dark hair and all. I, unfortunately, take after my biological father. My hair is somewhere between brown and blond, and my build is scrawny. I have my mom's baby blues, though, which is nice. Still, I'm not going to win any beauty contests. Haley might, if they didn't disgust her.

She snapped her fingers in front of my face. "Earth to big bro."

I mumbled some kind of a response, but I'm not sure if actual words came out.

"What the hell is wrong with you?" She leaned back, annoyed.

I shrugged. "Anything in the fridge? I'm starving."

Haley was staring at me now. "Sam, it's like four in the morning."

"So?" When she didn't answer, I got irritated and mentally called for Brooke. If anyone would listen to me and possibly get me a sandwich, it was her.

She appeared with a grin and her clipboard, but quickly lost the grin. "What's wrong with him?" she whispered to Ramon and Haley.

"Don't know," Haley said, but Ramon just gave her a one-shoulder shrug, the muscles in his jaw still working.

"Are you okay?" Brooke asked. When he shook his head, she patted his back soothingly. "I bet Mrs. LaCroix wouldn't mind if you took a few laps around the backyard and burned off some . . . energy."

Ramon nodded, and Brooke escorted him out; the twitching had now gone into the muscles in his arms. His fingers jerked.

I knew this should provoke a response in me. My friend was obviously having problems. But all that came out of my mouth was, "Man, I was hoping she'd make me a sandwich or something." Well, if you want something done . . . I started to get up.

Haley shoved me back down. "Yeah, not that I want to set a

precedent or anything, but I think I'll get it for you, lest you drink drain cleaner by mistake."

"Okeydokey."

The trio in the corner ended their conference. My mom's face was drawn, her eyes stormy with worry as James escorted her to us.

Ashley made it about two steps toward me before her BlackBerry buzzed. She cursed when she saw the screen. "I gotta go," she said to James. "Keep an eye on him, and I'll check in when I can." And with that, she opened up a vortex and disappeared, apparently in too much of a hurry to wait for the sparrows that usually accompanied her when she left. Maybe she was going to meet them halfway.

My mom slid past me and headed to the stove. The look she shot me was calm and reassuring, all trace of her worry gone, but I knew that if I got up right now and touched her, I'd feel the truth if I really wanted. An overwhelming wave of emotion would crash over me, so it's no wonder that I stayed where I was. "She's worried," I whispered to the table. I knew why, of course, but the details to things kept slipping away from me, like I was trying to grab an otter with oily hands.

Not that I'm into that sort of thing.

James settled gracefully into his seat. "Yes."

He, apparently, didn't feel like talking, so I spent the next few minutes staring out the window, looking away from my reflection only when Haley brought me a snack: cheese, crackers, fruit.

"Sis, you're an angel."

"You're welcome." She placed a similar plate in front of James. "I figured you might need a snack too."

He stared at the plate, making no move to eat anything. Haley frowned at him. "Look, if you don't want it—"

"No." The word came out too loud, and I stopped mid-chew to stare at him. My sister's frown became more of a scowl. "I'm just not . . . my sincerest apologies for my lack of manners. Thank you. This looks lovely."

Mollified, she took a seat. "You're welcome. If there's something wrong with my choices—"

"No, please. As I said, lovely, especially at this hour, and after we barged in unexpected." He quickly bit into a strawberry to prove it to her. And then another. "I think these are the best strawberries I have ever tasted."

"Why, thank you, James," my mother said from over by the stove. "I grow them myself. With Haley's help, of course."

"If I may be so bold, I would love to get either your or Haley's advice with our own garden. The gnomes aren't much help, and I'm having a bit of a problem with—"

I snorted and shoved a cracker in my mouth. James glared at me, eyes narrow, the silver becoming flinty.

"Ooooh, scary," I said, taking another bite. "You got some brown on your nose, by the way."

Haley stifled a giggle and, when it was obvious James didn't understand, leaned over, whispering something in his ear. I could tell when he got it, because his eyes narrowed even more.

"What?" I tossed a strawberry in my mouth. They really were good. Logically, I knew it was bad to make James angry. I'd seen how fast he could move. For some reason, though, I didn't seem to care. It didn't matter, anyway. James calmed down once Haley shook her head at him and patted his arm.

Whatever. I was more concerned about my plate, which had just been whisked away. "Hey, I was eating that."

Mom smacked the back of my head lightly and placed a mug in front of me. "Drink."

Since I was actually pretty thirsty, I did. The tea tasted weird. Sort of a burny, cinnamony, grassy taste. I pushed it away. James pushed it back.

"Either you drink it or I will pour it down your throat. Your choice, of course. I would like to add that I'm pretty sure your mother owns a funnel."

"Yeah, yeah," I mumbled, but I did what he said. Maybe if I kept drinking it, it would get better. It didn't. The more I drank, the more an unpleasant aftertaste of dirt surfaced. By the end, I was kind of sleepy. I pushed the mug away and laid my head down on the wood table.

I closed my eyes. Just for a minute.

The sun was streaming through the window and right into my face. I turned my head, but it was still bright. It felt like my brain was wounded and trying to bash its way out of my skull, and my mouth was dry and somewhat gamy tasting. All in all, an unpleasant start to the day.

"Good morning, twinkle toes."

I grunted into the couch cushion. "Morning, Mrs. W." The energetic, steely-haired Mrs. W used to be my neighbor. She was feisty, and wiry, and loud. She was also a witch and a friend of my mother's originally sent to spy on me. I didn't hold it against her, but this morning her chipper tone was certainly grating on my nerves. It seemed like she was conspiring with the sun to make me feel worse.

"Get up. You've got more tea to drink."

Ramon, who was curled up on the other couch, added, "And I'm supposed to remind you that your mother owns a funnel." He mumbled the words directly into the cushions.

I groaned and tried to burrow deeper into the couch.

Mrs. W yanked on the back of my hoodie and pulled me onto the floor. Then she nudged me with her foot. "I believe I said get up." Not an ounce of sympathy.

"I believe you did." I rolled onto my side, feeling my stomach roll at the same time. I scrambled to my feet and ran to the bathroom, barely making it. I heaved for a while, but I didn't have much in me. I knew better than to leave the bathroom just yet, though. I wasn't much of a drinker, but I'd been hungover before, and it felt a lot like this, only whatever was wrong with me was much, much worse. When my stomach didn't cramp again, I got up, my legs shaking and my muscles weak, and wobbled into the kitchen.

Mrs. W had a hot, stinking mug of tea ready for me. Generally, I like tea. Just not this stuff. I knew better than to say anything. I sipped at it while Mrs. W and Ramon drank their wonderful, delicious coffee. Those jerks.

"Once you've finished that, I'll take you home."

"Where is everybody?"

She leaned against the counter facing me. "Work, library, and before he 'took his leave' earlier, James mumbled something about having a house to run." Mrs. W shifted uncomfortably, and I knew there was something she was avoiding.

Before I could ask, Ramon said, "You better just show him—he's going to want to know."

I pushed my hand through my hair. "Right, the door. I want to see how bad it was."

With a nod, Mrs. W walked briskly out of the kitchen, and I—rather slowly and gingerly, like I'd been made out of blown glass—wobbled after her. Our journey ended at Haley's door. You could tell it was Haley's because she'd done a sort of collage on it with pictures she'd cut out of magazines. Mohawked rockstars and guys with a lot of eyeliner stared back at me, along with clippings from art mags and a small poster of the Dresden Dolls, which had probably been a full-spread article in its first incarnation. Here and there were blank spots where Haley had painted things—mostly vines, plants, and symbols. It was chaotic and beautiful.

At about eye level, she'd painted her name, but in that spot was now a ragged hole. The collage around it had been cleared, I could tell, the sudden empty spot looking cold and naked. I traced the hole with my finger.

When she'd said the door, I'd assumed the front door. Not her bedroom door. That made a world of difference. That frigid creep of fear was tiptoeing up my spine again. "Why didn't she tell me it was her door?" I asked. "Someone broke in—was a few fucking feet from my baby sister—why the hell didn't she tell me?" My blood, which had started to crystallize from the fear, heated up again—a boil of anger. Had I been a cartoon character, I think the resulting effect would have been steam shooting out of my ears.

"What would you have done, Sam?" Mrs. W said kindly. "It's not like an ordinary burglar broke in—we don't know how they managed it. We're not simply talking deadbolts here—this place is warded. But somehow they managed to sneak past all the wards and any mundane security. Without making so much as a peep or scratching a lock. Professional."

"That explains the chain lock," I said. A feeling of icy dread settled in my gut. Someone had been in my mother's house. A stranger had walked right up to my sister's door like it was nothing. "I would've sent some protection at least—maybe had James come over and assess the place. I mean, my house is pretty secure, and he set that up." I turned away from the door. I had to stop looking at the hole. I kept picturing Haley instead of the door. "What kind of knife was it?"

"A dagger of some sort. You'll have to ask Haley for details—I'm not sure where they put it."

Ramon, looking uneasy, said, "I can smell blood."

Mrs. W grimaced. "Yes, they wrote something on the door—Haley wouldn't tell me what." She glanced at me. "They were trying to keep it from you, but, well, I didn't think more secrets would do us any good."

"I see." My family was good with secrets, that was for sure. Mom had kept my necromancy a secret until Douglas had shown up. I wasn't a big fan of keeping things from my family because that seemed to only cause more problems, but I had no doubt that Mrs. W would have happily kept this from me if she thought it was a good idea.

As I followed Mrs. W back to the kitchen, I tried not to dwell on Haley's door. But someone had come after my baby sister. I felt the sharp pang of fear again. Later. I'd deal with it later. I didn't have all the facts anyway, and it would be better to come at the problem when my brain wasn't trying to wither and die and my stomach had returned to a more sedentary position. But I was sending James over, that was for sure. A chain lock was not enough by a long shot.

My head throbbed, and for a brief second, I thought I might see the return of my tea. "Can I have something for my headache?"

"You can have more tea."

"Thank you, but I'd rather have the headache." Resting my forehead against the table, I contemplated the floor for a while.

"I have yoga in an hour, kiddo, and if you think I'm going to miss the instructor's iron buns as he goes into downward dog, you are sorely mistaken. Let's pick up the pace."

Ramon shuddered over his coffee. "That's so wrong."

Mrs. W smacked the back of his head with the palm of her hand. "One does not wear spandex while waggling one's buns in front of a crowd without expecting some amount of ogling. It's human nature."

"It's objectification."

"No, it's appreciation. I'm not mentally turning him into a mindless fleshpot. He's a nice boy with a sweet disposition. It just so happens that I also admire his ass."

I groaned. "Can we stop talking about asses, please? How can you be a night owl and a morning person, anyway? It's disgusting and unnatural."

"I eat right, exercise, and every afternoon I do a shot of whisky before a twenty-minute power nap. Does the body wonders."

I lifted my head up enough to see if she was being serious. She was. "You must have been unstoppable in your youth."

"I still am. Now, drink."

Ignoring the whining and general complaining my body was dishing out, I sat up and drank. Between sips, I managed to not only keep the liquid down but to also ask Mrs. W why my body was acting like I'd beer-bonged a whole case of cheap beer. Until I talked with Ashley and found out why she'd done the "quiet, you," gesture, I kept my visitation to myself.

"That is a very good question. We're not sure. We can guess. You met up with something very powerful last night, that we're sure of. But whatever the cause, the effect is the same."

"A hangover?"

Mrs. W looked thoughtful. "Sort of, yes, but I'd liken it more to a spiritual hangover. It's like the thing you met was so full of magic and energy and all-around mojo that it over-whelmed you."

"So I was . . . soul drunk?"

She considered it before nodding. "About as good as any way to put it."

I downed the rest of my tea, gagging over the dregs. "This happen a lot?"

Mrs. W dumped the last of her coffee into the sink. "In my entire life, I've seen it happen once. An older man went into the woods to get in touch with Mother Nature."

"What happened to him?" Ramon asked, washing their

mugs and putting them in the drainer so my mom wouldn't come home to a mess. Ramon's been my friend for a long time, and my mom trained him well.

"When he didn't come back on time, we went looking for him. I found him in the water happily getting hypothermia, half drowned because he thought the glacial river was 'pretty.'"

"Ah."

"You ready to go?"

I nodded, then washed my mug in silence, almost dropping it twice. I was still shaking. Mrs. W removed it from my hands and gently placed it in the dish drainer. Then she herded us toward her car.

Whatever benefits I'd gotten from the tea were erased by the drive. I think Mrs. W had a secret ambition to be a stunt driver. Car rides from her always left me a little woozy, and even the mention makes Ramon downright pale. Right now, his eyes were closed and his hand had gone white-knuckled and clawlike from clutching his seat belt.

My house was at the end of a rather bumpy gravel road, and I'd never been so happy to see it. I leaned on my own car briefly to regain a little of myself. Something didn't feel right, and it took me a minute to figure out why. All my tires had been slashed. Great. And I had no idea who had done it. Oh, I had *some* idea. I looked at the Roman guys on the pediment, the Minotaur on the lawn, the gnomes suspiciously pointed away from me. Could be any of them. I would deal with it later. That was becoming a mantra of mine.

James was seated at the table reading the paper when I walked in. "I've already called a tow service. That thing needs a tune-up anyway. In the meantime, you'll just have to cope with the injustice of driving one of our other cars. A hardship, I know."

"Not now, James." My bed was sounding really, really good.

"Going to your room to mope, while wholly in character, is not the optimal choice at the moment."

"Yeah, well . . ." I walked off, leaving the sentence unfinished, a move sure to tick off James. I didn't care. Everyone else seemed pissed at me, so why not just add him to the list?

I threw myself onto my bed, letting my muscles relax, taking in the quiet. Wait a minute. I rolled to my feet. My bed was wet. Sniffing the comforter, I picked up the all-too-familiar smell of urine. Which was now on my shirt. After last night, I probably needed a wardrobe change anyway, but that wasn't the point. Fuming, I pulled on fresh shorts and a T-shirt, tossing the offending clothes into the hamper. As I did, I noticed something else. My room had been TP'd, and there was a scratching noise coming from the cabinet. Cautiously, I went to open it. A striped skunk darted by with a tiny—and I think drunken—garden gnome riding on its back and yelling "yippee-ki-yay!" as it went out the door.

I stood there, clenching and unclenching my fists, trying to decide what to do. Right.

I pulled the comforter off the bed and walked outside. I wasn't quiet about it. James, back in kitty form, came trotting after me, asking what was wrong. I ignored him, throwing the piss-stained comforter down on the grass.

The yard was quiet. None of the statues moved, no one looked my way, but that didn't mean they weren't listening.

"House meeting, right fucking now!" I crossed my arms and waited. Nothing. "James," I said quietly.

"Yes, Master?"

"I want a sledgehammer and a Dumpster."

A curt flick of the tail and then he morphed, pulling out his phone when he was done. And suddenly, but not surprisingly, my lawn came to life. The statues busted free in a cloud of dust, the gnomes slunk over from the flower bed, and the little gladiator guys slid down from their pediment. While I was glaring, Frank pulled up. He didn't say a word, just parked the car and quietly slipped into the crowd. Ramon rested his skateboard against the half-pipe and jogged over, an interested look on his face. They formed a semicircle around me.

"Sit," I said, pointing at the ground. They all sat. "I want to make something very clear, so I need you all to listen. This includes the shrubbery." I swear the bushes dipped a little in embarrassment. "Now, I've tried to be good-natured about everything, accepting all the harassment as well-meant hazing." I started ticking things off on my fingers. "The tires, short-sheeting my bed, taking staged incriminating photos of me in my sleep, and so on. Have to test the new guy, I get it. But I've had enough." I glared at them all, catching every eye until they knew I meant business.

"Like it or not, I own this house now. Like it or not, you guys are my responsibility. I've tried to be understanding, but apparently that just isn't cutting it." The Minotaur scuffed at the grass with his hoof. The gladiators from the pediment were also looking at their toes. Only the gnomes appeared defiant. "I know you guys had a lot of change this year. You've lost . . ."

I wasn't sure what Douglas was to all of them. A tyrant? A boss? A dear friend? I had a hard time picturing him in positive or glowing terms. Still, as with James, he might have been all they knew. And say what you will about Douglas, he apparently managed to run this household smoothly, something I was certainly having trouble doing.

I felt a grudging respect for Douglas in managing it, and some sympathy for my criminal housemates who had admittedly had their worlds turned upside down as well.

When you don't have much, you hold on like hell to the things you do have, even if they're rotten. That goes doubly for family, even if your family is Douglas. "You lost someone important to you. I am sorry for that. But this"—I motioned to the comforter—"has got to stop."

The group was silent, and I could tell my speech wasn't working. My anger was dissipating now, and more than anything, I just wanted to get the situation back in hand. I looked down at the gnomes. "You guys." At my address, they all leapt to their feet, puffed up their chests, and held their pickaxes, shovels, and hoes at the ready. One of them had a tiny lute. I didn't know they had a minstrel. Weird. I shook my head. "No, I don't want to fight. You have a leader, yeah?" The gnomes formed a huddle. After a few minutes of whispering and covert glances in my direction, they finally pushed forth a spokesman. He stuck his shovel defiantly in the ground, then took off his little red hat and held it in both hands.

"You have a name?"

"Twinkle."

"Twinkle," I said slowly.

"The Destroyer," he added.

"Your name is Twinkle the Destroyer?"

He nodded.

"Of course it is. Why wouldn't it be? Okay, Twinkle the Destroyer, I take it you guys have been popping my tires? Causing general mayhem?"

He nodded proudly. "Yes, though the Minotaur was conscripted for tire duty. He handled it with the soul of a warrior." He beamed at the Minotaur, who was managing to not make full eye contact with me. "We even set his pants on fire yesterday." He pointed at Frank, who shrugged sheepishly.

"You had a lot going on," he said. "I didn't want to add."

I turned my attention back to Twinkle. "You set my friend's pants on fire?"

"Yes. Death to the infidels!" The rest of the gnomes erupted into a cheer, brandishing their assorted lawn equipment with glee.

"Right," I said, pinching the bridge of my nose in frustration and praying for patience. "You know that means nonbeliever, right? So what are you accusing me of not believing in?"

Another pointy-hatted huddle. Twinkle came back to the forefront and shouted, "Death to the new guys and their non-jam-delivering policies!" They proceeded to high-five one another.

I leaned over toward James—back as a cat now and sitting on the porch railing—and whispered, "Non-jam-delivering policies?"

James flicked his whiskers in what I think was amusement, most likely aimed at me. "Douglas used to have me give them regular payments of jam, root beer, et cetera, to buy their loyalty."

"And you didn't tell me this because . . . ?"

"You didn't ask."

Touché. "You practically run the place, why didn't you do it?"

James sniffed in what I thought was a very haughty manner, his tiny pink nose stuck in the air. "I run the house, not the rabble. Do you expect me to do everything? My schedule is already filled to bursting with all the new people moving in, the extra shopping—"

I cut him off before he could work himself into a tizzy. I had a feeling that, had I been Douglas, he would have been doing all this without question. Maybe he was trying to get out of extra work, maybe I was too soft, but either way, the response was the same. "I guess not." I rubbed my hand over my face and considered. Essentially, the whole time I'd been here, the security staff hadn't been paid. I would have been harassing the management too, though I probably would have started with a discussion and not so much jumping straight to peeing on someone's bed. You have to work up to that sort of thing. Still, I had essentially staged a hostile takeover, which did kind of explain why they'd been going on the offensive. I didn't have time for this. I scanned the crowd and landed on . . .

"Frank." He got up from his seat on the lawn and came over. "I want you to get your clipboard and come back out. Quickly, please." After Brooke had received her new spectral-style clipboard, she'd insisted I get some for the house. It was easier to comply than argue with her, so I'd had to take her shopping at one of those big warehouses full of office supplies. I'd never seen anyone get so excited over Post-its and packs of highlighters.

Once Frank returned, I grabbed him by the shoulders and pulled him in front of me. "Okay, most of you know Frank already, but I'd like to reintroduce him as the head of human resources." I got a lot of blank stares. One of the little gladiators used his sword to scratch his head.

"This means that Frank will be your go-to guy. He'll oversee your problems, make sure you get paid—whatever you need, Frank will handle it." This announcement started a lot of chatter. I pushed Frank closer to the rabble. "He will sort this out." I gave him a quick pat on his shoulders. "Frank, sort this out."

To his credit, he stepped forward bravely, armed only with a pen and a clipboard, and said, "Now, what kind of jam do you prefer?"

I slipped inside the house.

11

EVEN HITLER HAD A GIRLFRIEND

While I shuffled aimlessly through the kitchen, Ramon made a beeline for the fridge and set to work eating his way through what appeared to be an entire roast chicken before I was even able to collapse into the chair across from him.

"You look tired," he said.

"That's because I am tired." I rubbed a hand over my face.

"Then take a nap." He placed a bone onto the platter and reached for a drumstick.

Sleep had become a treasured commodity to me the last few months. I'd been short on it before—I went to college briefly—but that wasn't quite the same thing. There's a difference between missing a few hours to finish a paper or cram for a midterm and losing sleep because someone is trying to kill you and your loved ones. Or losing sleep because you were kidnapped and stuck in a cage. And now I had a new nightmare to add to my list—a silver dagger buried in my little sister's door. At the rate I was going, I might as well stop sleeping altogether.

Recently, I'd also been losing sleep because of nightmares and the simple fact that the things that go bump in the night liked to come by and shoot the breeze on occasion. It's lonely being a ghost. My family aside—my estranged uncle Nick and two baby half-sisters were all part of team zombie— necromancers were rare. That meant the ghosties and ghoulies had few people to sit down and have a nice chat with. And from the sound of it, I was part of the tiny minority who weren't complete tools. So my sleep time was becoming more and more interrupted, unless I remembered to keep my medicine bag on constantly. Sometimes, though, that seemed like a cop-out. Lots of the spirits just wanted to talk or ask me to look in on their families or whatever, and so sometimes I left it off on purpose. I wouldn't want to go through any sort of afterlife without having someone to chat with. Brooke had been talking to me about setting up a regular time for spirits to stop by, sort of like office hours for a professor, but in nicer digs.

"Nap time would be awesome," I said to Ramon, "but I have to figure out what happened to Brannoc, who's threatening my sister, and probably five other things I haven't even thought of." I grimaced. "And I need to burn my sheets."

Ramon wiped his greasy fingertips on a napkin. "And if you don't rest your brain, you won't be any good at any of it. I know you, Sammy. You'll keep going until you collapse. An hour either way won't matter. Haley's out and about, and your mom is at her shop. They're safe. Go sleep, and I promise I'll wake you."

"And if I say no?"

Ramon snorted. "If I have to, I will pick you up and put you to bed myself. Before you try and argue, remember that I could juggle you now if I wanted to."

I sighed and got up. "Bullies, I'm surrounded by bullies. Fine, an hour," I said. "But that's it."

"An hour, and you can sleep in my bed. No one's pissed on my comforter, I'm positive." The implication being that no one would dare. Ramon chuckled evilly and went back to his chicken. I crawled into his monster-sized bed and considered how much my friends had changed and how it was all my fault.

True to his word, Ramon woke me in an hour. "Brid's here," he said, and then he left. I was groggy, but I felt a lot better than I had earlier. I crawled out of bed and went to go see my girl.

The sun was bright. It filtered in through the large pines, dappling the grass in the lawn. When I walked out, Brid was sitting on the newly installed porch swing, looking out at the scene before her, a thin layer of amusement perched over her otherwise sad face. And no wonder. The statue nymphs were lounging on the grass, weaving flowers into the Minotaur's hair. They giggled and braided while the large beast snored. The gladiators were playing Frisbee with a stone discus from the pediment, and the gnomes were conspicuously absent. Frank sat on the porch steps, his clipboard in his lap, a satisfied look on his face.

Even though Brid was smiling, I could see circles under her eyes and a slight pallor to her skin. I was not new to the signs of mourning. I took her hand, squeezing it to let her know that I understood what that kind of loss felt like. I'm not sure if that's what she got out of it—maybe she just got the part about the hand squeeze. But even that was better than nothing. I led her away from the house, figuring she could use some quiet time and privacy.

We took a walk down to the water. The coastal line of my property didn't have a beach as you might imagine it. No, it had more of a jagged-rocks-and-pebble-ridden-strips-of-land thing going on. I didn't mind. I loved the water, and I was still amazed and grateful that I got to live so close to it.

Brid and I took a seat on one of the bigger and less jagged of the boulders. The sun reflected brightly off the water, but a large pine tree hung over where we were sitting, creating a nice bit of shade. All in all, it was pretty perfect.

"This is nice," Brid said, getting comfortable. A sliver of sunlight cut across her tank top and shoulder, and I traced it with my finger.

"What's bothering you?" I asked. "I mean, besides your dad. Obviously I know what's bothering you on that front." Brid's level of preoccupation told me her sad demeanor wasn't due only to her father's death.

She popped her sunglasses up on top of her head so I could see her eyes and notice how her rueful smile didn't quite reach them. "I'm that transparent, huh?"

"Not usually," I said, "but sometimes I can figure you out."

She leaned in and brushed my hair out of my eyes. I needed to get it cut soon, but then again, if I did that, she couldn't brush it out of my eyes. Maybe that comes off as mushy, but I don't care. I will stoop to mushiness if it means I get to hang out with girls half as awesome as Brid, so there.

"We have to stop seeing each other."

Some statements come from so far out of left field that they poleax you. This was one of those statements.

"I'm sorry, but I think I misheard you. Did you just break up with me?"

"Not really, I mean, it's not like we were actually boyfriend-girlfriend, right?"

It was like snakes had shot out of her ears and she'd started drooling cotton candy. Who was this person?

"Yes, I guess I do think of you as my girlfriend."

She looked uncomfortable now. "Well, I mean, we never discussed it. You know, officially."

"Were you seeing anyone else?"

"No."

"And we were going out on dates and whatnot? Hanging out all the time?"

"Yes." Brid was practically squirming now.

"And it was you I was sleeping with? Not some evil doppel-ganger?"

She nodded glumly.

"Okay, so maybe I didn't pin you or buy you a 'Sam's property' T-shirt, but unless I completely misunderstand how things work, that kind of means you're my girlfriend." I was having a hard time keeping the anger out of my voice.

"You're right, I'm sorry." She picked up a fragment of shell and examined it. "I guess I thought this would be easier if I downplayed what we had."

"If by easier you meant to have me question every moment we've spent together, then yes, that's much easier." I was biting off words now, sarcastic and intended to hurt. It wouldn't alter anything, and it wouldn't endear me to her and make her change her mind, but sometimes you can't help saying stupid things. "Why?" I asked.

She had tears in her eyes now, and she was shaking her head. Brid wasn't one of those girls who turned into a faucet at the slightest provocation. So when she cried, you knew she was really upset. I was kind of glad, since I didn't want to be the only one hurting here, but it wasn't fun to watch her cry, either.

"I just can't do this right now."

Okay. What did that mean? "Am I taking up too much of your time? Is it because of your dad? Do you just need some space or something?"

She rubbed one of her eyes with the heel of her hand. "No, it's just—" She waffled for a minute, thinking. "You know how my parents had to get married? Because it was a good choice for the pack? I mean, it worked out great because they loved each other, but it was still a gamble."

"We need to get married?" I wasn't really following where she was going, and I was smacked upside the head with the realization that, should she prefer it, I would marry Brid without a second thought. That shook me to the core. I was too young. We were too young. Marriages at our age don't generally last. All the commonsense arguments, arguments I usually believed, began to stack up in an instant.

But.

I would ignore them if that was what she needed. Why? Because I was ridiculous for this girl, it was as simple as that.

Willing-to-crawl-through-broken-glass-clucking-like-a-chicken level of ridiculous.

"No," she said with a laugh. "What I'm trying to say is that sometimes I have to make choices with the pack in mind and not myself."

"And the pack wants to eat my face."

"Sam, do you know why we burn our dead?"

I shook my head. I knew precious little about her pack, even though I'd been trying so hard to learn. It seemed like, no matter what, I was always going to be behind the learning curve.

"Because of . . . your kind." It was hard for her to say it. Probably almost as hard as it was for me to hear it.

"Ex–fry cooks?" Lame joke, but I needed something to buffer what was going on. I got a little half smile for my trouble.

"Can you imagine what someone with your powers could do if they got ahold of one of us?"

Unfortunately, I could.

"So we build pyres and burn our dead—we have for centuries. Hundreds of years, Sam. You can't just overcome that kind of thing overnight, you know?" She tossed the shell fragment into the waves. "For the most part, they're coming around, but I can't push them right now. And like it or not, you're, you know, you. The pack had a hard enough time accepting my father, and fey hounds are a lot closer to werewolves than you are."

Oh, joy. Nothing like being discriminated against for something you can't change. "Like you said, they'll come around, right? Can't we just lay low until then?" There was a pathetic wheedling tone to my question.

"Maybe they will, but I don't know. It's hard to argue with them and tell them necromancers aren't evil after . . . what Douglas did to me." She swiped at her cheek. "I just took over, and I don't have the clout to rock the boat yet, Sam. The pack still needs stability. My father did a great job pulling it together, but the work's not all done yet. That's why Bran stepped down, and it's why I have to do this now."

I brushed my thumb along the lifeline on her palm. "What does Bran have to do with it?"

She made a face. "You've never wondered why he's not *taoiseach* instead of me?"

I shrugged. I'd always figured either her father had a good reason or it was some mystical werewolf crap I didn't know about.

"Bran and I, we're pretty evenly matched. In fact, he's got a bit more experience just because he's older, but, well, he's never hidden his preferences from the pack."

Preferences? It finally clicked. "Bran's gay?"

"You really didn't know?"

I shook my head. "Is your pack that homophobic?"

"They would have accepted him as *taoiseach*, no problem. He'd be a good leader, but he wouldn't produce any heirs, and that would invite trouble."

"You'd have another dynastic squabble. I get it." I was still tracing her lifeline, doing my best to avoid her eyes.

"Bran chose to step down because he cared about the pack." She lifted my chin with her other hand. Hazel eyes searched mine, and my heart broke. I understood her logic, but I'd be damned if I liked it. "I can't sacrifice any less than he has."

"You're worried that if we kept dating, it would cause the same kind of problem."

"Anyone I date right now, the pack will have to seriously consider. And you're powerful, yes, but I have to think about offspring. At some point, I have to provide an appropriate heir. Please don't see that as me being baby crazy or anything like that."

I smiled at her to let her know that wasn't how I saw her. I understood. I hated it, but I understood. "Any children we would have could end up like me." And if Brid and her siblings caused an uproar, I could only imagine what fey-were-necromancer children would do. Talk about diversity.

I pulled her to me, her back against my chest, my chin on her shoulder, her hands on mine as my arms went around her. "I love you. You know that, right?"

"You realize that saying that at this moment makes you a sadistic asshole, right?"

"Indeed I do."

"You're such a jerk," she said, but she pulled me closer when she said it.

We didn't talk much after that. I think too much had been said already. So we watched the waves crash, and the sun move, and held on to each other, knowing we might not get to do it again. Brid stayed until her legs fell asleep. Then she got up to leave.

I would have stayed until my legs fell off and the vultures came.

Despite the heart-deadening pain of it, I walked her to her car. "For the record, even though I understand your logic and want to make this easier on you, I think this is completely stupid." I opened her door for her. "For the record."

She hugged me good-bye, one of those long, painful squeezes of farewell.

"And in the spirit of honesty, I think it's only fair to let you know that I'm going to do my best to thwart your plan."

"I know," she said. Then she kissed me and left. I watched her drive away, moving only long after her taillights disappeared.

I'm not sure when Frank, Ramon, and Brooke joined me. All of a sudden, they were just there. I have the best damn friends in the world.

Brooke suddenly attached herself to my back, her arms wrapping around me. "Cuddle shark!" she yelled, snuggling in closer to me. I laughed, a broken sound that hurt coming out. I covered her arms with one of mine and squeezed back.

"Cuddle shark?"

"Yes," she said. "Very dangerous. You might, in fact, need to get a bigger boat." Then Ramon started humming the theme from *Jaws*.

"I love you guys," I said.

12

NO MORE MR. NICE GUY

Douglas shook. How long had it been since he'd felt something like this? A mixture of relief and elation so strong his whole body quaked with it? Not since his teens, surely. He twisted the key, popping the lock and stumbling into the room of his bungalow. Over the years, he'd purchased a few safe houses, places to lie low, should he need to. He'd just never needed them before.

The room was spotless, thanks to a cleaning service, but no amount of dusting and vacuuming can cover the smell a house gains when no one lives there. Musty like a decaying shell, that was what it reminded him of, that was what was left in a house without life to fill it up. And now with him staying here, he wondered if that would change. Would his half-life suffice?

Giddy, he turned the locks and rested his head against the door. It had been so easy. Too easy? No, those were just idle doubts. Sneaky things, plaguing him since he'd woken up. He'd never had them before Sam, and he didn't want them now.

He ordered Minion to start the fire, which the wooden-faced zombie did without too many mistakes. Douglas stood by the fireplace until the flames licked the edges of the wood, biting the smaller pieces first. Once it was big enough, he slipped off his bloody jacket and tossed it in. Slowly, he unbuttoned his shirt and did the same. After those were gone, he tossed in his pants, socks, and underwear. Blood might not be on them, but better safe than sorry. The last thing he needed was to smell like Brannoc. It was easier to burn away any chance of scent than to risk it. When everything was burned down to ash, he took a long shower. He cleaned every little bit of skin, scrubbed it until he was sure the blood was all gone. Once he was dry, he put on a fresh suit. It was like nothing had ever happened.

A good suit is like that sometimes.

The fire had died down and Minion had fallen asleep curled up on the rug. Douglas kicked the man awake and sent him to do a perimeter check, even though it was unlikely anyone had tracked him here, or even knew he was around at all. Mostly, he wanted time to himself.

He found a few scraps of unburned cloth around the edges of the coals. He pushed them back in and built the fire up. That done, he settled into a musty chair and played the evening back in his head.

How many nights had he waited for Brannoc to walk the grounds alone? Tonight he'd gone out and . . . what? Sensed that something was off? Animals a little too quiet? Douglas wasn't sure what had raised the fey's suspicions, but the result was the same. Brannoc had gone out to investigate. And Douglas had made just the right snap of twig, just enough rustle of branches, until the man had followed him to the clearing. The best part about being dead? He had no scent.

The coin had granted him a solid form, but it lacked that particular detail. It had freaked James out at first. That's the thing about creatures that rely on their superior sense of smell—trick the nose, and they're no longer superior.

Despite his nervousness, Douglas had drawn it out. Watching from the shadows as Brannoc stood in the middle of the moonlit grass twisting and turning, trying to figure out what was amiss. It must have driven him crazy, knowing something was wrong, hearing the very forest cry out against it, but not being able to understand.

Brannoc had never relaxed or let down his guard. No, not him. In the end, though, it didn't matter. Douglas had stepped from the shadows and sliced his throat before he could even blink an eye. It had all happened so fast. So much buildup and then suddenly it was over. Almost anticlimactic, really.

He'd stood over the corpse then, watched as the blood drained out. He was careful not to step into Brannoc's line of sight, tempting as it was. After all, what's the point of winning if you can't tell the loser who beat him? No glory. But caution won out. Douglas knew that death might not keep Brannoc from talking. He knew that better than anyone.

He cleaned his knife while he waited. It was weird. Brannoc had always seemed invincible. So big in the mind's eye. It must be much like the day when a child turns around to see that his parents, the people who towered over him for years, are really just . . . people. Weak and frail, and not as tall as he remembered. That's how Douglas thought it might be, anyway. He'd never had that opportunity. He hadn't seen his parents since they'd handed him over to his aunt.

But when it came down to it, Brannoc was still flesh and blood. And fey. Douglas had held up his knife. Cold iron—just a fancy way of saying iron that had been forged and purified away from its usual raw state. Faeries hated it. Ironically, if he'd stabbed any of the actual weres in the Blackthorn pack, they would have been able to heal it. One of the advantages of being a werewolf, he supposed.

Once he'd been sure that Brannoc was dead, he'd walked away. Slowly and quietly picking his way through the forest. No need to hurry, really. But he had to move before the temptation to wait, to stay and see the pack mourn their loss, overtook him. He had trekked the two miles back to his car—his shoes would be absolutely ruined—before he heard the first howl. First one, then many more. It covered the small sounds of his car as he slipped in and let Minion drive it back to the cabin. He was glad he had a getaway driver. The adrenaline coursing through his veins would have made it difficult to concentrate on the road.

Douglas threw another log on the fire, using the poker to prod the flames to greater heights. He'd sift through the ashes in the morning to make sure nothing was left. He'd have to dispose of the shoes some other way. Bury them? Throw them in the ocean? Give them to a drifter or a hobo? He would bag them and decide after a good night's rest.

For now, it was time to celebrate. Douglas grabbed his keys and went out in search of a good time.

13

SUMMERTIME, AND THE LIVING IS EASY

I was hungry, but my stomach was still kind of wobbly, whether from my magical overdose or from my meeting with Brid, I wasn't sure—not that it really mattered. The cause didn't change the effect. So I chewed on an apple as Frank went over everything he'd learned from the rabble. Brooke seemed to be taking her own notes, and Ramon appeared to not be listening at all as he leaned back in his chair. Or at least I started chewing on an apple. It wasn't long before James came in and began clattering around and putting more stuff in front of me: pita bread, veggies, and some sort of white dip. I sniffed the dip experimentally.

"What's this?"

"That is a Tuscan white bean dip." He didn't look at me when he answered, but continued to do his graceful kitchen dance. A glass of water and a glass of ginger ale appeared in front of me as well. Then a multivitamin.

"Am I both thirsty and in need of supplements?"

He continued to clatter and clang. "You've suffered a lot of stress and a major episode of . . . something. The ginger ale will help your stomach. Plus, you're still a growing boy, or so I'm told."

James was taller than me. The jerk.

"And you're still dehydrated—"

"How do you know that?" Frank asked.

James reached over and pinched my skin.

"Hey!"

He ignored me. "See how the skin isn't snapping back and the color is a little off?"

Frank stared at my arm and nodded. Then he took his turn pinching me. The skin stayed tepeed up for a few seconds, then slowly went back. I smacked his hand as he reached to do it again.

James sat down and snagged a carrot. "Basically, you have a metaphysical hangover. You need rest, which you've managed a bit of, and vitamins and water, and you haven't been getting enough protein, so I made the dip." He nudged it closer to me. "Eat."

"'Kay," I said eyeing James warily. He wasn't usually this nice to me. Was he actually starting to like me, or was he slipping arsenic into my dip? I slid the dish closer to him. "I bet it's good with carrots."

He raised an eyebrow at me, but didn't go for the dip. I might as well eat it. If I boycotted things because James might be poisoning me, I'd die of starvation. Besides, I had enough people actively trying to hurt me. I saw no need to add to the list out of paranoia. That didn't stop me from making Ramon smell it, just to be safe. There's not being paranoid, and then there's just being stupid.

I motioned at Frank's clipboard with a chunk of pita bread. "Gimme the skinny."

"Well, nothing they're asking for is too crazy. Basic needs stuff. Though they asked for access to some TV time, a communal computer so they can e-mail—"

"Gnomes e-mail?" Ramon sounded both amused and skeptical.

"Yeah, but I think the computer request was mostly from the Minotaur. The gladiators just wanted to use it to check hockey scores and stuff."

"Anyone else think it's funny that what Frank just said didn't seem weird at all?" Ramon asked.

Brooke rested her chin in her hands. "Nothing seems weird to me anymore." Ramon reached over and hugged her to him, kissing her cheek. She gave a little half smile and leaned into it.

"I was too busy trying to figure out why the gladiators wanted to check hockey scores, which just goes to show you how skewed my sense of strange has become," I said.

Frank shrugged, not looking up from the clipboard. "They're Canadian."

I swallowed my vitamin as quickly as possible, grimacing from the aftertaste. "But they're gladiators. Wouldn't that make them Roman or Greek or something?"

"I asked them the same thing. I guess the marble they're carved from comes from Canada. You can kind of tell if you talk to them long enough. They say 'eh' a lot. They don't seem to have spent much time in their homeland, so I think they are basing most of their culture on stereotypes."

"Maybe we should hold a Canada party or something," I said. "Like a little cultural festival. Then we should hold one for the gnomes, because they just boggle me entirely."

Frank snickered. "No kidding. Did you check out their names?" He pushed the clipboard over to me. Frank had methodically written down everyone's name and personal info and plugged it into a neat and tidy grid. Twinkle the Destroyer wasn't alone, it seemed. There were more gnomes than I thought. Pip the Bringer of Pain, Chauncey the Devourer of Souls, Cuddly the Inexplicable, Gnoman Polanski, Pith the Bitey, Gnome ChompSky, Gnomie Malone, Chuck the Norriser—the list went on.

"It's like a mishmash of violent imagery, TV, and political references."

"I told you, they like TV. I'm not sure they understand everything they see, though, so they don't fully grasp what they're stealing their names from. Like, I think Gnome ChompSky just thought it sounded tough, and Chuck the Norriser came from watching too many episodes of *Walker, Texas Ranger*. They believe Chuck Norris is a demigod."

"Who doesn't?" I asked. "Are they born with those names, or are they more like titles?" I had a sudden image of a baby gnome with "the Destroyer" on its birth certificate.

"No, they start off with Twinkle and Pip and whatever, and the other stuff is added on after their first battle." Frank scrunched up his face in thought. "It might be easier to just picture the gnomes as tiny little barbarians. From our preliminary discussions, they appear to be a warrior race. Battle glory, that's their number one. Makes them a bit bloodthirsty, actually."

I nodded slowly. "So they get titles bestowed on them once they prove their courage in battle. Hence the tough-guy names?"

"Yup. They tend to do the naming ceremonies upon puberty, so if there isn't a battle, they manufacture some sort of competition. They were a little hazy on the details there, but if the young gnome proves himself, he's awarded a new name and a hat."

Ramon laughed and tipped his chair back from the table. "Good thing they didn't watch too much daytime TV. You might have ended up with a slew of bloodthirsty gnomes named after talk show hosts and characters from daytime soaps."

I snorted and kept reading. "Okay, one of them wants to be referred to as 'The Darkness Known as Mittens.'"

"That's awesome," Ramon said. "We should all change our names too. From now on, I will only answer to Ramon the Invincible."

"More like Ramon the Assjack." I frowned at the clipboard. "Hey, some of them have normal names. Like Chad. And Stacy."

"Yeah, I asked about that. Apparently, Chad is new, so he hasn't had the 'opportunity to be tested in combat,' as he said."

"What about Stacy?"

"He said girls are scary."

My head was beginning to hurt. I handed the clipboard back to Frank. "Whatever. Just handle it—give them what they need. You know, within reason."

Frank nodded, but I could tell there was something else.

"Spit it out, Frank."

"It's just, well, they mentioned something you might want to take a look at."

I was instantly suspicious. "Like what? Am I going to get a jar full of Ebola virus or something?"

Frank shook his head. "I don't think so, but they weren't giving me much in the way of information. They just said you needed to check out the downstairs guest bathroom and it wasn't their fault."

"Well, that doesn't sound ominous at all, does it?" I got up with a sigh. Frank and Ramon followed, Frank out of duty, Ramon out of curiosity. Brooke skipped after us, ignoring all sense of decorum and foreboding, because she does what she wants, and right now that was skipping like a loon.

The guest bathroom was the one I'd had to use when I was first brought into the house as a hostage, so I tended not to use it. Ever. It had that clean, cold feeling that all guest bathrooms seem to have. I wasn't sure what I'd been expecting when I'd opened the door, but I was greeted—somewhat anti-climactically—by an empty bathroom.

I shuffled in and shot a look at Frank. "Okay, I checked it out. Are there any other random—" A soft scratching noise came from under the sink, where James kept the spare cleaning rags. I hushed everyone and leaned down to open the cabinet door. The memory of a gnome riding a skunk came to mind, and I moved so that I would be behind the door when I opened it.

There was a loud creak as I swung the door open, then a startled hissing noise as a creature the size of a ring-tailed lemur sprang forth and straight at Frank. The thing took Frank down to the ground, more out of his own surprise and horror than its physical force. Without thinking, I snatched it up by the scruff of its neck and yanked it back.

While it hung from my grip, twisting and growling, I was

able to get a better look. It didn't weigh a whole lot, maybe about as much as the average house cat, and it was reptilian in nature. Developed hind legs explained its ability to hurtle itself at Frank, and it had huge eyes, sharp fangs, and a rather feline face. Its arms had a flap of skin that looked like something a flying squirrel might have. Imagine if a lizard and a cat had a baby and then that baby married a bat and had another baby—you might get some idea of what I was looking at.

Pronounced canines jutted from its mouth, and the creature was trying to use them to take a bite out of me. I shook it gently. "Cut that out. We're not going to hurt you."

Yellow cat eyes focused on me as the beast appeared to be thinking over what I'd said.

"Okay," I said. "Good. Now I'm going to set you on the counter, all right? And we're going to get to know each other a little better. Sound good?"

Its head tilted in a curious manner, and its eyes darted between the three of us. I gently set it down on the counter and then backed away, giving it some space. Though it was feisty and obviously full of energy, now that I was able to get a good look at it, I could tell it wasn't well. Its coloring, a dusky brown with stripes in greens and blacks, had a dull appearance. The soft gray underbelly looked scratched, and I could see its ribs.

"Are you hungry, little guy?" I asked.

The reaction was immediate. He perked up, his giant ears swiveling forward and his nostrils flaring.

I leaned closer to my friends. "I'm not really sure what to feed him. Any ideas as to what he is?"

Ramon shook his head, but Frank looked thoughtful. "I'm not sure, but my guess is he's related to the chupacabra family. He looks pretty close to the drawings in one of the books I've been reading, anyway." He leaned in to get a closer look, but stayed outside the reach of the tiny thing's claws. "He should be bigger, though. Maybe he's a juvenile?"

I blinked at him. "You think I have a teenage goat sucker in my bathroom?"

"That would be a good name for a band," Ramon said. "Tonight, all the way from Wisconsin, it's Teenage Goat Sucker!"

Brooke snickered. Frank chewed his lip and ignored them. "Maybe? I have to look it up again."

"We have a problem, then," Ramon said. "In that he is a hungry goat sucker and we don't have any goats."

I smiled at the creature, making sure I didn't bare any teeth—some animals see that as a challenge. "We'll have to ask James where he got goats and stuff for Douglas's sacrifices. In the meantime, we can see if he'll eat something we have in the fridge."

We skipped the fruit bowl and the veggie bin because, based on folklore and his pointy teeth, I was pretty sure our new friend was a carnivore. After giving him a few bites of beef jerky, I was able to coax him out to the table, which is where James found us. Well, I say found, but it was more like James walked in and the chupacabra treed him. To be fair, James didn't know we had a new carnivorous buddy, and the chupacabra didn't know that this particular kitty was our friend. It was hungry, and James looked like lunch. He quickly morphed to human with very little prompting from me.

"What the hell is that?" James yipped, still crouched on the counter.

"According to Frank's research, it's a pygmy chupacabra." I tossed it a piece of Ramon's rotisserie chicken.

James watched as it snatched the chicken out of the air with its jaws, then bounced, eyes bright and fingers steepled, waiting for the next bite.

"I wasn't aware they came this far north." He clambered down from the countertop slowly so as not to spook the chupacabra.

I tossed some more chicken. "We don't think they do. Either he was accidentally transported up here with some livestock or something, like how a lot of nonindigenous animals end up where they shouldn't, or Douglas ordered him."

James negated that idea. "I would have known. He didn't want them around."

"Why wouldn't he want one?" Brooke asked. "It's so adorable."

He frowned. "Something about it being disruptive." He shook his head. "All I know is that chupacabras were certainly on the banned list. They're pretty useful, though. He'll keep the pests down, at least."

"He really likes beef jerky," Brooke said.

Ramon shrugged. "Everyone likes beef jerky. Even *Sam* likes beef jerky, he just won't admit it.

I wiped my greasy fingers on a napkin before tearing another big piece of chicken off the leg bone.

"Well, Douglas isn't here now, which means the ban doesn't apply anymore, so can we keep it?" Frank asked, throwing

James some serious puppy-dog eyes. Brooke joined him, batting her eyelashes and balling her fists up by her chin. They both looked pretty pathetic.

I expected James to say no outright, but he didn't respond right away. He eyed the creature thoughtfully and watched him eat.

"That might not be a bad idea, actually." He reached to grab a piece of the chicken to toss, but the creature's eyes narrowed as he growled at James, his ears flattening against his skull. James's eyebrows shot up in surprise as he leaned back quickly, his arms raised in surrender. "As you can see, they are fiercely loyal and highly intelligent. He could probably live off the local wildlife, but maybe we should get him some food of his own so the neighborhood cats don't start disappearing."

"Pygmy goats!" Brooke clapped her hands. Then her face fell. "No, pygmy goats are cute. I can't stand it when things get all Animal Planet."

"Guinea pigs might be more his size," Frank said. "Or chickens."

James gave him a flat look. "No, I'm going to get him food twice his size. I'm so glad you brought it up—otherwise, I never would have figured it out."

"Play nice," I said, cutting them off before a fight could erupt.

"I think I will name him Precious," Brooke said, "because he's so freaking cute! We can call him Preshie for short."

I could see Brooke already imagining the little guy in sweaters and Halloween costumes.

"Shouldn't we call him something like Paco or Taco or Juan?" Frank asked.

"Why?" Ramon crossed his arms. "Because he's from Mexico? Isn't that kind of racist?"

"Maybe we should just call him Sven," James said. "I like 'Sven.'"

"How is that racist? Besides, how do you know he's from Mexico? Chupacabras have a bigger range than that." Frank mimicked Ramon's crossed arms, a smug look on his face. "Now who's being racist?"

Ramon looked closely at the little guy as he ate. "Maybe he's Jewish. I mean, if Sammy Davis Jr. could convert to Judaism, why not a chupacabra? We should name him Harry Mendelbaum."

I held up my arms in protest. "You're all racist. Now shut up. We'll call him Taco von Precious of Svenenstein. There, everyone happy?"

"Isn't *von* the same thing as *of*?" Frank asked. "Wouldn't that be kind of redundant?"

"You're redundant," I said. "Besides, I'm basing it solely on the fact that it's fun to say, so I'm keeping it."

Ramon sniffed. "Just for all that, I'm calling him Stalin."

"You want to call everything Stalin." I tossed a chicken bone onto the plate. Taco eyed it hopefully, but I wasn't sure if it was good for him or not. "No bones for you yet, my precious."

"If you start baby talking that thing, I'm going to hurl." Ramon, apparently, was completely immune to Taco's preshie charms.

"Quiet, you," I said.

His belly bulging, the chupacabra finally looked sated. A

pink—and slightly forked—tongue came out to lick the remaining chicken grease off his lips. I knelt down to see if he'd let me pick him up, and he skittered up my arm and onto my shoulder. He was, well, I'm not sure if the term is entirely appropriate, but he was purring. More of a hum than anything else, but he was obviously happy.

I took Taco back to the bathroom, making Frank grab him some old blankets and a water dish. He seemed curious at first as to what we were doing, but once he understood, his ears perked up. I coaxed him back under the bathroom sink for now, figuring he'd be more comfortable there, since he was used to it.

"This house is strange," Frank said as I closed the door on the happily curled-up Taco. "Do you think we need to get him a litter box?"

"What, your parents' house didn't have a chupacabra?" I asked. Frank gave me a withering look. I punched him on the shoulder, but in a friendly way. "Hey, beats working at Plumpy's, yeah? They just had rats there."

"Beats living with my parents, too." Frank frowned. "I wonder where he came from. I better ask around. Hey, weren't you supposed to meet Haley today?"

I looked at the clock. "Oh, crap, is that the time? I was supposed to pick her up thirty minutes ago!" I ran and grabbed a car before anyone could say anything. No one had slashed my tires, and the bushes only took a halfhearted swipe at me. Things were beginning to look up.

Haley was seated on a brick half wall, swinging her legs and reading a book when I pulled into the library parking lot.

I hadn't realized how tense I'd been until I saw her. The entire drive I'd been picturing worst-case scenarios, so it was a tremendous relief to see her safe.

She looked a little goth today—dark hair braided on each side of her head, black boots, black and red skirt, skull tank top. I used to think that was the scene she was into. Finally it occurred to me that she was just being Haley. She wore exactly what she wanted to wear, completely incognizant of where those clothes put her on the social spectrum. My sister was one of those rare high school kids who simply didn't care. She didn't need extra definitions to feel whole: cheerleader, jock, punk, whatever. For her, being Haley was enough.

It was pretty obnoxious.

She didn't look up from her book as she opened the door and climbed in. The bookmark hit the page only when she put her seat belt on.

"Nice ride, Latey McLaterson. What happened to your Subaru?"

"I'm a jerk. Jerks are late. And I don't want to talk about it."

She stowed her book and turned in her seat to glare at me. "I could have taken a bus there by now."

I nodded as I turned the car onto the road. "Yes, you could have. But would a bus pay for the flowers we're going to get and buy you an apology coffee?"

Haley relaxed farther into the seat. "You are forgiven, especially if the apology coffee comes with a groveling pastry."

"Of course it does. The two are practically inseparable."

Haley picked out an arrangement that she deemed suitable, and we drove to the cemetery. I've always felt oddly at ease in graveyards, but over the last few months, that feeling of comfort has deepened. Now it's more like the sensation of homecoming. Nothing quite like the knowledge that death welcomes you with open arms to give you the warm and fuzzies.

Haley put the flowers next to Haden's grave, and we sat down on the grass and stretched out a bit in the sun. We didn't always talk. Sometimes we were silent, sometimes we chatted to him, sometimes we just said "hey, Dad," and then chatted amongst ourselves. We felt he didn't care. He was just glad for the company.

Haley and I were silent for a while. It was nice to sit out in the sun and listen to the birds and the bugs and the muffled sounds of the city. It was the best I'd felt all day.

Haley flopped onto her side. "Have you ever wanted to, you know." She wiggled her fingers at the grave.

I plucked a piece of grass and shook my head. "I don't feel ready for that. Besides, it doesn't really seem right, calling him up for no reason. Kind of, I don't know, disrespectful. Does that make any sense?"

"Yeah, it does." She leaned her head in her hand. "I want to picture him happy and content where he is, and I don't want to interrupt it to say something stupid like hello."

I pulled my T-shirt up a little to get a breeze. It was getting on in the day, but still pretty hot. "I miss him. I know that's a stupid thing to say—I mean, of course I miss him—but I wonder if things would be, you know, easier if he was here right now."

Haley nodded. "Do you ever wish he was your actual dad?"

She winced. "Wow, that sounded cruel. I meant in the biological sense."

My sunglasses slid down my nose, and I pushed them back up with one hand before I answered her. "Yeah." I didn't add on that it would be nice to fully belong somewhere. Or that I'd have liked to have had Haden my whole life, not just a handful of years. She knew that. Besides, it seemed selfish. I should be grateful that Haden had come into my life at all.

My sister put her hand into the grass, letting a ladybug crawl up onto her index finger. It sat there, content to be close to her.

"I'm glad he wasn't. I know that sounds selfish and makes me kind of an ass, but if things hadn't happened how they had, you wouldn't be you. You wouldn't be Sam. Sure, you might have looked more like me, and you might have been nice enough, but I like who you are now. I like my weirdo brother who talks to ghosts."

"I'm not sure whether I should say thank you or punch you in the face."

Haley blew on the ladybug, and it took flight. I watched it fly lazily up until I lost it in the glare of the sun.

"You should thank me," she said. "And then you should buy me my apology coffee. I'd like my apology iced and my groveling to have cherry filling."

"As soon as you describe the knife found in your door." I smacked my hand on the ground. "Damn it, Haley, *your* door! You deliberately let me think it wasn't as serious as it is."

Haley cursed. "Mrs. W ratted us out, huh?"

"Yes," I said. "But that's not the point. I thought we all agreed. No more secrets, wasn't that what we said?"

Haley fixed me with a stare. "No, I think that's what you said." She heaved a sigh. "I get why you're pissy, but honestly, it's no big deal. It was probably just my friends pulling a prank. Didn't seem to make sense getting you all worked up over it."

I sat up and tipped my sunglasses onto the top of my head. "You don't really think it was your friends, do you?"

Haley deflated a little. "No, not really. But we can handle it, Sam. There was nothing special about the knife. Just a basic, cheap, plain *athame*. No scrollwork, nothing. It's not a big deal, and it seemed silly getting you involved in it."

I scowled at her. "Uh-huh, and how do you know it's not directed at me?"

"My door, big brother. My name written in blood, not yours." She tossed a clump of grass at me.

"My baby sis, baby sis." I threw the grass back at her. "Fine, what's done is done, but at least let me send James over to check your security or something."

Haley gave in with a shrug. She seemed a lot less worried than I was about the whole thing, but then again, it was Haley. Even if she was as freaked out as I was, she'd never show it.

Iced coffee, on a hot day, can perform miracles. So can talking things out with your little sister, if she is anything like mine. You know, too smart for her own good.

"So," Haley said around a mouthful of Danish. She took a sip of her coffee to wash it down. "What you're saying is that on top of Brannoc being murdered, the pack is a mess, they're seemingly angry with you, Brid dumped you, you've been drugged with magic or something, and there's an insurrection at your house?" She ticked these things off on her fingers. "My, you have been busy. No wonder you were late."

I threw my straw wrapper at her head, which she dodged. "No reminder of transgression after consumption of apology coffee."

She held up her hands. "Fair enough." She gazed thoughtfully out into the café for a few moments. "Well, it sounds like the insurrection has been quelled for now, yes?"

"If by quelled you mean they aren't openly trying to bite my face off, then yes, it has."

"We'll put the strange whacked-out experience you had on the back burner for now as well. Interesting, but maybe not quite so relevant as the rest of it. And I think the pack will calm a bit once they get some sort of answer, so what you really need to do is make headway on the whole Brannoc thing, yeah? And then maybe your girl will take you back?"

"I guess. I mean, I'm no detective or anything, but I feel bad because they do need help and they came to me—"

"And you blew it."

"Hey, now."

Haley held what I refer to as her shushing hand out at me and took a long sip of her coffee, biting the end of her straw in thought. "Don't you know a detective?"

"Yeah, sort of." Detective Dunaway had been assigned to Brooke's murder. Because of which he now knew what I was. It had thrown him a bit, to say the least, but overall, I think he was happy to get an explanation for all the weirdness in her case. Sometimes finding out you're not insane is enough, I guess. I wouldn't classify him as a friend—an ally maybe. He'd threatened to lock me away if he found out that I had anything to do with Brooke's murder, but I don't think that him being angry at her death and his willingness to punish the perpetrators was necessarily a bad thing.

I grimaced. "It's not a bad idea, but I don't think the pack would be too hip on me bringing a human police officer onto their land."

"Well, they probably won't like my other suggestion, either."

"Which is?"

"Bring your Council."

I choked on my coffee. "Oh, man, Haley. They'd like that even less."

"That seems unlikely. Brannoc was Council, wasn't he?"

I wiped my mouth with a tiny café napkin. "Wouldn't it be a bit like showing up with a whole posse instead of just a deputy?"

Haley rolled her eyes. "Not if you play it right. They want to be reassured, and showing that you're bringing in all the big guns to find Brannoc some justice, well, why wouldn't that soothe them? Sam, you need experts on this, and I love you, but—"

"I'm so new I have that new-car smell about me?"

"Yeah. Plus, isn't it, like, their job?"

I opened my mouth to shoot her down, but had to close it. She was right. It was their job. Besides, Brannoc was Council. It would look bad if we did nothing, right?

"You're right."

She snorted. "Don't sound so surprised."

"I'm not." I ran a hand through my hair, feeling the cold damp where my sweat had chilled. Gross. I wiped my hand on my shorts. Haley watched with amusement but said nothing. "But I have no idea how to get ahold of everybody."

"How do you usually?"

"I don't. We have set meeting times, and I just show up. They haven't really called me in for too much yet." I had a feeling they were waiting to see if I could handle it before they did.

"Don't they have a phone tree or something?"

"Haley, that's ridiculous. This isn't the PTA."

She swirled the ice in her cup, a skeptical look on her face. "Fine. Why don't you ask Ashley, then?"

I mumbled at her, then shut my eyes. I tried to not think about how silly I looked and relaxed. Breathing deeply, I let the sound of the café die away. With each breath, I pulled in the quiet and then let it out, taking my anxiety with it. Once I felt calm, I pictured Ashley, right down to the inky ponytails and the gray eyes and the grin she got when she was making fun of me, which was always. Then I pushed that thought out. That's the only way I know how to describe it. That's how it feels, like you put an image into a little boat and shove it out onto the air.

The bells on the door tinkled, and I opened my eyes. Ash, in her usual Catholic schoolgirl attire, slid into an empty seat next to us.

"You rang, Master?"

"Shut up. I get enough of that from James."

She looked at me, then she looked at the empty spot in front of her, then she looked wistfully up at the menu.

I sighed. "Fine, I'll go get you something. Haley, fill her in."

By the time I came back with Ash's drink and scone, Haley was wrapping it up. Ash settled her snack in front of her and put a little paper napkin on her lap. I guess you can be dead and still care about getting crumbs on your skirt. She smoothed out the napkin. "Why don't you just call the phone tree?"

Haley didn't say "I told you so," but she didn't have to—I could see it on her face. I ignored her, of course.

"Fine," I said, "where is it?"

"James probably has it. Call a meeting and ask about your human cop then."

I frowned. "You don't think they'll nix the idea?"

She broke off a piece of her scone, examining it while she thought. "There's no harm in asking. Dunaway hasn't gone running to the papers about you yet, and he might have ideas that we won't." She popped a bit of scone into her mouth. "The Council is full of experts, but none of their expertises are detecting. Maybe you can sell it like that." She broke off another chunk of scone. "If you play it right, it might actually help soothe some of the pack's ruffled . . . well, I was going to say feathers, but maybe I should say fur."

I leaned back in my chair, which wasn't easy in the scrawny wooden thing I was in. "You think?"

She nodded. "It will make it clear that you're trying everything you can think of. That you're putting yourself at risk by revealing to the Council as well as the human authorities a weakness—that you can't do this on your own. It will show that finding out who killed Brannoc is more important."

"Of course it's more important."

"Yeah, but this will show it."

Haley leaned in and held out her hand. "Give me your phone, and I'll call James." I did as she said, watching her walk outside to make the call, thankful that while I seemed really good at getting myself into messes, I appeared equally good at surrounding myself with people who would help me out of them.

I dropped Haley off at home. I couldn't exactly take my little sister to a Council meeting, now, could I? Ashley vamoosed as soon as we'd hit the car, but promised to come back later. For about five minutes, I drove in silence after Haley got out. But the quiet allowed too much time to think about what might go wrong and what already had. I turned up the stereo after that, too loud for ruminations, but not so loud that blood came out of my ears.

The gnomes were watching *Walker, Texas Ranger* when I walked in. They were getting popcorn everywhere, which was going to send James into fits. Frank was with them, though, and monitoring their behavior somewhat, so I didn't say anything. I needed to shower and change. I couldn't go to a meeting in a T-shirt and shorts—it would give James an embolism.

On the way, I stopped by his room to check in. He had curled his long frame into a chair and was clutching a throw pillow to his chest. Oddly enough, he was also watching TV. It looked weird. I guess I'd always assumed that James listened to opera and read classic novels on his breaks. He seemed like that kind of person. I didn't even get a chance to knock before he waved me in without looking in my direction.

I hadn't really spent a lot of time in James's room, but I had noticed that, more often than not, he was human when he was in there. He didn't go into kitty default mode until he left. Maybe it was a comfort thing?

His room was cozier than I had imagined. I think I'd expected antiques and hard Victorian furniture. He did have a four-poster for a bed, but the blankets were broken in and comfortable looking, a patchwork of inviting blues, reds, greens. The room was tidy, but the shelves were full of books, knickknacks, and random odds and ends. The furniture was some kind of warm-looking wood, again looking old and broken in. And though he didn't have any posters, the walls were all painted in mural fashion. Trees around the bed, their branches reaching up onto the ceiling, where a night scene was painted very *Starry Night* style. His room was beautiful and functional, and when I sat on the bed, I realized that I didn't know very much about James.

He didn't say anything right away, so I remained quiet and continued to look. A small framed picture stood on his nightstand. Without thinking I picked it up. What could only be a young James—who else had silver eyes?—stood under the branches of a weeping willow. He didn't look more than twelve, but he was dressed smartly even then, though a trifle out of date. The photo looked like the early versions of color photography I'd seen. Douglas was next to him, a hand resting on the boy's shoulders. Douglas was smiling a little. It was creepy. James wasn't smiling. I guess he'd perfected his somber face at a tender age.

"I set up the meeting. And I ordered your new furniture." He said all this without looking away from the screen. He was damn near mesmerized.

I squinted at the TV. "Um, are you watching *Murder, She Wrote*?"

"I find it to be . . . soothing."

I laughed, turning it into a cough when James turned to glare at me. Pounding my chest, I made an apologetic face. "Sorry, something in my throat."

The glare intensified. "Go ahead, get it out."

I held up my hands in mock surrender. "Nothing from this party."

Ramon sauntered in eating an apple. "Is that what I think it is?"

James sighed and released his pillow. "Do I need to hang a no-trespassing sign on my door?"

Ramon ignored him and sat next to me. "It's cool, I just didn't realize you were an eighty-year-old woman. Hey, that's Tom Selleck! Is this a crossover episode? He looks all *Magnum, P.I.*"

"It is."

"Sweet. My mom loves *Magnum*. She has all the seasons." Ramon stretched out on the bed, and we watched the rest of the episode in silence. At first I think our presence annoyed

James, but eventually he relaxed. I realized that he'd probably never learned how to hang out with a group of people before. Until my hostile takeover, it had been just him and Douglas. And, occasionally, a psychotic werewolf named Michael, and I couldn't really see him appreciating Jessica Fletcher and her exploits. I think Michael's only hobbies had been weightlifting and admiring his "guns." It would be hard for James to adapt to having a legion of people in the house after that.

Once the credits rolled, James morphed back into kitty form while I went over things so I could figure out how his phone calls had gone and how to prepare for the meeting. Surprisingly, Ramon insisted on going with me.

"I don't need to go to the actual meeting, but I want to go with you to the Den afterward." He hesitated, which was unlike him. "I think you could use the extra muscle right now. Your cat here is impressive, but the more the merrier on this one."

"Technically," James said, standing up and arching his back, "I am a *pukis*, not a cat, but I agree."

Ramon threw his apple core into a trash can. "The pack is mass confusion right now, Sammy, and I think we should do what we can to avoid . . . incidents."

"Incidents." I laughed. "What a nice euphemism for 'let's see if we can keep them from ripping off Sam's arm and beating him to death with it.'"

I was hoping they'd argue, that they'd insist I was being overly dramatic. They didn't. Instead, both of them eyed me levelly, and I knew they were thinking exactly that. I ignored the leaden feeling those looks caused in my stomach and got up.

"All right," I said. "That makes sense. Let's dress to impress, then, fellas."

TURN AND FACE THE STRANGE
(CH-CH-CHANGES)

The Tongue & Buckle had just opened up for the early crowd when I walked in. Zeke patted us down, waving us in one by one as he finished. The meeting wasn't due to start yet, so I pulled up a stool at the bar with James and Ramon flanking me. Aengus plopped a stout in front of James before getting requests from Ramon and me. I was just surprised to see James drinking something that wasn't tea or water.

We sat in the quiet of the bar for a few moments. There were only a couple of other patrons, so the murmur of voices was low. I decided to practice a little while I waited. Dropping my head so it looked like I was staring at my coaster, I closed my eyes and let my mind open up. I still wasn't really used to the sensation. It feels kind of like your skull dissolves and your mind flows out over the room—a freaky cerebral version of echolocation. I took in the Tongue & Buckle and the people in it.

"What do you see?" I heard James say softly.

"Magic. Lots of it. And it's . . . old." I wasn't sure how I knew that, but that's how it felt to me. The Tongue & Buckle pulsed with it. The magic had seeped into the very wood.

"The customers?"

"The one by the door, he's human. I can tell by the coloring of, well, his aura, for lack of a better word. The two in the corner . . ." I frowned. I didn't recognize their coloring, but it was different enough for me to know that they weren't human. "I don't know what they are."

I heard the soft *whoosh* of James scenting the air. "Fey of some sort. Not sure which, exactly."

Someone walked in front of me, and whoever it was, I was impressed. "Wow."

A palm slammed down on the wood before me, and my eyes snapped open.

"Cut it out," Aengus said.

"Holy crap, Aengus, what *are* you?" Aengus was the only member of the Council who remained a mystery to me, at least as far as his creepy-crawly status was concerned. I knew he was powerful, of course, but I hadn't had a real grasp of what that meant until now.

"An irritated bartender. Now, mind my customers' privacy, will you?"

My cheeks burned. "Sorry, I didn't mean anything by it."

He just grunted and walked away.

Ramon sniggered. "Great start."

"Shut up." I tried to imagine a day when I was so integrated into my new world that I'd stop making horrible faux pas, but it was a hard day to picture.

"James, when you can, I'd like you to stop by my mom's house and check their security."

He didn't look up, just swished his half-full pint glass in a lazy circle. "Why?"

I explained what had happened as briefly as I could. "I'm just worried about them—and I know how good you are with security. You keep me alive, at any rate." I didn't add that he seemed to like my family a hell of a lot more than he liked me. I was pretty positive he'd protect them based solely on that affection and not so much on my request.

He stopped his swishing to take a long drink, and I swear for a brief moment his face looked mournful. Before I could be certain, the look was gone, and he was back to stone-faced James. "Of course," he said, his voice soft.

No sharp words or verbal jabs. Huh. I considered asking about that, but felt it might be best to just leave a good thing alone.

The other Council members filtered in, but I stayed where I was. There was someone I had to meet first, but before that someone could show up, the last person I wanted to see entered the room. She was also the first person I wanted to see. Ah, the inconsistencies of human emotion. Brid came over and stood near me awkwardly, obviously not sure if she should hug me or just say hi. I nodded at her, suddenly bone weary.

"I didn't expect you here," I said.

Brid shoved her hands into her pockets. She was dressed up for the meeting, charcoal lightweight slacks I'd helped her pick out, the emerald of her tank top making me notice the green flecks in her hazel eyes, even though she had a sort of 1930s paperboy cap on. And of course, combat boots, the better to walk on my heart with, damn it. I wiped my face with one hand.

"Can you at least have the decency to look like crap for a while? I feel like you're making this harder on me than necessary."

Her lips twisted into a soft half smile. "As long as you do the same."

Next to me, James snorted. "Don't think you'll have much of a problem there."

I elbowed him.

Brid leaned in, her eyes closing, her nostrils flaring. When you date a girl who spends a lot of time as a wolf, you get used to being scented. I guess it might be weird for some, but I thought it was kind of cute.

She sighed, her eyes opening. "This is hard," she whispered. "I wasn't ready to see you, I guess." She leaned over, nudging me with her side, brushing up against me, a very wolflike mannerism.

I wrapped one arm around her, pulling her into a sideways hug and planting a quick kiss on her forehead. "Yeah, most people aren't forced to have meetings with their exes only hours after dumping them. But I had to call it. You understand why. Couldn't you squeak out of this one?"

"Maybe," she said, resting her chin on my shoulder. "But it would be easy to let things slip, and even easier for someone to challenge me for my spot if I didn't immediately come in and establish dominance."

She seemed so tired and worn. It was hard to look at her, knowing I couldn't do anything to help. And knowing she wasn't really mine to help anymore. No, that wasn't right. It sucked, don't get me wrong, and I wanted nothing more than to try to talk her into forgetting our whole breakup conversation earlier, but . . . first and foremost, she was my friend. And you help your friends, even if it fucking breaks your heart to do so.

"I'll try to keep it short," I said. Then I sent her on in while I waited for the detective and thought about how much of a pain in the ass it is to be a good person sometimes.

Dunaway was just how I remembered him. Short brown hair, clean jaw, and somehow able to look both good-natured and like someone you wouldn't want to tussle with at the same time. He seemed bigger than he actually was. I wish I could project that much authority, but I just don't have it in me. In fact, I think I actually look smaller than I am.

I got up and shook his hand and smiled. I couldn't help it. For some reason, I liked Dunaway, despite the fact that he'd once threatened to lock me up and toss the key in a lake.

"I'm not a hundred percent sure why I'm here."

My grin turned sheepish. "You might be here on a wasted errand, but I had to try. I'm going to go in there and talk to some people."

"People like you?"

"Sort of. If all goes well, I'll be back out to get you in a moment. If not, I'll buy you a drink for your troubles."

Dunaway shoved his hands into his pockets. How was he wearing jeans in this heat? Then again, I was wearing a suit jacket and slacks. Summer weight, sure, but still not the best for this temperature. It was a little scary how quickly I was getting used to being dressed up all the time. Well, all the time in comparison to before, when it was never.

"I'm not guaranteeing that I'll do . . . whatever it is you think I'll do."

I shrugged. "Fair enough. All I ask is that you keep an open mind."

He agreed, and I pointed him to the empty stool between James and Ramon. I saw the detective shake hands with Ramon and introduce himself to James as I walked into the back. It was amazing how comfortable he looked there.

I'd never addressed the Council before, having only been to a few meetings. I still didn't really feel like I belonged. I was younger than everyone in just about every way possible. You know how occasionally there are ten-year-old geniuses so smart that they jump ahead to college? Imagine that kid's first week on campus, and I think the feeling is pretty similar. Except minus the genius part. I'm more like an idiot savant, really.

We didn't have a podium or anything, but standing in front of everyone made me wish we did so I'd have something to hide behind. No use thinking about it now. I ignored my sweaty hands and tried to address the group with what I hoped sounded a little like confidence.

"Am I correct in assuming that we all know what has happened to Brannoc Blackthorn?"

Everyone nodded to varying degrees, but I gave them a sketch anyway, because they might be missing some key facts. It was hard to do, especially since my eyes kept being drawn to Brid sitting in Brannoc's chair. I tried to just give them the details, black and white, because if I thought about it too much, I'd choke up. We sat in silence after I finished, all of us lost in our own thoughts. Finally, I cleared my throat and shifted nervously. This is where it was going to get tricky.

"I think we can all agree that Brannoc went above and beyond for the Council." I smiled self-consciously. "Even I could tell that, and I'm new."

Kell chuckled, and a few others nodded.

Best get to the hard part. "To that end, I want the pack to know that we're doing everything possible to figure out what happened. I brought someone here today, someone I think can help us. But . . . he's human."

Pello laughed, and I got raised eyebrows from Kell and Ariana. Aengus kept a blank face. I couldn't tell what Ione was thinking—she was hiding behind her hair again.

Kell tapped a finger to his lips in a thoughtful way, then leaned forward slightly. "Explain."

I summoned in Brooke, thinking it might be best if they heard about him from two sources, even if those sources were connected. I told them how Dunaway had handled Brooke's case and how he hadn't tried to destroy me even after he saw Brooke's talking severed head. Brooke went over Dunaway's presence at her "reinterment ceremony" (as she put it) and how he had listened to her carefully, even though it had to have been the first time he'd talked to a reanimated head.

"Look, I know this is a big leap of faith, but he knows about our world already, and he hasn't tried to kill me in my sleep yet or tell any tabloids," I said.

"He could be biding his time." Ariana leaned back in her chair as she said this, all coiled, deadly grace. She was beautiful in an I-can-literally-rip-out-your-still-beating-heart kind of way.

I shook my head. "He strikes me as the type who would face things head-on if he wanted to. I have no doubt that if he thought I really was responsible for Brooke's murder, I'd be in jail by now. He'd find a way." I shoved my hands into my pockets. At least they were thinking about it and not laughing my idea away immediately. "Look, I know this is a big risk, to all of you, but I think he can help, and . . . I let the pack down. They asked for assistance, and I failed—I know that. Please help me do something to set that right."

They talked about it for a while. Kell made some phone calls, apparently checking with sources on Dunaway's character. After about twenty minutes, surprisingly, they let me bring Dunaway in.

The detective walked into the Council room like he met supernatural creatures handing out secret missions every day. I introduced him to everyone, not mentioning what they were. If they wanted to tell him, they could, but for now, first names were enough. Dunaway nodded and half smiled until I was done. Then he grabbed an empty chair and flipped it around so he could be right next to the table. He pulled out a pen and a notebook and said, "Now, how can I help you?" When he noticed a few of them staring at the pad and paper, he gave a rueful half smile. "If I decide not to help, or if you guys change your minds, you can rip up my notes, but it doesn't make sense to not take them and then make everyone repeat themselves later."

The room relaxed visibly, and I suddenly knew that Dunaway would be helping us. For some reason, it made me feel a whole lot better.

15

TAKE IT EASY,
DON'T LET THE SOUND OF YOUR
OWN WHEELS MAKE YOU CRAZY

Brid ran through the forest, the warm evening air burning in her lungs as she jumped over rotting logs and ducked under hanging branches. Nothing like the sharp smell of pine and the angry cawing of crows to remind you that you were alive. And yet Brid felt like she was dead. Oh, she knew she wasn't. Her blood flowed and her breath whistled and her muscles moved, the picture of life and health.

But that wasn't what told her she was still with the world. She had to look inside for that, past her hollow core, beyond that center of nothingness, to her brittle edges. A bundle of nerve endings exposed to the cold, that was what she felt like. Those disconnected nerves, the pain floating, with nothing to filter or transfer it away. And every time she considered this, she remembered it was because her father was dead, and her heart tore all over again. That was how she knew she was alive. Not the sunshine, not the sound of her feet hitting the ground, but the pain.

She should cry, shouldn't she? An image of herself bawling while curled up on her bed emerged in her mind. Yes, that seemed right. Maybe curled around a pillow, clutching it painfully to her chest. That was what grief should be. Not this dead thing.

Was this what it was like? Did her father feel this now, this terrible, empty, static space? She couldn't ask him. Sam had failed her there.

Brid came to a stream. It was hot enough out that she wouldn't mind swimming or wading through it, but she didn't want to slow down. She felt like running. She wanted the earth under her feet, the sound of long grass whispering as she flew by. More than anything, she wanted some part of herself to remember what it was like to move. Not stalled down in negotiations, not stuck handling the grief, and not chasing her tail trying to find her father's murderer. If she ran, at least her body still had motion, even if her brain was mired under responsibility. Brid turned along the stream and followed it deeper into the trees.

Sweat dripped down her back and along her hairline, but she ignored it, wiping it only when it came close to her eyes. She wasn't ready. She had to face that fact. When her dad had made her the next in line, it wasn't meant to happen for years. Instead it had been months. Years—time enough to learn what she was supposed to do and how to handle problems like these. Maybe after her father gracefully stepped down or died from old age. Not like this. Never like this. She could almost hear his voice in her ear. "Things seldom go the way we plan, girl."

But she didn't know what to do! And the pack expected results. They wanted blood, and she had nothing to give them. They had scoured the scene and could find no weapon, no sign of any other person, no smell except of forest and of her father's blood. Nobody had said it out loud yet, but they were all thinking it: it was like a ghost killed him. If there was another explanation, she couldn't think of one.

Which made Sam's performance all the more troubling. If it was a ghost, he should know, right? Ghosts must leave . . . something. She growled in frustration. No one knew. Her father's gentle voice surfaced again: "You've got to give him time, little one. He's new to this, remember?"

That wasn't the point, she wanted to argue. But you couldn't argue with the dead. Unless you were Sam.

How could he have given them nothing? Anger boiled up in that empty place inside her now. The first time she'd counted on Sam in her new role as *taoiseach*, and he'd let her down. It hurt.

The soft crinkle of a leaf gave her brothers away. They flanked her without a word, matching her pace as she flew along the stream. Sayer and Roarke ran a little behind, though the dark-haired Sayer soon pulled up on her left. She had always enjoyed their quiet strength and the way they seemed to be able to communicate more in their silence than most people could with their words. The twins were like a buttress to her, holding her straining self above the darkness.

Sean stayed on her right, but it was strange to see him quiet. Out of the corner of her eye, she watched him as they ran. His mouth held a straight and stubborn line. She didn't realize how much she'd counted on his easy smile over the years until she saw that grim expression on his face. His eyes were dark, and he hadn't shaved. She realized that what was disturbing her most wasn't Sean's lack of levity, but the reflection of herself that she was seeing in him. Her hair might be longer, her features more delicate, but that same determined look of grief was there.

As one, they turned away from the stream and started to head deeper into the forest. She didn't know how long she'd been running or how much longer she would have continued if Bran hadn't stepped out from under one of the bigger pines. She wished she could keep going. Run until she hit the ocean. Then she would lope across the waves until she hit more land or sank trying.

But with Bran came the reminder of responsibility. She had to think beyond herself and past her grief. She was the *taoiseach* now. It was her duty.

Bran started to say something but stopped and shook his head, choosing to pull her into his arms instead. Since he was normally serious, Bran was the only one who didn't seem completely ravaged by the loss of their father. This didn't mean he didn't feel the same way, only that he held his grief tight to him, a solitary pain. Her older brother wasn't very demonstrative, especially for a were. Still, whenever Bran handed out one of these rare offerings, she remembered how comforting they were. An enveloping anchor of warmth, making her feel small and loved, reminding her of soothing moments after skinned knees and heartbreaks. Bran had done his best to fill in for their missing parent when their mother had passed. Now he was going to have to fill in for two. She squeezed him tight. Bran let her get what she needed, and for that she was grateful.

When she finally eased away slightly, he said, "Have you finished your run?"

"Never," she said.

He nodded, understanding. They all did. Wolves were patient creatures for the most part, but they preferred running, given the choice. "The rest of the Council is here."

"I don't know what they're going to find," she murmured. "We looked already."

"We looked as weres. Now they will look with their own eyes. It can't hurt."

Just the idea of seeing Sam again was painful. Earlier had been bad, but this would be worse. She'd have to stand apart from him here. No reassuring herself that he wasn't really gone. With her pack around her, she had to remember she'd said good-bye.

"It can always hurt," she said.

Her brother leaned back and arched his eyebrows at her. "I know you feel raw, and I know the pack is begging for swift retribution. But you must remember that you are *taoiseach*, not them. You're the leader, and they are to follow what you decide, not the other way around. Don't let your emotions sway you. The pack doesn't need you armed with a torch and pitchfork screaming for vengeance."

"I think that's the most I've ever heard Bran say in one go, so you better listen," Sean said. Bran reached out and cuffed him.

"It's absurd that they think Sam has something to do with it. He's about as bloodthirsty as a bunny rabbit," Sayer said from his perch behind her.

Sean snorted. "It's completely ridiculous."

Brid turned her head so she could look at him. "Is it?"

"Yeah, it is, and I can't believe you're listening to their crap. You know better," Sean growled.

Brid jerked back, shocked. Sean had never reprimanded her. Not ever. It stung. The pain might be less, she supposed, if her brother wasn't dead-on.

"You're right," she said, "I guess." She stumbled over the words. "I'm just angry, and Sam is, well, he's . . . a convenient target." And it was so much easier to be angry than heartsick. "So many of the pack are screaming for blood. There's a lot of fingers pointing in his direction right now, and I can't say that I totally fault their reasoning."

Bran kissed the top of her head, ignoring the sweat. "Wolves are vilified for taking down a lamb, but the wolf doesn't know it's poaching. He just knows the grumble of his stomach and the whine of hungry pups. You can't get mad at the wolf for being a wolf."

"What are you saying?"

"Sam can't help what he is, so it's not fair to hold it against him."

"Life's not fair," she mumbled into his shoulder. "If it was, Dad would be here."

Bran loosened his hold and stepped back, his hands on her shoulders, his eyes on hers. "Our people are frightened and scared and focusing on the first culprit they can. Fear, left unchecked, can spread like a virus. You need to stop it and stop it now. Address their doubts, make a show of looking into Sam—doing your due diligence—but don't let your imagination run off with theirs. There is no proof that he did anything to our father. When farmers fear for their livestock, they take down every wolf indiscriminately—don't let the pack do that. Maybe someone like Sam did this, but not Sam."

Sean softened next to her. "Sam couldn't have done this, Brid. He can't even kill a bird when he's supposed to. He's still bothered by what he did to Douglas, even though the rat bastard tried to kill him. And he liked Dad, you know that."

"I know," she whispered, tears filling her eyes. She wouldn't cry. Not anymore. "But it doesn't look good for him. What is a necromancer who can't speak to the dead?" Being mad at Sam was so easy. A convenient outlet, yes, but that anger masked other things, like her fear, because if she wasn't mad at Sam, then she was afraid for him. Brid didn't like being afraid.

Bran squeezed her shoulders. "What good is a *taoiseach* who does not lead?" He used his thumb to brush away a tear, letting her know that her seconds-old promise to herself had already been broken. "Give him another chance," Bran said softly. "Let one of the complainers watch over Sam and the Council with us. It will be the quickest way to show the others that you aren't ignoring them, but you aren't in the grip of their fear, either."

"You should have been Alpha," she mumbled.

"I am your adviser, which is exactly what I should be, and nothing else." He pulled her back toward the house, one arm around her shoulders. The rest of her brothers followed, a comforting weight at her back.

16

I REMEMBER YOU

Douglas ran one hand over a stack of CDs and the other over a row of vinyl. It had to be in here somewhere. He often moved it around, trying not to keep it in one place too long, and he was sure the last place had been the music library inside the duck figurine.

Minion looked into the fragile belly of the duck for the third time. "It's still not here, Master." He shook his head in a slow, confused fashion. "Strange things are afoot at the Circle K."

Douglas wondered—again—if calling Minion had been the best idea. He closed his eyes and looked out into the room, searching with his powers. He didn't have all day, either. Sam would come back eventually. The various security measures had ignored him, either because they weren't set against Douglas—and why would they be since he was supposed to be dead?—or because they weren't meant to keep out spirits. Or zombies. Minion had snuck in without any problem at all, and Douglas hadn't slipped the coin around his neck until he'd shut the library door. He was corporeal enough without the coin to manage getting it on, but it took a concentrated effort.

So they had to search and get out before Sam came back from his Council duties. The boy would sense a ghost, surely. He grimaced. Of course with Sam, you never could tell.

He opened his eyes, his scan once again finding nothing. Frustrated, he flopped into his chair. Technically, he supposed, it wasn't his chair anymore. The dead can't own anything, and all of his belongings were in Sam's ownership now. Douglas could petition the Council on the grounds that he wasn't truly dead and get it back, but that would rather defeat his purposes. He could always buy a new chair.

He looked around the library. A feeling of regret filled him. When was the last time he'd felt anything like that? He couldn't remember. Douglas hadn't been prepared for how much he'd miss his house. His home or, really, if he was being totally honest, his sanctuary. This was where he should be, not some seedy cabin in the woods with no lab, no music library, no James, and only the idiot Minion for company.

"For heaven's sake, Minion, put the duck down. Wherever it is, it's not here."

Minion carefully set the duck on the table. "What should I do, then? Would you like me to get you something?"

Douglas waved him away. "Keep looking, I guess, but leave me alone."

He was not used to being at a loss. Usually, he was the gentleman with the plan. Every little detail cataloged and put in its place. But now he had no place, and the details were everywhere.

Where could it have gone? James would have mentioned Sam finding it. Maybe one of the others? There were simply too many unknown factors. For a second he was tempted to just kill them all. It would be so much simpler. But then all his plans would go to waste, and he couldn't have that. You can't rule a kingdom with no one in it.

Douglas closed his eyes and drifted. He was in a field. Somewhere in the South. He couldn't remember where. They moved around a lot when he was young and still training. But the air was hot and sticky in a way he wasn't used to, he remembered that. He was . . . what? Ten? Twelve? So long ago, he could only register it as young.

Shiyomi and Auntie Lynn were across from him. Shiyomi was his age, a tiny girl they had purchased somewhere. He didn't know before then that you could buy people, and though he'd never seen anything so gauche as money changing hands over the deal, he understood that they owned her now.

She was petite, like a bird. He wondered at her, her black hair, shiny in any light. Her skin was a little darker than his—tan and soft looking. Often, he found himself wanting to reach out and touch her. To see if her skin was as soft as it appeared. Shiyomi didn't smile much and said even less. She'd broken down to the power of the fates long ago. All the fight was gone. They had a lot in common.

After she'd traveled with them for weeks, he found himself taking care of her. Making sure she ate, brushing her long hair and tying it with ribbons. She was his responsibility now, and he found himself enjoying his task. But he really hadn't understood her purpose.

He'd helped her pack that morning, filling the small bag that came with her. There wasn't much: a change or two of clothes, a hairbrush, a tired-looking cloth doll. And the egg. That was a newer purchase. Douglas had caught her eyeing it—where had they been? The East Coast? He didn't remember where, only that the store had been enveloped in the smell of dust and incense. The jade egg was tiny, not much bigger than a quail's egg. Beautifully carved cherry blossoms trailed down the sides, swept up in an imaginary wind. He'd picked it up then, felt the cold of it in his palm.

He held it out to her.

At first, she didn't move. With his palm slightly cupped, he moved it closer to her. Hesitantly, she reached out for it. She smiled at him, and it made something in his chest loosen. He smiled back. Then he used his pocket money to buy it for her.

They'd become friends after that. Never really speaking—her English was either poor or nonexistent—but enjoying the silence together. Sometimes, when she was really scared, she'd hold his hand. Feeling her frail hand in his made him realize how much he missed touching another human being. Auntie Lynn wasn't the comforting type.

And in Shiyomi's other hand, the one he wasn't holding, was always the jade egg.

But that morning in the field, she'd had only the egg. Douglas was across from her, too far to reach. Auntie Lynn had her hand resting on the girl's shoulder. A sluggish wind was pushing at his aunt's hat and curling Shiyomi's skirt around her calves. Wind does not discriminate—it touches everyone, everything. He liked that about wind.

In his hand, the one that was now used to holding Shiyomi's, was his aunt's spare ritual dagger, her *athame*. He should have known or understood as soon as he'd stepped out onto the field and felt it. Old death. This was all overgrown grass now, but it had once been a burial ground—he knew that as soon as his feet hit the soil.

Auntie Lynn held Shiyomi. His friend wouldn't look at him, but she didn't shake or stare at him accusingly. Like him, she'd been broken and given herself over to the quiet space where no fight remained. Or not like him. Where he'd thought there was nothing, a small spark stood up and weighted his arms, his feet, his heart. He couldn't move, and his aunt was getting angry.

"What did you think she was for? A living doll for your amusement? She is as much a part of the ritual as the knife in your hand, and just as replaceable." She laughed then. Auntie Lynn's laugh was joyless and unpleasant, sickly as winter grass. He wouldn't move, and he wouldn't cry, but he couldn't stop that laugh from crawling inside him and squatting.

The laughter died when he continued not to move. She pursed her lips and stared at him. Not angry. You have to have passion to be angry, and Auntie Lynn was a cold, calculating thing. She sized him up and cocked her head. Then, quick as a snakebite, she had her own athame out and had drawn it across the girl's throat. A thin shallow line blossomed on that fragile skin before Auntie Lynn released her and let her crumple to the ground. Then she cleaned the knife off on Shiyomi's faded dress.

"Because of you, her death will be without purpose. We will raise nothing today. I do hope you've learned your lesson."

Then she turned and went back to the car.

Douglas was left standing, his knife still in his fist. He walked over to the girl, leaned down, and brushed back her hair. Shiyomi, *his* Shiyomi. He held her hand and said nothing. It took her a while to die. Auntie Lynn had left the cut shallow. Had Douglas done it himself, her death would have been much quicker. Still, he stayed squatting until he felt her life leave. And he cried.

It was the last time he would ever do so.

When it was done, he closed her eyes, and he took the egg from her loose grasp. He asked the earth to open, to take what was hers. He couldn't leave Shiyomi to the scavengers, so he tucked her into the soil as he had tucked her into bed so many times. Under his breath, he sang an old song—an almost-forgotten lullaby his mother used to sing. When he was done, only the empty field could be seen. He hoped that, in the summer, flowers would grow there. But that was beyond his control. Douglas couldn't create life and make things blossom. He only had power over the withered things.

Sticking the egg into his pocket, he walked slowly back to the car. Auntie Lynn sat unconcerned, cold and waiting, behind the wheel.

The next time he got a girl, he did the cut himself. No one cried, and Auntie Lynn took him to dinner afterward. She'd been proud of him. He cut his steak into little bites and felt nothing. The spark was gone.

Douglas came to with a start—Minion was leaning over him, concerned and confused. Had he been sleeping? Could he even sleep now? He didn't know. But it was time to leave. Time to return to his cabin. The egg wasn't here. It must be somewhere else in the house, but he couldn't look for it now. He'd have to be patient and come back another day.

Minion held up a random CD. "How come you don't have any of mine?"

"I like myself a little too much for that."

"Oh," he said. "Okay. We're leaving now?"

Douglas nodded. Yes, they were leaving now.

17

HELLO, IS IT ME YOU'RE LOOKING FOR?

After the meeting and a couple of phone calls, we all left the Tongue & Buckle and headed over to the Den, except for Brid, who'd left early to prepare the pack. We carpooled, making us the oddest entourage in the history of the planet.

It was hard, standing in that clearing, knowing that was the last place Brannoc had been. Everyone from the Council, as well as many unhappy pack members, watched me as I stood there, which made it even harder. Now that we were all here, I wasn't sure what to do. Ramon stood off to the side with Dessa. He'd talked me into letting him swing by and pick her up. She was a seer like her mom, though I didn't think she was nearly as sensitive, which would be a good thing in such a charged area. Her mom might be overwhelmed. I'd argued at first, despite this, but Ramon felt she would bring something sorely needed to the table, and I ended up agreeing. So it was all hands on deck.

Some of the wolves weren't friendly. I could feel their animosity from here. Well, standing and doing nothing wasn't getting me anywhere. Everyone else was moving. Ariana was walking through the field slowly, touching the occasional patch of grass. Pello was off to the side, talking to a tree. Hopefully, the tree was talking back and Pello wasn't crazy. Ione was muttering to herself in what I also hoped was a constructive manner. Aengus and Dunaway were talking to Bran, Brid, and the rest of her brothers. The weres appeared shell-shocked. Sean, especially, since I wasn't used to his face looking so sober.

James stood near me, his arms behind his back, looking very unconcerned. I knew him well enough to know it was an act. He was keeping too close an eye on the pack to really be that nonchalant. True, it was his duty to watch over me, but I liked to think there was some genuine concern there.

Kell stood off to the side, analyzing the crowd as much as the scene. I'd been surprised when he joined us. I kept expecting to see him burst into flames or collapse into ash, or whatever happened to vampires when they encountered sunlight. Instead he stood, somewhat anticlimactically, under a strangely masculine parasol.

Kell sauntered over when he caught me looking. "Nice day," he said.

"I guess."

"Confused?"

"On so many levels, I've stopped counting. Why aren't you . . ." I made a sort of exploding gesture with my hands. "No offense."

He smiled. "I'm old enough that I can manage the sunlight a little. I don't like it. We're nocturnal by nature, and I don't do well in direct light, but a little sunblock and some shade, and I do all right. Modern science is amazing, don't you think?" He smiled and twirled his parasol. "You are aware that some of the pack want to string you up, yes?"

"Yes."

"But you're here anyway."

"Yes." I squinted into the sunlight.

"Do you mind if I ask why?"

Despite the fading sunlight, it was too hot for what I was wearing. I slipped out of the suit jacket and button-up shirt to the white tank beneath. Better. I threw the clothes behind me. James caught them one-handed with a frown.

"Because it's my job. Or maybe because I owe the pack. And because Brannoc was my friend. Pick one." I shrugged. "Pick all—either way, sitting here isn't helping me any."

I closed my eyes and concentrated. The air around me shifted, and I knew without opening my eyes that both Ashley and Brooke had shown up.

"Huh," Ashley said, looking around. "You actually got Haley's plan to work. Good job, Sam."

"I knew he could do it," Brooke said. She leaned over and kissed me on the cheek. "Go get 'em, tiger. I'm going to go over and make sure they're playing nice with Dunaway." She didn't skip over, but I could tell she wanted to.

Ashley wasn't nearly as chipper. She was frowning, tapping her foot, her arms crossed. "This place is weird, Sam."

"I know. Do you think it's all from . . . you know."

She scrunched her nose. "It's possible. I'm not sure. Some of it feels like hers, but there's something else here, too. Another layer. Either way, this soil is practically soaked in strange magic." She looked over at me, worried. "And with that kind of unknown . . . I'm not sure you should be trying anything out here, Sam. Too many variables. The outcome will be unpredictable."

I sighed and held out my hand. Without speaking, James handed me the old silver athame. He didn't like me trying anything out here, either, but he stayed quiet because James had already reached the same conclusion as I had. I didn't have a choice. If I came out here and did nothing, the pack would lose what little respect it had for me, and things would get dangerous. I really wanted to avoid getting eaten. I didn't want to die, period, but I especially didn't want to be chewed to death. More than basic survival, though, I wanted to find out what had happened here. I owed Brannoc that, at the very least. There was also Brid to think about. I didn't want to jeopardize what was left of our relationship by screwing this up again. Things were going to be hard enough with pack dynamics changing in ways I couldn't understand and the emotional bomb of losing her father.

"I know, Ash, but I have to try. Ione is on standby with herbs and whatnot, and I've got you with me. It's the best I can do."

She recrossed her arms with a scowl. "I understand. I don't like it, but I get why you have to do it. I'll help you this time and see if we can't get a better result."

Impulsively, I reached over and hugged her one-armed, kissing her on the cheek. "Thanks, Ash."

She shoved me off with a mock growl. "Just try not to get yourself killed."

I let go of her and took a deep breath. Positioned my feet shoulders' width apart, and straightened my back. I took a few more steadying breaths, holding up my arm and the knife. I wasn't really used to cutting myself yet, but given the alternative, which was stabbing something else, probably to its death, it was preferable. I felt a tap on my shoulder. Sean was standing next to me.

He nodded at the knife. "Given your state last time, I thought maybe I'd volunteer."

I blinked at him. "Huh?"

He rolled his eyes and held out his arm. "I don't want you passing out and bleeding all over our nice field."

I didn't like the idea of someone else taking my place. "It's silver," I said. "It will take you longer to heal it."

He shrugged. "Not as long as you, and not as long as them." He jerked his head back at some of his pack members. Sean was a hybrid, which meant his allergy to silver wasn't as severe. That didn't mean I was any more cavalier about slicing my friend with a knife.

Kell leaned forward. "If I can interfere for a moment, I suggest you take him up on it, Sam. Bleeding will weaken you, and Sean's willingness to volunteer shows the pack that he doesn't believe you have anything to do with this mess. I believe the current vernacular is 'win-win.'"

He was right, of course. I nodded slowly. Sean held out his arm. "I'm sorry," I said. Then I slashed the blade. The world held its breath for me as Sean's blood fell. My back became rigid, and I gasped as it hit the grass.

Sometimes, a location can become steeped in death.

Douglas's basement is one of those places. I'd never really encountered it outside, since the ground is porous and more forgiving, but since Brannoc's death was so fresh, all that blood and energy was still there. It hadn't been this responsive the last time I'd tried to contact Brannoc, but It was possible that using Sean had made it worse, his blood calling out to Brannoc's. Either way, I was flooded, and the magic took over.

When it comes to magic, the human body is a lot like a conductor. It flows through you, and you direct it where you need it to go. Like electricity, sometimes you get a surge and it's too much for the conductor to handle. With electrical energy, you have fail-safes—breakers flip, and things turn off. It's not so different in humans. There was a power surge, and my breaker flipped, only it felt a lot like getting hit by a Mack truck. Then floating darkness and a firm feminine voice telling me *no*. The flower lady was back, and she wasn't taking any guff from lil' ol' me.

I awoke to James smacking me. Jolting up, I desperately pulled air into my lungs. Sean knelt next to me, shaking my shoulder. "You scared the crap out of us." I stared back at him blankly, my teeth chattering. There was a grumbling next to me, and I looked over to see a big-ass bear. Apparently I wasn't the only one out of control here. Ramon snarled at someone and parked his big bear butt at my side. Comforting . . . sort of.

After a few false starts, I got out the question, "What?"

James had his blank face on, but to me that was beginning to be a sign that things weren't well. Brooke hugged me, and Ashley hovered, looking pissed.

And it was the angry little Harbinger who answered me.

"You passed out. Then you got cold and stopped breathing. Ods bodkins, Sam, your lips are blue!"

James wrapped my suit jacket back around me, and I pulled it close. He finally pushed the hovering crowd out of the way and scooped me up.

"James Montgomery, you're my hero," I chattered.

"With all due respect, you need to shut the hell up, Sam." He set me on a big boulder that had grown warm in the sun. It felt awesome. "Look around now and tell me what you see."

"Hey, you called me Sam. My actual name. Not Master or dumbass—"

"I have never in my life called anyone dumbass."

"Are you sure?"

"Yes. Now, focus."

I held my jacket and tried to covertly take in my surroundings. Brid was off to the side with members of her pack. She seemed torn between staying with them and coming over to me. At least, I hoped she was torn. Some of her pack looked worried. But a few of them looked mad as hell. There was a lot of grumbling going on, and angry faces. A few had shifted into wolves, pissy ones, and it was them Ramon was growling at.

"Great, now what did I do?"

"Look."

Frowning, I continued to scan. Oh. Oh, boy. Stanley, the giant undead bull elk, came up and nudged my shoulder. James had to dodge his antlers. I stroked the elk on his cheek and nose. "Hey, buddy."

As I petted Stanley, I realized a few things. One was that he was glad to see me and happy that I was okay. The other was that he wasn't alone. In my stupor, I had accidentally raised a lot of . . . things. That surge had to go somewhere, and my unconscious self had sent it out. The clearing was now populated with squirrels, raccoons, birds, a few deer, and worse, wolves. I put my head against Stanley's nose and hoped those weren't werewolves. But I didn't have high hopes on that one. What can I say? When I screw up, I screw up big.

"Shit."

James absently scratched Stanley between his antlers. "Indeed. You need to do something about this now."

"No wonder some of the pack look pissed," I said. Keeping the jacket loose around my shoulders, I stood up, leaning on Stanley for support. Even though I was warmer now, I still felt tired and abused.

As I walked into the center of the clearing, I noticed that everyone else had backed away a bit. Unintentionally I'm sure, but it made me feel like a pariah. Of course, it could have been the giant were-bear by my side, but for some reason, I didn't think that was it. The animals naturally came up to me, and the few that didn't watched my every move. One of the wolves, a big gray and white beast, walked over, and the rest of the creatures parted for her. I knelt down so I could look her in the eye.

You need help. Her voice whispered in my head, an unheard alto. It was weird to not actually hear something outside, but to have it bouncing around on the inside of my skull like a Ping-Pong ball. As with everything else I seemed to do lately, it was creepy.

Yes, I whispered back. She seemed to nod, and the wolves spread out, smelling and searching. I let them do what they do best.

One of the pack, an angry but somewhat familiar looking guy of medium build, broke away from the crowd. "This is outrageous!" He shouted the words, his red face reminding me of a volcano only a heart's beat away from eruption. Spittle flew from his mouth. A speck hit my cheek, and I wiped it off with the heel of my hand. The eruption had begun.

"Eric." This from Bran, a warning tone in his voice. Brid was clutching her brother, but she remained silent.

Ah, yes, Eric. My number one fan. Of course he was here. We were a thunderstorm and an industrial accident away from the best day ever. I wondered if I should have Ashley run over and give me a wedgie just to complete the experience.

Not to be swayed, Eric kept his eyes on me, his voice pitched for all to hear. "No, someone needs to stand up for the pack. Someone needs to stand up for your family. This"—he waved at the wolves that I'd raised—"is adding insults on top of what he has already done. If this doesn't prove that he cares nothing for us, what does?"

Okay, now, I'd felt pretty bad over the last few days for screwing up, but this time . . . well, this time, with the help of my furry clue-sniffing undead lackeys, I was actually doing something helpful. So I got angry. I left Ramon's side and marched over to Eric.

"Look, buddy, I don't know what your freaking problem is, but has it occurred to you that I'm trying to do my damn job?" I waved out at the crowd of creatures. "This is what I do. This is how I help."

He got in my face and started jabbing a finger into my chest. "Then we don't want your help, if this is what it looks like. First you bring a human among us, and now this? I don't like your kind, and I'm not the only one. They can't be trusted. *You* can't be trusted." He drew the last word out, practically hissing it.

That's our Eric. What a charmer. Ladies, try not to swoon.

I stared down at his finger. He'd left it stuck to my chest, poking just a little too hard to be comfortable. I felt the rage blossom in my rib cage and spread out like a sea anemone. The tentacles reached for that offending finger. I like to think that I'm a pretty mellow person. I try really hard to understand where people are coming from. To show a little sympathy or empathy where I can. But even I have my limits, and I had been pushed a touch too far the last couple of days.

Very softly I said, "You need to remove your hand and back away."

"Or what?" And he shoved me. A little push is all, the small ubiquitous shove that prompts so many schoolyard scuffles. But it was enough.

I felt the animals stop what they were doing and come up behind me. And I felt the things that couldn't rise. The ghosts, the spirits, the energy, call it what you will, but it was all there, and it was for me. And I took it. I looked up at Eric, and I felt the burning in my eyes, the unveiled wrath and fury. "Or I will remind you why I am Council and you are not."

And I shoved him back. Not hard. Enough to put him off balance and get him out of my face, but not to hurt him. Yet.

I let my jacket fall. I didn't need it now. My skin felt like it was burning up. And for the first time, I think I really understood what it meant to be Council, and that I was right to be there.

I advanced. "Do you know what that means, or do I need to break it down for you?" The wolves that I'd raised flanked me, growling softly. "It means that I work for the law, I work for justice, no matter what you want. You think I give a damn if I'm pissing you off or offending your fucking sensibilities? I don't. This is what I do. This is what I am. I won't apologize for it any more than you should for sprouting hair and drooling on occasion." I jabbed him in his chest. He wanted to fight. I could feel it. Some of it was directed at me, but mostly it was just built-up aggression. But you know what? We'd all been having a shitty week. That didn't mean we got to take it out on whomever we wanted.

The crowd around me felt like it was at a tipping point. If we got in a fight, an actual physical altercation, it might do more damage than Eric wanted. There were a lot of high emotions floating around. But I had a feeling that if I didn't throw a little smack down on this assjack, it would be opening up the floor for all kinds of challenges. I couldn't afford that. And even if I wanted to, it wasn't like I could take Eric in such a way physically that would dissuade others from trying. Skinny necromancer versus full werewolf? No contest. Tokyo under the rampaging feet of Godzilla. But I didn't need to hit him. I just needed to scare him.

The pack had gotten pretty comfortable with me. I'd been around for a while, and I'd never done anything really spooky in front of them, and it had made a few of the dumber ones like Eric careless. There's a reason why Zeke is careful when he frisks me at the Tongue & Buckle, though. He's always thorough, I don't mean that. But when it comes to me, he makes sure his skin never touches mine. Smart people are careful around someone like me.

I opened my hand and changed the poke to a full palm on Eric's chest, my fingers touching the skin not covered by his tank top. Some people had natural defenses, or a stronger will, but Eric was clear as a bell. The were was pissy on so many levels. Losing his pack leader was only part of the problem. Strengthwise, he wasn't too high on the totem pole. He wanted more of a position than he had, and he thought by stepping in like this, he might get it. And it might impress a certain redhead as well. Jealousy and anger are never a good combo.

"Oh, Eric. How little you understand your own people." I'd barely been trained in my gift, and most of that training had been of the nuts-and-bolts variety. I'd found, though, that there was more to it than raising the dead. Sometimes I could give someone a little mental *push*, and they would go along with what I wanted. I had used it accidentally on my biological father's wife once when I was trying to get information out of her. It was not something I liked to do, and I got the impression that not many necromancers had this particular ability, which made asking for help with it a touch awkward. Douglas could do it. I didn't really want to think about that, though.

I took Eric's emotional welter and untangled it. Then I showed him each piece, one by one. Every petty anger, every little jealous thorn. Most people would have a hard time if someone showed them the weaker parts of themselves—the things that make us fragile and ashamed, but also make us human. It's even harder on a young male were. Packs have hierarchies. Strength, cunning, intelligence, speed—these things are prized. Strong at the top. Weak at the bottom. For a guy like Eric, tiny flaws would seem like chasms, huge and insurmountable. They would need to be conquered. Ground out. So I slowly revealed all of his, and then I pushed how I felt over that. *Here*, I said, *here is where you went wrong. Here is where you are flawed and broken. Weak.*

After a minute, he tried to fight. He twisted and smacked my hand away. "Don't touch me!" His voice had a note of hysteria in it. He kept trying, though, I had to give him that. "You!" He didn't jab me that time, but poked at the air instead. "You freak! I don't care who you are. You raised *her*, damn it!"

He pointed a shaky finger at the big gray-and-white wolf, the one I'd talked to earlier. She was sitting calmly behind me. I looked at her in question, but she was regarding the whole scene with faint amusement.

What's he going on about? My voice a whisper in her mind. Spoooooky.

She snorted. That was even weirder than having someone talk in your head. *Eric, same sniveling pup. I had hoped he would grow out of it. I was fond of his mother.*

He's had a rough week, even if he is being a total dumbass.

Now that I was talking to her, I felt the anger dissipating. I bet she'd been a force to reckon with when she was alive.

Now, you, I like.

Thanks?

I felt the grim smile in her words. *Tell the pup this: how dare he interfere with the investigation into the death of my mate? It is my right to assist. Does he presume to tell me how to channel my grief? I may not call the shots anymore, but that doesn't mean I'm outranked by that whelp. This is still my pack, death does not change that, and he should kindly understand his place in it.* Along with her words came the visual of the way she wanted the words delivered. And, believe me, I could see where Brid got her feisty behavior.

I walked calmly up to Eric, who had backed away, and punched him in the gut. The move surprised him, or I wouldn't have gotten away with it. While he was still gasping, I grabbed him by the throat. Then I whispered her words into his ear. I mimicked her grim smile as I did it, too.

"Now, I admit I don't know the lady as well as you, but even I know she wouldn't have showed up if she damn well didn't want to." I shoved him away. He cowered, unmoving. I hadn't made a friend there. Oh, well. You can't be friends with everyone. "Now, shut the hell up and let me do my damn job."

And I walked away. No one moved. The enveloping silence was a little unnerving. If I'd felt like a pariah before, it was nothing to how I felt now. The she-wolf padded after me.

Too much, wasn't it?

With some people, you just can't be subtle.

I sighed. *Thank you for everything, Mrs. Blackthorn.*

You're welcome.

I returned to my warm rock and sat down. The animals went back to their respective roles, sniffing out the clearing and trying to figure out what had happened. Someone walked up behind me, and I turned to see Dunaway, a little half smile on his face.

He sat in the grass next to me and watched the animals. "That's pretty impressive," he said.

"Mmm." Now that I was calming down, I was starting to feel the drain of it all.

"Can you explain what you did that pissed off everyone so badly?"

"Are you going to charge me with assault?"

Before he could reply, Bran said, "He had the temerity to do what we asked him to do, just not in the way they expected. Next time we ask him to call the dead, we'll be more specific." He smiled as he said it. If I'd had the energy to rise, I would have hugged Bran right then and given him a big ol' kiss on the cheek.

Dunaway shook his head. "Has to be more than that. No way I was the only one here that knew what he could do."

"No, but they hadn't really seen Sam at his impressive best." He tilted his head to the side in thought. "You shouldn't be able to do that, you know. We burn our dead. But you did it all the same." He looked over at his pack. "They haven't thought of that yet, but when they do . . ." He shook his head as if to clear it, returning his full attention to Dunaway. "And a few of them objected to the specific wolves he chose to raise."

I kept my eyes out over the clearing. "But you're not mad."

"I know my mother. No way anyone could make her do anything she didn't want to do, even from the grave."

Dunaway chuckled softly. They chatted behind me, but I tuned them out, listening to what the animals had to tell me.

Both Bran and Dunaway seemed perfectly happy to wait for me. After a little while, the she-wolf came back over.

You're not going to like what I have to tell you, she said.

I stared at her derisively. *Brannoc has been murdered, your daughter dumped me, lawn gnomes are pissing on my sheets, and the pack is about to tear me limb from freaking limb. Exactly what kind of outcome were you expecting that could possibly be construed as even partially happy?*

She cocked her head to the side.

What?

Are you done wallowing in self-pity yet?

Not even close.

Her ear twitched. *I can wait all day, you know, but I don't think you can.*

I sighed. *You're right, my apologies. What did you find?*

Whatever killed my husband had no scent.

That's what they've said, but everything has a scent, right? Or can it be masked or something?

If it was being masked, then we'd smell what was masking it, but there is nothing.

I frowned. *Nothing? How can that be?*

Exactly. Between that and the traces of magic, we have come to a conclusion. The only way it could be *is if it* wasn't.

Run that by me again?

Whatever it is, it's not alive, and it's not dead, which means—

Which means that it has something to do with someone like me.

Most likely.

But a necromancer would leave a scent trail, and I doubt a ghost could do this. . . .

I said you wouldn't like it.

I leaned back and sighed again. *And yet, I still didn't think it would be as bad as it has turned out to be. I'll talk to the rest of the Council, see if we can figure this out.*

Dunaway's gaze moved from me to the wolf and back to me again. "What is it?"

The detective had his arms crossed and a concerned look on his face. I felt strangely grateful for him all of a sudden. He was probably one of a handful of people here who wouldn't want to exterminate me on the spot after I told them what I'd found.

"I thank you for your help, Detective, but I'm not sure what you can do. It seems our suspect pool is . . . well, I'm not sure what it is."

"Then it seems like you most certainly do need my help. How did you put it? 'Shut the hell up and let me do my damn job'?"

I couldn't help but grin at him. "Rightly so. It seems whoever or whatever killed Brannoc had something to do with a necromancer. Which brings the suspect pool down to a dead man and myself, since we're the only ones in the state of Washington. The only other necromancer I know is in Mississippi, which probably alibis her out. Oh, and I have an uncle about someplace."

"You know where I can find him?"

"Haven't the foggiest."

"And this other one, you're sure he's dead?"

"As sure as if I'd killed him myself."

Bran choked a little on that.

Dunaway's eyebrows rose. "You're including yourself on the list?"

"I would be remiss if I didn't."

He nodded. "You're in quite a pickle, then."

Bran cocked his head to the side.

I answered his unasked question. "If there are four necromancers, and one is dead, one is on walkabout, and one is out of state . . ."

He straightened, understanding. "Then right now you're the most likely suspect."

"Sometimes I hate my life." I had James bring the rest of the Council over so we could share our findings. Ramon, still in bear form, joined us. It was kind of funny to see a bear sit down and listen, a curious look on his face. If I hadn't been so screwed, I'd have laughed.

I filled the group in on what the wolves had told me.

Ariana spoke first. "Could a spirit have done this?"

I thought on that a moment. Ghosts had injured me before. Douglas had sicced a whole pack of them on me in his basement. But even under his expert hand, with many of them, the most they'd done was scratch and terrify me. Sure, it had hurt, but Brannoc was bigger, stronger, and there was no way they could have killed him.

"I don't think so," I said, looking at Ashley.

She shook her head. "There's no way."

"Whatever it was, it happened fast," Pello said.

"Why do you say that?" Kell asked with a twirl of his parasol.

"I spoke to the tree spirits. Their concept of time is different from ours, but still, they felt Brannoc's death—him being fey and all, they're a little more sensitive to him. They said it was like one moment he was fine and then, suddenly, anguish."

"We knew it had to be fast," Ariana said. "Brannoc was a warrior. To have him go without a fight . . ." She crossed her arms, scowling.

There was silence as we all mulled this over. Dessa cleared her throat and looked at me questioningly.

"What is it, Dessa?"

"I tried to see what had happened here, but the magical interference is so heavy—remember when you first came to my mother and Brooke was causing too much static for her to get a good reading?" I nodded. "Well, it's the same here. Too much death magic. But, if I had a focus maybe, something of Brannoc's, and your witch would help me?" She looked at Ione hopefully.

"Of course," the witch murmured, already reaching into the kit she'd brought with her in case I'd gone off into the land of the soul-drunk again. "What may I help you with?"

Dessa had us scoot back, creating a half circle around her and Ione. Then she made some of the more upset wolves leave. Her tone made it clear that she expected to be obeyed. Dessa was a little scary sometimes. A few hesitated, but Brid backed her up, ordering the wolves away. I had my undead friends fall back to the tree line, getting them as far back as I could.

Ione lit a bundle of sage then, walking slowly in a wide circle around Dessa who stood, eyes closed, body relaxed. The witch sang softly to herself as she walked. When she was done, she handed the smoldering bundle to Pello. He walked it back over to us, and the smoke made Ramon give a bear sneeze.

Brid offered herself as a focus. The three girls held hands as they walked through the area again, covering all the ground inside the circle, Dessa slowly putting one foot in front of the other until she jerked to a stop, her head snapping up.

"It happened here." Her voice was eerie, and her eyes looked faraway. "There was only one—the fey—and then suddenly there were two. He came from nothing. . . . He is . . . nothing. Just power. So much power."

"But it was a he?" I asked.

"Yes," she said.

"Did he leave the same way?" Ashley asked.

"No." Dessa pointed out toward the woods. "He left that way. I can taste his joy. His . . . excitement." She shook her head and dropped Brid's and Ione's hands before she ran to the bushes and got sick. I went after her, Ramon shuffling behind me.

"Are you okay?" I asked.

She held her hair back in one hand, her hands shaking. "Yeah, I think so. It was just . . . awful, Sam. It was so awful. He *enjoyed* it. Killing Brannoc made him so happy—I . . ." She shook her head, closing her eyes. "I've never felt anything like it."

Ramon nudged her with his nose, and she gave him a sickly smile. "I'll be all right," she said. "It's just going to take a minute."

I left her with Ramon and headed back to the group.

"She okay?" Ione asked.

"Yeah, she just needs a break. I guess we all do. So, what did we figure out?"

"Whatever killed Brannoc has to do with death magic, but there was no necromancer present, or we would have found some trace."

"So you're off the hook, Sam," Brooke said with a smile.

"Not necessarily," Dunaway added softly. "If I understand correctly, you have more than ghosts at your disposal." He eyed Ashley inquiringly.

Inky little eyebrows raised, Ashley looked at him in surprise. "You think I did this? No way, José. I may transport spirits, but I do not kill people. So, yeah, I could have appeared and talked to Brannoc, but I couldn't have stabbed him. My boss would have my ass—that's not something that gets by him. And even if I could have, then why would I run off into the woods? Why not just call another portal and disappear again? And anyway, Dessa said it was a guy." She gestured to her skirt.

"She's got a point," Kell said.

"So we're no closer to figuring out what happened than we were when we got here," I said, defeated.

Dunaway shook his head. "Not so. We've ruled some things out. Sometimes, Sam, canceling out a theory is the best we can do. Now we know that you didn't do it, and the other necromancers seem just as unlikely. So, what else has this death magic besides you guys?"

Everyone turned to look at me. "Hell if I know, people," I said, throwing my hands up in frustration. Once again, I just didn't have the knowledge people needed. Well, that wasn't entirely true. I did have *access* to knowledge that might help. "But you might be able to find out," I said to Dunaway. "I can give June a call—she's the necromancer in Mississippi. And my predecessor left all kinds of notes. I guess I need to hand you over to Frank, see if you can't find something."

He nodded, putting his notebook away. "I think we're done here, then," he said.

We all thanked him, and our group started to break up and head to their respective vehicles.

Bran patted me on the shoulder. "Good work."

"Thanks. You think it will make the pack back off a bit?"

He scratched his chin. "A few of them, but many don't trust you, and this might be a little nebulous for them. Until something concrete happens . . ." He shrugged.

"Great." I was exhausted and sore, and it kind of felt like I'd done it for nothing.

Bran shifted on his feet. "Before you send them back, do you think you could let her come over and say hi?"

"That's up to her, but I'll keep it up a few more minutes. After that, I'm going to have to put them back." It was either that, or I'd pass out soon.

Bran nodded gratefully and led the she-wolf over to her pack. I started returning the others, making sure to let them know how happy I was with their performance and how thankful we all were. I wasn't sure if they'd remember that in a few seconds, but it was important to be respectful nonetheless.

Soon it was just the she-wolf and Stanley left over. He came up and gave me a nudge. Apparently, I'd made a friend. The big bull elk wanted to come home with us. His nose felt soft under my fingers as I patted it. "Sure, buddy, but you might have to wait until later, lest we scare the normies."

He seemed to accept that, as he sauntered off into the forest. I watched him go from my spot on my rock. Warm as it was, I couldn't help but notice that I sat by myself, while everyone else had formed into knots of people. Family surrounded Brid. The rest of the Council had vamoosed. But not a single person was over by the spooky kid. I kicked myself for the self-pity. It wouldn't help. Besides, I'd been the loner before. I knew what it was like to sit by myself at a lunch table, trying to pretend that I'd planned it that way. That I was alone on purpose.

James joined me. "You need sleep," he said. "And food. You've been spreading yourself thin."

"I need a lot of things," I said.

Ashley came over with Brooke. "Look," she said, "I have to go—I'm late for an appointment, but I'll return when I can." A portal opened up behind her, a kind of swirling mist. Sparrows flew out of it and picked her up. Tiny wings making no noise, they took off and the vortex blipped out of existence.

"Man, she totally knows how to make an exit," Brooke said.

I pulled on James's sleeve. "If I don't go home and sleep

soon, I'm going to keel over." James nodded and took care of it. Sometimes, I didn't know what I'd do without him. Other times, I wanted to shake him. Good thing this time it was the former. I just didn't have the energy to shake anyone right now.

18

MR. SANDMAN, BRING ME A DREAM

Douglas had never spent much time in dreamland. In his childhood, sure, but as he'd gotten older, it seemed like his ticket to the place had been revoked. Sleep was a dark and static time when nothing happened. Since he'd died, though, his pass had suddenly become valid again and the conductor was making up for lost time. So once again he found himself dreaming of the past. . . .

"You're sure you want to do this, then?" James looked on anxiously from the chair. Though the aging process was certainly slower in James than human children, it had still seemed like he'd only gotten the boy yesterday and now he was teetering into adulthood.

Douglas pushed back his hat with his wrist, avoiding the parts of his hand that were covered with chalk. James handed him his handkerchief, and Douglas used it to swipe at the sweat beading on his forehead. He passed it back and stared at his work. He'd drawn and redrawn the symbols until he was positive that they were exactly right.

"You have doubts?"

James pulled up a chair and sat carefully, trying to not

disturb his duster folded over the back of it. The jacket was new, a gift from Douglas, and James was very protective of it. He crossed his legs, his hands folded neatly in his lap. "You know full well that I do."

"The theory is sound."

"Theory. The notes you looked at belonged to a man who died trying. As did almost every other reference you found."

Douglas sat back on his heels. "*Almost every* being the important part of that sentence. They made mistakes— mistakes that I most certainly will not make."

James studied his nails. "Do you know what *hubris* means, Master?"

"Seeing as how I've handled most of your education, it is a safe bet to assume that I am familiar with most of the words in your lexicon."

"You are purposefully misunderstanding me."

"Yes, I am." Douglas stood, wiping his chalky hands on a rag. "Life is a series of calculated risks, James. I happen to think that this one is worth it."

The *pukis* sighed, his posture straight and even, despite his despondency. "You could at least choose an item that was less . . . I don't know. Obvious?"

Douglas took the jade egg off the shelf. He had very few items from his past. This egg and his aunt's knife were probably the only remnants he still had, if you didn't count his books. He folded the cool piece of jade into his palm. His heart still squeezed a little when he looked at it. For that feeling alone—something that was becoming more and more rare—he would have kept the egg.

James continued the argument they'd already had several times. "Anyone familiar with fairy tales will figure it out." He shook his head. "While you're at it, why don't you start yelling *fe, fi, fo, fum* and climbing beanstalks?"

"That's the wrong giant in the wrong fairy tale."

James threw him a look that said he was missing the point.

Douglas sighed. "Even if they are familiar with it, they would still have to guess that I did it in the first place, and few will fathom that. For most it will be . . . unthinkable." The egg remained cold in his hand. "And no other object will do."

Defeat sagged James's shoulders. "You've made up your mind, then," he said softly.

"I have," replied Douglas. "I really have."

He stepped into the circle and began the rite.

Douglas came to with a start in a chair pulled close to the fireplace. The fire itself was long out, the hearth cold. Minion slept on the rug at his feet, the half-chewed remnants of several pieces of wax fruit spread around him. Douglas sighed. At some point, his life had gone off track. He wasn't sure *how*, but he was pretty sure the *when* had been when Sam had entered into the equation. But that would be fixed soon, the number refigured to change the outcome.

He just needed a little more time.

19

OUR HOUSE IS A VERY, VERY, VERY FINE HOUSE

My mom called on my way home. She used to call about once a week to check up on me, but since Douglas kidnapped me in the spring, the calls had become more frequent. If I hadn't known better, I'd have said she was worried about me. I sleepily caught her up on what we'd found out. Then I told her James would be stopping by to check her security. I didn't lecture her or get mad that she'd tried to hide it from me. She was well aware of how I felt about keeping things from each other, even if the intentions were good. We'd had enough of that, I'm sure. But I wasn't going to shrug off a threat to my family like it was nothing, either. Not after everything that had happened.

I must have fallen asleep in the car shortly after the phone call, because James had to wake me up when we got to the house. Everyone was outside in a ring, shouting. Night had fallen, and despite the tiki torches and the bonfires they'd lit, I couldn't quite see what was going on, as some of the bigger creatures were on the outside and they had gnomes and gladiators on their shoulders, all of them covered in war paint and chanting, "Two men enter, one man leaves!"

Every bone in my body ached with fatigue, but you can't

just walk past something like that. I walked up to one of the gladiators who had climbed up onto the shoulders of the Minotaur. They'd altered one of those beer hats with the tubes to fit onto his giant bull head. One tube, I assume, went to the Minotaur, and a gladiator was holding the other tightly in his little fist. Since the gladiators only came up to my waist, the Minotaur could easily hold one on its shoulders, even though it was made of marble.

I tapped him on the shoulder. "Hey, uh—"

"Dave!" he shouted.

"Dave, right. What's going on?"

"Welcome to the Thundergnome!" he crowed, never taking his eyes off the action.

"Thundergnome?"

He nodded, taking a sip off his beer tube. "Sometimes they don't like to wait for battle situations to bring in a new gnome, so they do something like this." He shouted something about the combatants and their parentage. "As a gladiator, I have to say I approve, eh. Maybe after this they'll give us a go, you think?"

"One can dream," I said. I thanked him, waving off his offer of the beer tube before moving to the other side of the action to see what was going on.

Once I was able to see, I noticed Frank—at least the shoes looked like his—covered in gnomes, wrestling on the dirt. He appeared to be holding his own. Some things are just so surreal that they don't even register in your brain as weird. I shrugged and left Frank to his gnome wrestling and went to find my bed.

I'm not quite sure when I passed out, but it was full dark when I got home. My sleep was pretty deep, though. I kept having weird dreams about searching all over the house for glowing chocolate eggs like some sort of demented Easter bunny. Then I had to go to the zoo and put Ling Tsu the panda back to rest, only someone kept moving the zoo. I finally woke up in a sweat sometime midmorning. For a few minutes, I just sat on the edge of my bed, scratching the sleeping head of Taco, who'd curled up in a ball by my feet in the night, and tried to wake up. It didn't work. I knew it had been a dream—I'd put Ling Tsu the panda back after I'd killed Douglas—but I was having a hard time shaking it. Finally, I pulled on a T-shirt, getting tangled up in a rather embarrassing fashion with my pouch necklace somehow, before yanking on some shorts and stumbling downstairs, Taco padding after me. Though I felt better after my long sleep, I was groggy as all get-out.

I grabbed a soda and a seat at the kitchen table before collapsing facedown. Frank, I noticed after a moment, was doing the exact same thing. James was bustling around the kitchen, chipper and neat as a pin. It was rather obnoxious, really.

"Bad night?" I mumbled at Frank.

He groaned. "Never, ever accept anything out of a gnome's flask."

James sniggered.

"Quiet, you." I poked Frank. "Just ignore smarty-pants over there."

"No," Frank said with a sigh. "I should have known better. But I was trying to bond with the guys, you know?"

I did know. When I used to work with Frank at Plumpy's, he'd done his best to get to know the rest of the crew and fit in. It was kind of adorable in its awkwardness.

"Plus, I lost, like, fifty bucks betting on the gladiator fight after mine, and I can't get all my face paint off, and Dunaway is coming over after his shift so he can go through our library, and I look like I made out with Rambo." He twisted his face so I could see the dark smudges of paint under his eyes.

"I hear cold cream does wonders," James said. "And you should never bet against Dave. He currently holds the title amongst the other gladiators, if I remember correctly." He sipped his tea. "Maybe you shouldn't bet. You appear to be a poor judge of character." Even James's voice was perky. Morning people are annoying. If he kept smiling and sipping his tea in that jaunty manner, I was going to grab an orange out of the fruit bowl and chuck it at his head.

Frank squeezed his eyes shut against the light streaming into the kitchen. "James, I generally consider that I'm poor at everything. It saves time."

James frowned over his tea. "That's no way to look at things."

I smiled into the crook of my arm. It's hard to pick on someone when he rolls over like Frank tends to do.

"As long as none of them peed on my sheets again," I said with a laugh.

"I don't think they will. I'm pretty sure everything is smoothed over now, so there's really no reason to add to the long list of awful stuff they've been doing. At least I found out how Taco got here. The gladiators ordered him out of a catalog.

I think they saw the regime change as a chance to get a long-desired pet."

James stirred his tea. "Ah yes, that rings a bell. That's how it came up originally. The gladiators wanted one—something about playing fetch with their stone shields. Wouldn't work with a dog, but chupacabras have strong jaws."

"Is that why Douglas didn't want one?" asked Frank. "He hates fetch?"

James shot him a withering look. "No, he didn't want one because they disrupt magic. If you let Taco loose on the grounds and aren't careful, he could bust all the protective wards and who knows what else. They are the rodents of the magical world."

I took a sip of my soda, thinking. "Wait, Frank, go back a minute, what long list of awful stuff?"

He grimaced. "It's best if you don't know."

"You're probably right." I looked around the cheerful kitchen with its perky yellow walls and white curtains, and it really wasn't helping things. "Ugh, I can't handle this kitchen anymore. James, I'm beginning to think you painted it this way so none of us would linger, except you did it before we lived here. If anyone needs me, I'll be on the front porch."

When Ashley materialized, I was seated at the table on the porch, enjoying the weather and examining the jade egg I'd stashed in my pouch. Even in the summer sun, it was chill to the touch. Ashley wasn't wearing her standard Catholic school-girl chic. Her hair was pulled back into ponytails as usual, but that was the only thing that was the same. Flip-flops, short shorts, and a tank top with what appeared to be a glittery purple unicorn on it took the place of her usual outfit. And she had on purple, heart-shaped sunglasses. It was all very un–Ashley-like.

"What's with the gear?"

She hopped into a chair, crossing her legs and propping them on another chair. "Kinda stands out, don't you think? School uniform in the summer months?" She yanked a sucker out of her mouth to talk to me.

"That's never really stopped you before. And that doesn't mean you have to wear purple sparkly unicorn shirts."

"There is nothing more universal, Sam, than a girl in a unicorn top. Besides—" she held the tank out to show me the rest of the shirt. There was some glittery script under the rainbow the unicorn was galloping on. It said BITE ME.

"Ah," I said. "That makes more sense."

She popped the sucker back into her mouth, shoving it into her cheek. "Whatcha got there?"

I rolled it over to her. "I'm not sure. I think there's something going on with it. I mean, I found it in a weird place in Douglas's house, like he was hiding it, and it's cold all the time, so I figure it's got some sort of Creepy Douglas Death Magic on it, but I'm afraid to monkey with it, since I don't know anything about it."

"This whole house is weird, so how can you say it has a specific weird place?" Ashley snatched the egg off the table. "Let me see that." She peered at it, a grimace slowly forming on her face. "You're right. It's almost like . . ." She shook her head. "Never mind. You said you found this here?"

I nodded.

"That would explain the oddness of it, then. I'm suspicious of anything that comes from this house. We've got enough to deal with for now, though, so I say stash it in your pouch. That should neutralize or hide whatever it is. We can come back to it in the short window of time after this crisis blows over and before the next one begins."

I tucked it away as she bid. Ashley can get kind of bossy when you argue with her, and since I didn't know what else to do with the thing, I'd do what she said for now. With Ash, you pick your battles carefully.

Ashley threw her sucker stick onto the table. "Okay, now that we got all that out of the way, we can get to the important stuff—namely, we can try to figure out what happened the night of the bonfire."

Frank and James came out to join us, the former flopping down in a seat next to me while the latter swirled into cat form before leaping up and settling himself regally on one of the chair cushions.

"This view used to be so lovely before that wooden abomination was constructed." His eyes flicked back and forth as he said this, following Ramon on the ramp. Ramon was human again and putting his skateboard to good use. I was glad someone had energy this morning.

I started to reply, but was interrupted by Taco crawling up my leg and settling in my lap. He eyed the feline with interest before James hissed at him. I smiled and scratched Taco's head, causing him to close his eyes and purr in his odd little way.

With a wary look at the content chupacabra, James began explaining my state when he took me to my mom's house the other night, mostly for Frank's benefit, though Ashley had missed the last part, since she'd had to take off. Taco rolled onto his back and offered up his belly for some scratching. I complied while James finished with his recitation.

"James, would you mind repeating all that to somebody?" Ashley asked.

"And what do I get out of that?" he asked, his lids drooping lazily as he looked at her.

"How about I keep petting Taco so he doesn't start looking for a kitty snack and you don't have the embarrassing recurrence of me vomiting all over your shoes? How's that for compensation?" I asked.

"No need to get nasty," he said, not looking at me. "I was kidding. Sort of." He added the last bit when I stopped petting Taco and glared at him.

Ashley pushed her sunglasses onto the top of her head. "Sam, this should be somewhat official, so would you mind opening a portal for me? I'd like to discuss this with Ed."

I hesitated. "Ash, last time I did that, it took a lot of blood." I shuddered inwardly. The last time I'd seen Ed, I'd been in Douglas's basement, exhausted, battered, and confused. The summoning had been an accident, and it almost got me killed.

Ashley patted my shoulder. "You were untrained and scared. Plus, you have access to more power now. I don't think you'll have a problem at all. Just try it like you're calling me, and we'll go from there."

Even though she'd been fairly helpful this week, it was

weird to have Ash be nice to me. Not that she wasn't a sweet person or anything; it's just that her sweetness was usually covered in wasps, like a soda left out on a particularly hot summer day. You know the kind that bite and sting you? And maybe you don't notice them in your soda and you take a drink because it's hot and you accidentally swallow one and it stings your esophagus and you have to be taken to the hospital because you find out that you're allergic to wasps? But no matter how much pain you're in, the soda was still pretty sweet and refreshing because it was so hot, and you don't regret drinking it, even if it did have a freakishly high cost.

It was like that.

"Okay," I said slowly. "I'll give it a shot." I closed my eyes. My breathing slowed. Deep breath in through the nose. Hold it. Out the mouth. I continued this pattern until everything inside me felt still and calm. Then I pictured Ed. I'd only seen him once, but you don't forget Ed. He was around seven feet tall, golden-skinned, with the silvery-black head of a jackal. Yeah, he was pretty easy to pick out of a lineup. Once I had his image firmly in place, I pushed my power at it. I knew it had worked before I even opened my eyes. I think it was the sound of Frank choking on his drink that gave me the first clue.

When I looked, Ed was standing next to Ashley, who was smacking Frank on the back trying to get him to stop choking. Ed had his arms crossed and was looking rather amused by the whole thing. At least, I think he was amused. Kind of hard to tell, actually.

After all the commotion had passed, Ashley brought Ed up to speed. He leaned against the railing and settled in, nodding at James to retell his story. He asked a few questions, which caused another choking fit with Frank, since no one had warned him that Ed spoke telepathically. Once Frank had stopped sputtering, Ed made Ashley tell him about last night. When the story was finished, he turned to me.

And you remember nothing?

I went to speak, then frowned when nothing came out. It wasn't like I didn't remember anything, but it was disjointed, like trying to remember what happened after an evening of hard drinking. Things flashed and surfaced, but then quickly sank down again. I told them what I did remember—a lady by a fire, flowers, laughter.

Ed tapped his fingers on one of the copper cuffs that adorned his biceps. *It would take a lot of power to disrupt what you were trying to do, and an intimate connection to the deceased.*

"So what can do something like that?" I asked. Taco continued to purr, his eyes closed. He didn't care what we were talking about as long as I kept scratching him. He didn't seem much like the rodent of the magical world to me.

Ashley socked me in the arm, then she thought about it and punched me again, just for good measure. "Why can't you stop having weird things happen to you? Seriously, it's like you're a strange-magnet. Cut it out!"

Ah, there was the Ashley I've come to know and love. Ed was apparently used to these kinds of outbursts from her and ignored it.

We are talking about something above my pay grade. Perhaps an elemental spirit or a creature of that nature. Ed's ears twitched. I'm pretty sure if I hung around Ed long enough, I'd be able to tell what he was feeling all the time just by watching his ears. *It would have to be something powerful,* he said, scratching his chin. You would think his thoughtful expression would sit oddly on such a canine face, but it didn't. He looked wise, and I could see why the Egyptians had carved the images of his race onto pyramids. Ed was that badass.

"Could anyone at the Den have done it?" Frank asked. He leaned forward, his elbows on the table. One of the gnomes was crawling around his shoulders and muttering.

No, not anyone that you have mentioned. These were heavy workings. What is that creature doing?

"I think he's measuring me for a proper gnome hat."

Ed's nose wrinkled. *But you are not a gnome.*

Frank blushed. "I know, but they've sort of made me an honorary general or something."

I almost laughed, but then the gnome—I think it was Twinkle, it was kind of hard to tell them apart sometimes—stood up, put his hands on his hips, and beamed fiercely at us. Since it appeared to be a serious source of pride for the gnome, and since I didn't particularly want my room trashed again, I quelled my amusement.

"Excellent, Frank," I said. "Good job. You're finally moving up in the world." I eyed Twinkle gravely. "Is this the kind of event that warrants a celebration?"

The tiny gnome nodded solemnly, but proudly too. "'Tis. A promotion of rank is always marked by much revelry. But his should be doubly so. It's not every day we let a non-gnome wear the hat." He patted Frank's ear affectionately.

I smiled. "Then it will be doubly done. Can you let me know what you'll need? It would be bad form to have Frank set up his own party."

Frank blushed even more, but Twinkle seemed happy that I was taking the whole business seriously. "Aye. We can do that." He tipped his hat at me and disappeared into the bushes.

Your house is very entertaining.

"Thanks, Ed."

Frank raised his hand.

I rolled my eyes. "We're not in class. You can just talk," I told him.

He lowered his hand slowly. "Could something like Ed do it? I mean, you said whatever killed Brannoc came out of nothing. Maybe that same force is keeping you away?"

Ed's ear twitched, and he looked thoughtful. *The power is there, but like Ashley, I would have to answer to our overseer, and he would not be amused with such interference.*

Frank processed this. "Well, that tells us something, right? Ed is considered a heavy hitter, isn't he?" He peered up at Ed. "What did Ashley call you? An upper-level entity?"

"Yeah," Ash said, "he's got some juice." She pursed her lips. "So what we're looking for is probably not mortal, something big, something from a higher plane, like a demigod or something associated with a major pantheon." She looked at me and narrowed her eyes. "What kind of shit storm did you land us in this time?"

"I would like to point out at this juncture that this is not my fault in any way."

"It never is," she said with a sigh.

We sat quietly for a minute, all of us deep in thought. I sifted through my brain trying to come up with any little tidbit or memory, anything that might get us closer to what was going on.

"The flower," I blurted out. Everyone turned and looked at me. I got some blank expressions and a few worried ones.

"The flowers are very pretty this time of year," James said hesitantly.

"No," I said, frustrated. "When I came back that first time, I had a flower with me. I remember, because I put it on Brannoc's pyre. But it was nighttime, and the flower was fully open, and I didn't pick it. The flower was with me when I came back."

"That's something," Ashley said.

Frank got up and dusted off his jeans. "Enough for me to get started," he said.

"On what?" I asked. I was grateful for his enthusiasm, but to me it didn't seem like much to go on.

"Research," he said. "I can cross-reference higher-level entities with flowers, see what we can come up with. Not everything is associated with flowers, right?"

No, but many of them are.

"It will still give me somewhere to start. And as we learn more, I can narrow it down. James, can you come down to the library? You might be able to help me."

"I need to go to Tia's house first." His whiskers twitched. "Sam has asked me to go and assess their security."

"Oh. Okay. After, then?"

James nodded and Frank left. It was amazing to me to see how much self-esteem Frank had gained in the past few months. When I'd first started to work with him, he seemed like such a shy and lost little kid. He was pretty young, but not so young that his shyness made sense. As I got to know him better, I started to understand. I don't think Frank had ever had anyone show full confidence in him. His parents were indifferent at best. He'd often stay for days at my old apartment, and they didn't seem concerned that their minor was gone for some pretty major stretches. It wasn't that he was unloved, but they certainly seemed preoccupied. So to see Frank starting to come into his own, well, it felt good.

I wondered what his gnome name would be.

Ashley sniffed, wiping away a pretend tear from her face. "Our little boy is growing up so fast."

I pulled her pigtail. "Shut up. I'm proud of him."

"Me too," she said. "Isn't that what I just implied?"

A very entertaining house. Ed seemed to be enjoying his time here tremendously.

James cleared his throat. "If I can add something?"

"Sure?" It was best to make it a question with James and leave full judgment on whether his adding something was okay only after he actually added it.

"You might also want to talk to the pack and see if they have a patron god or creature or something associated with them. That could save you a lot of time. You know, assuming they'll talk to you."

I blinked at him. Sometimes, it's easy to overly complicate

things. "You just earned yourself ten brownie points," I said, grabbing my phone. I walked into the yard so I could make my call with a little privacy, when I noticed an unfamiliar car pulling up. I didn't know what kind—Ramon was the car guy—but it was sleek, expensive looking, and had darkly tinted windows. Because of that last bit, I was only mildly surprised when a large umbrella poked out and unfurled, followed quickly by Kell.

He advanced, looking coolly sophisticated in his three-piece suit and wearing his wide and toothy smile. I didn't know how old Kell was or if vampires lived as long as I thought they did, but I wondered if he was as smooth and charismatic before he died. Since he was the only vampire I knew, I couldn't tell if it was just him or not. He managed to look suave even walking under an umbrella on a sunny day, so I was inclined to think he'd been dead at least long enough to get some practice making that look completely normal.

"Good morning," he said. "Mind if I approach? I'd much prefer the porch if it is all right with you and your guests."

"Sure," I said, pocketing my phone. We walked back to the porch.

Once under the overhang, Kell collapsed his umbrella. He greeted the group as he did, seeming to know everyone there, which surprised me. He stopped on James. "That's a nice look for you," he said, indicating James's kitty status. "Very svelte." Kell's mouth twitched as he said it, a small smirk on his face. James simply nodded in greeting and then ignored him. It would take a lot more than that to shake him up.

Kell made himself at home, pulling up a chair and sitting at the table.

"To what do we owe your visit?" I asked.

"Council business. We need you to accompany Pello up to the mountains."

"Yeah, 'cause last time I helped, I did so well. I'm still finding seaweed in uncomfortable places."

Kell tilted his head. "Really?"

"Well, no, not as such, but you know what I mean. And seriously, don't we have enough with Brannoc's death and all?"

"Seriously," Kell said, "current tragedy aside, we still have a job to do. The world continues to turn, even after we die."

"That seems a little heartless," I said.

"Brannoc of all people would have understood," he said, "that we cannot allow ourselves to wither and fade just so we can adhere to convention. We mourn while we work." He tapped me with the umbrella. "Now, get properly dressed."

"What does that mean?" I said, starting to rise. "Like a suit or something?"

"Like good shoes and a water bottle. You're going hiking."

20

I FEEL THE EARTH MOVE
UNDER MY FEET

"Kell wasn't joking," I panted, stopping to pull out my canteen and drink. Pello offered me his handkerchief, and even if it hadn't been covered in filth and spots of . . . something, I wouldn't have accepted it. Everything Pello owned fell into the category of "I don't know where that's been and I don't particularly want to, either."

"No, thanks," I said. "Got my own."

Pello tucked his away without using it. He wasn't sweaty, despite the uphill climb and his beer gut. Ramon, who had come as my escort and additional muscle in case I needed it, wasn't breaking a sweat either. We'd also brought Taco, who was bounding from rock to fallen tree and racing through the dappled sunshine in blatant disregard of the leash law. The sunlight and fresh air, I figured, would be good for him, but I'd fed him before we left. I didn't want him taking down Bambi on our first trip to the great outdoors. He sprang merrily after a butterfly and didn't look winded in the slightest.

"Hey, what gives?" I asked. "Why am I the only one suffering here? There's no way in hell Pello is in better shape than me." I quickly added, "No offense meant, Pello."

The satyr grinned lecherously at me. "I get plenty of car-di-o." He punctuated the word with some questionable thrusting.

"Okay," I said. "Never do *that* again. And I call bullshit. So serious answer, please." I took another swig from my canteen while I waited. It had taken us over an hour and a half of driving plus a ferry ride to get to Olympic National Park. We'd been hiking and walking for over an hour on a wandering trail, and I was beginning to wonder why whoever we were meeting hadn't just come to us like everyone else.

The air felt somewhat cooler underneath all the old-growth pines towering above me. Despite, or perhaps because of, everything going on, it was really nice to get outside. Another butterfly flickered by, floating past a mass of ferns to a small open nook. I'd have to come back here when I wasn't concerned with my friend's murder and my own potential demise at the hands of his pack.

Pello gave a half shrug. "I am at my best in the forest. This is where my power lies." He affectionately patted the thin, peeling white bark of the paper birch next to him.

"So if we were urban hiking?" When he gave me a blank look, I added, "It's exactly what it sounds like—hiking through city trails." Downtown Seattle had steep hills that were appealing for that sort of thing. Not that I did it. I'm not much of a hiker, urban or otherwise. A leisurely stroll through the woods? Yes. A ten-mile uphill death march? No, thank you.

"I would be in your sorry state," he replied with a grin.

We started moving again, and I snagged a few huckleberries off a bush while we walked. When we were younger, my parents would take us out hiking and camping all the time.

If we were good, and if we were diligent enough about picking—but not eating—enough huckleberries, my mom would make pancakes in a griddle over our fire. There were few things better after a day of hiking than waking up to pancakes with those tart red berries. Bellies full, we'd spend the rest of the morning sitting on downed trees or large boulders by the lake, fishing for rainbow trout.

I flicked a berry at Ramon. "What about you? You've never been what I'd call a forest denizen."

Ramon grunted. "Maybe not before, but I am now. Besides, after weeks of trying to keep up with the pack, I've just got more endurance for this kind of thing." He thumped his chest with one hand, Tarzan-style.

Sometimes, if I wasn't thinking about it, I forgot what had happened to my best friend. That we'd both changed over the spring. The remembrance was always followed by a wash of guilt. I was born to be this way, but Ramon's state was completely my fault. He'd gained it by trying to save my scrawny ass.

I flushed and looked down, concentrating for a moment on the crisscrossed formation of roots at my feet. "Right," I mumbled. "Sorry."

Ramon either didn't want to talk about it or felt that apologies weren't necessary, and he didn't answer.

"I'd forgotten how pretty it is out here. We should come back. I'll bring Brid, and you can drag Dessa along. We can double date." Oh, wait. My gut bottomed out even more. "Never mind. What I meant to say was, 'You can bring Dessa up here, and I'll follow you crying and being a big, whiny baby.' *Très* romantic, no?"

Ramon glanced at me. "You were really serious about her, huh?"

Taco came back to me then, a suspicious feather sticking out of his mouth. I plucked it and held it up in front of him. "No poaching. Got it?" He managed to look hangdog for approximately two seconds before I felt bad about scolding him. I picked up a stick. "You wanna play? Here." I threw the stick. "Fetch!" Taco didn't need any encouragement—he took off like a shot.

I turned back to Ramon. "Yeah, I mean it hasn't been super long but . . ." It was hard to put it into words. Brid was, well, she was amazing. But it was more than that. We had fun together. And as cheesy as it sounds, we fit.

Ramon finished my sentence for me. "But you're stupid for her."

"Ridiculously, boneheadedly so, yes." I gave him big puppy eyes. "She completes me," I said in an eerie singsong voice. Taco came back with the stick, a look of grave importance on his face . . . that lasted until I tried to take the stick back. I grabbed for it, and he danced away, stopping just out of my reach. I managed to snatch it (when a bug distracted him) and tossed it again. We were going to have to work on "dropping it."

After a minute of digesting what I'd said, Ramon nodded. I examined him closely. "What, that's it? A nod? No 'you're too young' or 'you're still at the infatuation stage, so give it some time' kind of speech?"

Ramon stopped and put his hands on my shoulders. "Look, you're my best friend in the whole world, so I'm only going to say this once and then we're going to forget I said it, because we're dudes and we don't like to talk about feelings—"

I snorted. "Please. You cry like a baby every time we watch *Old Yeller*."

He pointed a finger in my face. "That's different. That's a dog. Now, listen up. You're my best friend, and I love you, so obviously no girl is ever going to be good enough. That being said, you're not going to do any better than Brid." I opened my mouth, but he cut me off. "Not because you're not awesome, but because she is."

"Wait, what?"

He shook his head. "If anyone is perfect for you, it's that girl. I've seen you guys together and, well, I think you're meant to be." He paused, thinking. "Getting stuck in that cage might have been the best thing that ever happened to you."

I cocked my head at him with a grin. "Aw, you're a romantic! I can't believe I never realized it before. That's adorable."

He jabbed his finger in my face again. "Shut up. I don't know what you're talking about. This conversation never happened." He turned away and kept walking.

I jogged to catch up. "Oh, don't be like that. C'mon. Ladies love a sensitive guy."

"I take it all back. I hate you," he grumbled. He gave me the silent treatment after that.

Pello was leading, and once we'd gone a few minutes in and the trail was out of sight, he paused to take off his necklace. The odd-looking charm he usually kept around his neck was actually a purchased glamour—an object that changed the perception of the people around you. It made it possible for the satyr to live in an urban environment. With it, he looked like a dirty, overweight, dreadlocked skeezeball hanging out in one of the parks sleeping under trees or hitting on underage girls. To me, he'd always looked like a washed-up Dead Head with his flip-flops, ripped jean cutoffs, and stained Hawaiian shirt open and framing his rounded gut.

Without the charm, he looked exactly the same until you got to the gut, below which you found fur and hooved feet instead of the usual scrawny legs and sandals. Unfortunately, he felt more comfortable going pantsless. On meeting days, Ariana made him wear a Utilikilt that she had purchased for him so she wouldn't have to see anything she didn't want to or worry about where his naked ass had been. Her next goal was to get him to utilize the kilt's "modesty snaps," or at the very least learn to cross his legs. It was an uphill battle.

I wouldn't have cut off-trail without Pello. I wasn't that experienced as a hiker, and the woods were full of lots of things that weren't fuzzy bunnies and happy butterflies. As I was thinking this, the forest gave me an example in the form of a seven-foot thorny menace referred to as devil's club. It's an aptly named thorny plant, and it can grow in large, dense clumps that I don't recommend walking through unless you are a masochist or happen to have a sharp machete on your person.

I was well versed on this plant. My mom cultivated some of it behind her house. Devil's club is related to ginseng, and it's used in a lot of herbal remedies. Despite being a literal pain—I spent a good deal of my childhood nursing wounds from harvesting that plant—it was kind of beautiful. The leaves resemble those found on the maple, and they can grow really big. In the summer, the plant blooms with these tiny flowers that later turn into bright red berries.

We tried to slip around the plant, but even though we were aware of it, we all got a few things tangled in its leaves. One particularly thorny bit snagged my arm and drew blood. I hissed at it as I pulled the leaf slowly away from my flesh. It was a slow process because I didn't want the plant leaving any barbs behind, and I knew from my mom's garden that the plants are actually quite delicate. I didn't want to harm it, even though it was making me bleed. I lectured it under my breath as I detangled myself.

"Sorry, guys," I said, focusing on my task. "This is going to be a second." Getting no response, I glanced up at my companions. Both of them were about five feet away, their backs to a large conifer. They managed to both be looking up with identical looks of amazement on their faces. Taco, concerned, had climbed up onto my shoulder and was eyeing my battle with the plant.

"What?" That was all I needed, something else going wrong.

Ramon licked his lips. "The plant."

"What about it?" I asked, frowning.

"Look at it."

"That's what I've been doing." I went back to my careful extraction. Apparently I'd snagged part of my backpack on it as well.

"Dude, *chico*, look up."

I paused my extraction and did what I was told. The giant plant was . . . cowering. I'm not kidding, that's what it looked like: a giant, leafy, scolded child. And that's what I'd been doing exactly—scolding it. I stood there for a moment, surprised and bleeding and a little amazed. I'd seen ill-mannered plants act this way around my mother sometimes. When Tia LaCroix walked through a forest, you could bet nothing snagged her favorite shawl. This plant was treating me like my mother. But why now? If I had a bit of witch in me, why hadn't it come out earlier? I gave a mental sigh. Yet another question to put into the "hell-if-I-know" pile.

While I was staring at the plant, a giant crow—and I mean *giant*—landed on a branch above me. I'd never seen one so huge. Taco hissed at it. The crow seemed unimpressed.

"Holy shit," Ramon said. "That thing could carry off babies."

Pello stared at the crow thoughtfully. "Crows are harbingers and omens. Big juju stuff."

"My mom said a ton of crows showed up at my birth. She said one was the size of, well, that." I nodded at the crow. "She even named me after them—my middle name is Corvus."

"Well, then, I suggest you be nice to it," Pello said, and he turned and started walking farther into the trees.

The bird was uncharacteristically quiet, apparently happy with its silent vigil.

"Ramon, can you get that container out of my bag? The one we packed for Taco?" It was full of roast chicken and sliced ham. Ramon handed a chunk of ham to Taco so he'd stop looking at us in an accusatory manner, then placed a particularly large chunk of chicken on a branch for the crow. The crow didn't move, but I felt we'd done enough, so he repacked my bag and wiped his greasy fingers on my shirt.

The crow apparently appeased, I returned my attention to the devil's club. "It's okay," I told the plant. "I'm not mad. It was my fault. You were just protecting yourself." The nettle, slowly, as if expecting a blow at any moment, started to pull away. I winced, an involuntary hiss escaping my lips. The plant immediately snapped back to where it had been. Not ideal. I repeated, as soothingly as I could, that it was still okay, and then I slowly pulled my arm away from the spines. My skin was bloody and irritated and stinging, but I'd had the forethought to put some of my mom's balm in my backpack, so once I'd rinsed it, it would be okay.

The plant still looked . . . scared. I know plants don't have faces or expressions or anything, but it still managed to convey that emotion to me.

I patted a leaf gently. "Good boy," I said. The plant perked up. I smiled and gave it another pat before stepping away. The devil's club pulled itself taller, its leaves spreading a little farther out, its tiny flowers opening up a bit more. If the plant were a person, I'd say it was puffing itself up with pride. My grin still fixed on my face, I backed away.

"Let's get out of here before anything else odd happens." Ramon and I started walking again, ignoring the giant crow and the weird plant as best we could.

We caught up with Pello and stopped under a big tree somewhere in the middle of the woods. I was completely lost by now, so hopefully nothing untoward would happen to

Pello while we were out here, or I would have to learn to live off the land. I settled into a cozy spot amidst the roots and drank some more from my canteen.

"So, who or what are we meeting here, again? And is there anything I need to know? Like, for example, anything I might blurt out that could be found offensive?"

"I'm sure you'll do fine. We're very understanding." I turned at the sound of the deep voice and saw . . . hairy knee-caps. I looked up. And up. And then I swallowed hard. "We do have some river nymphs, though. Pretty harmless for the most part, but they can be temperamental. Not nearly as calm as the dryads."

Ramon, who was sitting next to me, was having a reaction similar to mine. We were both staring with a glazed look at the biggest guy I'd ever seen. He was about as tall as Ed, but where Ed was lean, this guy was built . . . well, the term *brick shithouse* comes to mind, though I've never quite understood what that meant. He was big in scale, not just tall. And he was covered from head to giant toe in reddish brown fur. Oddly enough, he was wearing an olive green forest ranger's uniform.

Ramon whistled. "I bet you would've made a mean line-backer."

The hairy man smiled, and his teeth were like giant off-white boulders. Realizing I was staring, I tried to stop, but I couldn't. "You're a, um . . ." I couldn't quite bring myself to say it. Even after all I'd seen and all the creatures I'd met, he was unbe-lievable.

He chortled at my reaction, then squatted down in a

movement slightly more monkey than man and offered me a hand, palm up, like you do with scared animals sometimes so they can smell you, which is both weird and a good way to lose a finger if the animal is scared. I gave him five instead. That really tickled him, and he tousled my hair while continuing to chuckle. "I believe the current moniker you've given us is Bigfoot. We'll just leave it at that." He helped me up. "But you may call me Murray." He tapped the cursive stitching on his shirt. It said MURRAY. Go figure.

Somehow the mundane nature of his name helped me pull my brain back together. "Is that your actual name?"

He helped Ramon up. "No, but my language is hard for *hashmuk* to say."

I tried to repeat the strange word he'd said, but it was oddly guttural and accented, and I couldn't repeat it. I gave up. "What is . . . whatever you just said?"

"*Hashmuk*. It is what we call your kind. Roughly translated it means 'skittish naked badger.'"

"Funny," I said. "We're usually compared to monkeys."

He scratched his chest. "Never seen a monkey." He motioned for us to follow. We fell in behind him, Pello introducing us as we walked. Though I could tell Murray was slowing his pace for us, I still had to jog occasionally to keep up. He led us to an open area by a stream and motioned for us to sit.

We spread out by the stream, unpacking our respective lunches carefully. Murray got out his lunch—some fruit and what smelled like smoked salmon.

"If I ask you some questions, do you promise to not throw me in that stream?" I asked. He nodded and kept eating.

"Are you actually a forest ranger?"

"Yes."

"Doesn't that cause problems?"

He pulled a long chain out of his pocket. At the end of it dangled a charm similar to Pello's. Ah. "So you just look like one of us to them, eh?"

The slowly spinning charm caught Taco's attention. He started to stalk it, his ears flattened to his skull and his tail twitching. Murray, an amused smile on his face, twirled the necklace some more.

"Better put that away," Pello said through a mouthful of food. "Otherwise that chup there will bite right through it."

Murray shrugged. "I can always replace the chain."

Pello shook his head. "No. Chup as in *chupacabra*." At Murray's blank look he added, "If he bites it, the magic will be toast. They're disruptive." Murray quickly stashed the necklace, but handed a piece of salmon to Taco when the little guy let out a dismayed chirp.

All the stuff James had said about Taco clicked into place. That was why Douglas didn't want them around—who would if one snap of the jaws would undo any magic you'd been working on? Besides us, I mean.

Murray patted the pocket where he'd put the necklace. "Yes, well, at any rate, it works fairly well. They think I'm a very large man with a strange diet. Often I am referred to as a 'health nut.' Occasionally, I buy snack treats as camouflage. Cheetos work well, as I can get the neon powder everywhere but not actually have to eat them." He shuddered.

"How can you not like Cheetos?" Ramon asked.

"How can you like them? They are not food, and they smell *wrong*."

"I like them," Pello said, raising his hand.

Murray snorted. "I have seen you eat old tires and tin cans. I do not consider you a good spokesman for Cheetos."

I settled into my spot in the grass. It was days like these that reminded me why I loved the Northwest so much. The sun was warm and pulling out the smell of grass and clover. The thick scent of some kind of flower wafted over. The combination with the sound of the stream burbling and a slight breeze rustling the trees made me aware of the life all around. The idyllic moment built a fierce joy in me, and I welcomed it. For a brief spell, I forgot about Brannoc, Haley, murder, the Council, and death. I felt the warm wind and the grass under me. It was wonderful.

And like all perfect moments, it couldn't continue. I took my sandwich out of its container with a sigh. James had prepared everything carefully, making sure that I knew to pack everything out and not leave a single scrap behind. Not that I would have anyway, but now I knew why he was so insistent.

"Beautiful, isn't it?" Murray eyed me knowingly.

"I can certainly see why you like it here," I said.

Ramon leaned back onto his elbows. "Yeah, man. Beautiful."

I rested my sandwich on an upturned lid and pulled out a container of fruit salad. "But I doubt you had us come up for the view."

"Wouldn't that have been nice, though?" Ramon asked

quietly. He wasn't looking at us, but gazing out over the stream instead. I knew what he was getting at. Seemed like everyone wanted a little piece of us lately. Or more specifically, a little piece of me. Ramon, Frank, they were just casualties. The guilt that welled up at that thought was beginning to feel familiar.

"So what can the Council do for you, Murray?"

He didn't answer right away. He examined his food carefully, like he was trying to find something inside his grapes that might help him out. "I am part of what you might call an experiment." He plucked a dark purple grape. "That's not quite right. Part of a flagship program, maybe would be a better way to put it. Whatever term you wish to use, I am one of the few of my tribe to try and blend with yours. For a long time, we tried to remain apart. We kept to the woods and watched your kind from a distance. We were happy this way, but with the forest shrinking and the *hashmuk* coming closer, we couldn't stay hidden much longer. Your kind propagates so quickly."

"Yeah, we're like bunnies that way."

He grinned his too-big teeth at me.

"So is the program not working?" Ramon asked.

Murray shook his head. "No, it is actually working quite well. We've found several forestry positions to our liking. My brother is planting trees for a nonprofit, and his wife helps monitor and conserve the local salmon population. It is most satisfactory." His voice was full of pride as he said it.

"Wonderful," I said, stabbing a piece of pineapple with a

fork. "But I'm assuming you didn't call us out here just to give a status report." I looked around at the clearing while I chewed. "Not that I'd mind if you'd do so occasionally."

Murray nodded. "Indeed, it has gone so well that others are willing to try it. To live closer to town."

"Then what's the prob?" Ramon asked.

"We . . . in order to live with your kind, we need something we have never needed before. We need money." He patted the pocket where his charm was. "Besides the glamour, which hides our physical differences, we have to purchase a second one to obscure our scent during certain . . . seasons." Had his face not been covered in hair, I'd have said he was blushing.

"Seasons?" Ramon looked as confused as I felt.

Pello flopped down by me and stole a piece of my fruit salad. "He means rutting season. His kind gives off quite the pheromone-laden stench in the springtime. You know, it's how they attract a mate."

"Ah," I said. "I can see how that could be problematic."

Murray nodded emphatically. "Your kind either complains or gets a little too . . . friendly." He frowned at me. "My cousin Gary tried to work for UPS. More so than the rest of us, he is comfortable in urban settings. He seems fascinated by your culture. The combination of his scent and their infamous uniform, well, it was just too much for some humans. For a species that ignores its sense of smell so heavily, you certainly perk up for that sort of thing."

Ramon grunted. "I've always wondered about those

uniforms. I mean, they shouldn't be attractive ... all that brown, but somehow they are." He plucked at his own shirt. "Maybe I should apply for a job. . . ." He mumbled the last bit almost to himself.

I shrugged. "Like I said, bunnies. I assume you're not making enough at your jobs to pay for the charms?"

"Most of us, no. And besides the charms, we have to purchase food since we don't have enough time to gather it anymore. Then there's lodging, clothing, and we must pay for your paperwork."

"Paperwork?"

"You need things like social security cards and IDs to work. Kind of hard to get those things when you were born in the forest and have no paper trail."

"Oh," I said, "I see. Legal stuff. So what, exactly, do you need help with?"

Murray shifted around uncomfortably. This was hard for him, I think. "We wanted to see if maybe the Council would give us a grant? My brother, the one who works for the nonprofit, learned that sometimes the *hashmuk* government gives money to things that will help out other *hashmuk*."

"And you wanted to see if the Council would do the same for its people, yes?"

"Yes," he said, and his voice was passionate now. And since he was arguing for something that would help his family and friends thrive, I guess that made sense. "If only the Council would help with our charms, we could manage the rest."

I considered this. His request wasn't outlandish. I didn't

know how much the charms cost or whether or not the Council did grants. But if it would help Murray and his people, I didn't see the harm. I looked at Pello. "Do we do grants?"

"I imagine so," Pello replied thoughtfully. "We'd need to bring it before the entire Council, though, to see what we could do."

"Well, yeah, I figured." I stood up, brushing off my hands as I did so. I stuck one out toward Murray. He grabbed it with a grin and shook it. "I will do what I can for your people," I said.

His smile widened. "I know you will." Then he pulled me in for a bear hug. While he was squeezing the life out of me in a happy fashion, I considered how things might go if the Council denied his request. This embrace might turn quickly into another kind, one that I wouldn't walk away from. And as I tried to spit some of the Bigfoot hair out of my mouth, I considered, should the situation sour, sending Pello to deliver the message for me. Cowardly, perhaps, but death by Bigfoot didn't seem appealing, either.

We started packing up then, and Murray pulled me aside. "There was something else. It might be nothing, but you remember that cousin I mentioned?"

"Sexy Gary?"

"Yes, well, after the job with UPS . . . failed, we transferred him closer to the city. He works for the parks department out there. Anyway, there's an area he oversees that has been feeling some general upset. He's not sure what's going on, but it's like something nasty moved into the neighborhood, and it's causing a ripple effect."

"You want me to look into it?"

Murray nodded. "He's not sure what's out there yet, as he hasn't isolated the source, but he says whatever it is, it feels unnatural."

I scribbled my number on a scrap of paper and handed it to him. "Okay, have Gary give me a call, and I'll see what I can do." He thanked me, and we finished gathering our gear. When I looked over at Ramon, I noticed he had a wistful look on his face. He'd never been what I'd call the outdoorsy type, but judging from the expression he was wearing, I think that had changed. I wondered if that was another side effect of his transformation or just a naturally occurring thing. Was it his choice or brought on by the new life I'd shoved on him?

Murray walked us back toward the trail. He shuffled nervously, and I could tell he had something else to tell me.

"Spit it out, Murray. I promise I won't bite." As if to emphasize this, Taco chose that moment to climb up on my shoulder, curl around my neck, and pass out. The hike had him all tuckered out.

"I have already asked for so much, but I was wondering if you'd do me one last favor? There's a volunteer here—he's been helping me over the last few weeks—who wanted to transfer over into Gary's territory. I would drive him myself, but I figure you're already going that way. . . ."

"You want us to give him a ride?" I thought about the size of our car. "I'm not sure he'll fit."

"He is not like me. He is like you. *Hashmuk*."

I nodded in understanding. "Sure, I mean, we're already

going that way." I took a sip from my water bottle. "Murray, you could have come in to the Council to tell us all this. Why didn't you?"

He managed to look a bit sheepish. "I figured it would make a better argument if you saw what you were investing in." One big arm swept out to take in the whole forest.

And it was beautiful, but he was missing the point. I shook my head at him. "No, man. I mean, yeah, the forest is great, but we wouldn't really be investing in that," I said. "We'd be investing in you and your people, and I think you guys would have been enough. This," I said, doing a smaller imitation of his arm wave, "is just a wonderful by-product." I patted his shoulder. "That being said, I won't mind hauling my cookies out here for future discussions. It's loads better than sitting in a chair in the back room of a pub, even if it is a nice pub."

A few minutes later, we broke back onto the trail. Waiting for us was an older guy, probably about my mom's age, with summer-tanned skin and darker hair. He hopped up when he saw us and dusted himself off.

"They will take you," Murray said.

The guy grinned, still dusting off his shirt. "Thanks. You don't have to take me all the way to the park. There's someone in the city I'd like to visit first. . . ." He'd been shaking hands with the others, but trailed off when he got to me. Despite his somewhat awkward staring, I grabbed his hand to shake it and . . . suddenly understood why he'd stopped.

Even though he'd been out in the summer sun, his hand

felt cold to me. Ice cold. Necromancer cold. And when he finally spoke again, a few things fell into place.

"Samhain," he whispered. He was bigger than me, and the hair was darker, but the resemblance was undeniable, though it still took me a minute to place him. Not that surprising, since I hadn't seen him since I was a baby.

"Uncle Nick," I replied. We stood there, locked in an incredibly awkward moment. The silence dragged on and on and on. "I'm not sure how to react right now."

Ramon snorted. "Good thing you have me, then." And he punched my uncle straight in the eye. He was a trifle enthusiastic about it. Nick crumpled to the ground, unconscious.

"You might have hit him a little hard, Ramon."

"Sorry," he mumbled, picking up Nick and chucking him over his shoulder in a fireman's carry. "Still getting used to my new strength. Only meant to tap him one, you know?"

I patted his arm reassuringly. "I'm going to buy you the biggest milkshake we can find, oh, buddy of mine." Nick's head wobbled in agreement as Ramon adjusted his inert form on his shoulder. Maybe not the homecoming my uncle was imagining, but he'd kind of earned it.

Murray looked confused, and Pello looked worried.

Ramon gave a one-shouldered shrug in response. "He hasn't been the best uncle to my boy here."

"But we're still taking him with us?" Pello asked.

"Oh, yeah," Ramon said. "We just had to get that out of the way first."

I grinned.

Murray looked first at Ramon and then at my stupidly grinning face. "You seem like such nice boys, but I think that, in the future, I will try not to cross you."

"I can honestly say that's probably very wise of you," Ramon said, returning to his march as he began whistling a merry tune, Nick's head bobbing in counterpoint the whole way.

21

I GOT CAT CLASS, AND I GOT CAT STYLE

Douglas was drifting. He didn't dare keep the Stygian coin on all the time. It was unlikely that anyone would think to search for him—that was one of the positives of being dead—but if they did, the coin would make their job easier.

The problem was, when he didn't wear it, he had a hard time staying anchored in the here and now. It was so easy to drift into the past and away from what mattered. Douglas had spent most of his life as a focused kind of individual, so he found this development disturbing, to say the least. He didn't particularly enjoy remembering the past. . . .

The driver had been chattering incessantly since he'd picked Douglas up from the train station.

"So after I got back, I spent all my clams on this beauty. Hits on all sixes, she does. How 'bout you, young man, you in the war?"

"I was . . . at school." Nicely vague. You couldn't really tell people you weren't out performing your civic duties because you were too busy raising the dead. Something about his tone put the driver off, and the rest of the trip, while not entirely silent, was at least free from questions.

Douglas was surprised when the taxi took him to a middle-class neighborhood. The merchandise he'd come for was top end, which meant wealth. Sure, unexplainable wealth sometimes led to questions or made one stick out, but conversely he knew that this was the kind of neighborhood that asked questions. The houses, lined up in neat little brick rows, were close enough for gossip to slither easily amongst them.

None of his business, he supposed. He asked the taxi driver to wait, slipping him the fare he owed already to keep the car idling. Then he stepped into the cold spring rain, buttoning up his overcoat as he did so.

He used the brass knocker, noticing that the paint on the door was chipped and worn. Negligence, or more camouflage? He'd have to inspect carefully in case the former was a habit. Purchasing something that would get sick and die ran counter to the purpose of buying a live assistant in the first place. Not that Douglas had ever had an assistant. Since Auntie Lynn had died—and didn't that thought bring a smile to his lips?—he'd been content to be on his own. But a few years had gone by now, and while he didn't feel lonely per se, he figured that an extra set of hands would be useful.

A beleaguered old woman opened the door and ushered him in. She shambled into the back, beckoning him to follow. Taking in her tattered skirts and head covering, Douglas decided she originated from somewhere in Eastern Europe. Without a word, she deposited him into a room where a man sat drinking brandy by the fire. The man was much younger than the woman, but there was some resemblance, enough to make Douglas guess that this was her son.

"Mr. Smith, I presume?" He smiled at the obviously fake name. This man was no more a Smith than he was a kangaroo.

"Ah, Mr. Montgomery!" The man stressed the *Mr.,* a small jibe at Douglas's obvious youth, and grabbed him roughly and joyously by the arms, kissing his cheeks briskly. "It is fine to see you! As they say, at last we meet!" He let go and waved him to a moth-eaten chair. "Come, come! Enjoy the fire! May I offer you a refreshment?" Smith's eyes narrowed as he said this.

This is where things got thorny. To refuse would be rude. To accept could prove folly. What if the man poisoned his drink? That way he could pocket the money Douglas had on him for the sale, dump the body, and then keep using the merchandise as a lure. Not a wise business practice in the long run, but Douglas had no evidence to suggest that the man in front of him had any more wisdom than a wooden post.

Then again, if he didn't accept, he was showing weakness. He took a small brandy, watching as the man poured himself some from the same bottle. Douglas's shoulder relaxed a fraction, and the man smiled. They drank to health and wealth before the man sat and got down to business.

"You wish to see him now, yes? Why waste time with words when you could judge with eyes." The man shouted something in another language, and not one of the ones Douglas was familiar with. Eastern European, he was sure now, but beyond that, he couldn't guess. A few seconds passed and then the old lady returned, followed by a young boy.

"He's still learning English, but he speaks it well enough," Smith said.

Douglas ignored him and focused on the child. He looked no more than ten, possibly a little younger, though it was hard for Douglas to judge such things, as he hadn't spent much time around other children while he was growing up. Tall and thin, either due to a growth spurt or being underfed. Considering the boy's worth, he'd be surprised if it was out of neglect, but then again people abused things of worth all the time. Carriage drivers beat their horses, lords beat their servants, and husbands beat their wives. It was a very human thing to do.

The child waited calmly, and if being scrutinized bothered him, he didn't show it. Douglas looked him over slowly, even going so far as to examine the boy's teeth. And still he stood there, hands behind his back, silver eyes watching Douglas calmly.

"They say you speak English?"

"Yes," he said, with a similar accent to Smith's.

Douglas nodded. "What is your name?" From his research he knew that if the boy answered, it would tell him that he'd been owned before. The man could have taught him not to answer, of course, but Douglas felt he should try anyway. He could most likely tell if the youth was lying.

The boy regarded him with amusement, like he'd performed a funny trick. "I do not have a name yet. We are named by our first masters, and I have not had one."

"What do they call you, then?"

This amused the boy even more. "Boy. You. It does not matter."

"Have you mastered both forms?"

The amusement was transformed into a look of approval, making Douglas feel like he'd finally asked a proper question.

The boy reached up and took the small hat off his head, with a smile. Then, without a word or movement, he shifted like smoke. A dragon the size of a puppy fluttered in his place. He zipped around the room with a tiny roar, stretching his wings out, barrel-rolling with obvious joy. This went on for a minute or two, then the dragon hovered closer to the ground and shifted again. It was like watching the sands of an hourglass pour out from the shape of a dragon to a white-and-black kitten.

The kitten mewed at him, the quicksilver eyes large in the minute face. Though the sound was the scratch-crackle of a kitten, the message was unmistakable. A sort of "See? Now ask for something difficult." The kitten began cleaning its paw and ignoring him completely.

Douglas fished a quarter out of his pocket surreptitiously before tossing it quickly into the air. The silver flashed as it flipped; the picture of Lady Liberty on the newly minted coin flopping to the flying eagle so quickly that they were a blur. It never hit the floor—it didn't even make it to the top of its arc. The kitten so focused on cleaning between its toes became the dragon in a blink, caught the coin, and turned into the boy before landing. The quarter, Lady Liberty side up, sat in his pink palm, which he held out to Douglas.

He leaned in and curled the boy's fingers around the coin. Before he could say "keep it," the coin was gone, secreted away in some pocket or hidey-hole.

Smith grunted. "So? You made a decision, or are we going to do the parlor tricks all day?"

Douglas put a hand on the boy's shoulder and pulled a stack of bills out of his inner suit pocket. He tossed them at Smith. "The price that we discussed."

The man grabbed the money greedily, and Douglas could see the urge to count it out making the man's fingers twitch. Only the fear that Douglas would take it as an insult kept him from doing so. Though still young, his reputation was already spreading.

Smith pocketed the cash and, without looking at the boy, said, "Go get your things." The boy didn't move. The man scowled. "I said go get your things."

"You are not my master," the boy said, matter-of-factly. "You are not even my caretaker. Money has changed hands, and so have I."

The glower deepened on Smith's face, and his skin took on a reddish hue. The tart behavior might have angered Smith, but it pleased Douglas to no end. After all, a good companion should have a bit of spine to him.

Before Smith could start yelling, Douglas gave the boy a small push and told him to get his things. Without a second look at the angry man, he did just that.

"Don't you want to know where we are going?" Douglas asked. They were in the car and well away from Smith's house. The boy hadn't said a word.

Without taking his silver eyes off the scenery flashing by the window, he said, "Would you like me to ask?"

"Boy—" Douglas said and then stopped. "I can't keep calling you that."

"Then give me a name." They might have been discussing the weather for as much interest as the child showed.

He put his hands in his lap and watched Douglas. He showed no interest, no sign that he was invested in the conversation at all, but Douglas felt this might be a ruse. Perhaps a test to see what kind of master he would be, that this naming would set up the paradigm that they would follow from now on.

Having come to this conclusion, Douglas had an idea how to handle the situation. "What would you like to be called?"

When the boy looked at him, he had the same expression that he'd had earlier when Douglas asked whether he could change forms, the one that said he'd done something properly.

He thought for a moment, hands folded calmly in his lap, his eyes looking to the heavens. "James," he said. "I've always been partial to 'James.' When we were staying in London, there was a man who sold sweets in the shop on the corner. That was his name. He always gave me an extra bit of licorice. I had to smile for it, though." He mused on that for a moment. "Do they have licorice in this country?"

"They do."

The boy digested this. "May I have some?"

Douglas nodded in agreement. "I won't even make you smile for it." He held out his hand. "Welcome to the family, James."

James shook it solemnly before letting it go and returning to his vigil. "So, Master, where are we going?"

"We're going home, James. We're going home."

GET OUTTA MY DREAMS, GET INTO MY CAR

Uncle Nick came to sometime on the hike down. He didn't look super happy, but then again, he didn't complain either. He kept an eye on Ramon for the rest of the trip, even though my friend was just smiling and whistling. I scratched Taco's head and tried to hide my own smile.

Ramon offered to drive, since he wasn't nearly as worn out as I was. Or as angry. He didn't have a license yet, but Pello was a poor choice, and I was exhausted. No one asked Nick. I'd have to add sending Ramon to the DMV to my to-do list. As I curled up in the back seat, my brain already going fuzzy with sleep, it occurred to me that if we'd done this hike last year, Ramon would have been as beat as I was. Floating on that thought was the fact that I was probably the only one in the car—besides my uncle, and I was choosing to ignore his presence—who could still be considered human. If I could still be considered that at all. I was still human, wasn't I? It hurt to think about, and I was too tired, so I stored it for another day. I put it right under the festering guilt that the reason my best friend was probably out of the human category was completely on my head.

My uncle was letting me ignore him, which was difficult since he was sitting right next to me. Ramon had to be in the front to drive, of course, and it was hard for Pello to sit in the back with his goat legs. I had a pretty complicated relationship with my uncle Nick, considering I hadn't seen him since I was an infant. When I was only a few hours old, my mother and Nick had decided that it would be best if I could remain under Douglas Montgomery's radar. So out of fear, they bound my powers and didn't tell me about it until recently. It had made me extremely vulnerable, and though I kept telling myself that they did it out of kindness, I still got mad sometimes.

I know the two aren't completely analogous, but my binding reminds me of a spiritual chastity belt. You know, the big metal underpants that noblemen used to put on their wives and daughters when they weren't around to "keep them pure for their own good"? Apparently, their own good meant no physical comfort and the risk of infection, and added a strange hitch to their step. Mine didn't involve something so humiliating as metal underwear, but spiritually it was the same thing. They cut me off from a natural part of myself, hobbling my growth. Yes, they did it because they thought it was their most viable course of action, but I bet those noblemen thought the same thing. The phrase "for your own good" always makes me hesitate, because sometimes it is, but usually what they actually mean is "for my own good."

Ramon broke the tense silence. "So where are we taking you?"

I caught Nick glancing at me from the corner of my eye. I didn't look over.

"Tia's," he said. "If that's okay."

I felt my jaw tighten involuntarily. Taco, who had been sleeping in my lap, rolled over and growled softly at him.

"You're angry, and you have every right to be, but we did what we thought was best."

"I know," I said. "But that doesn't mean I have to like it." Then I childishly turned away from him, curled up around Taco, and went to sleep.

I was in the basement again. That's how I knew it was a dream. No way in hell I'd voluntarily be down there hanging out. I was sitting in an old wooden chair, staring at the cage. Douglas was in it. He looked like I'd last seen him—hole in his throat, blood staining his front, but his manner was calm as he stared back at me.

"Let me out," he said. "I can't search in here."

I shook my head. "No way, bucko. You put yourself there, not me."

"You think this can hold me?" He knocked the cage door open with a shove.

Fear seeped into my core, but I stayed in my chair. "You can't do that," I said. "You're dead." Douglas laughed his cold, creepy laugh, and we were suddenly in the Tongue & Buckle drinking at the bar. Our pint glasses were filled with blood, and I didn't want to drink mine.

"You have to," Douglas said. "It's part of who you are."

I shoved the glass away, and it shattered on the floor. Aengus came up carrying a jar of pickled eggs, which I've never actually seen in a bar, but for some reason I associate them with bars anyway. He looked down at the spilled blood with a sigh and handed me the jar of pickled eggs. They were a sickly greenish color, and I gagged.

"Don't just sit there," he said, tossing a bar rag on the counter. "Come clean up your mess."

"It's not my fault," I said, even though I had shoved the glass.

Aengus shrugged. "Still a mess. Still needs cleaning." Then he walked away. I tried to get up and walk over to the other side of the bar, but the jar kept getting heavier and heavier. The floorboards cracked and gave way. I was underground, the roots grabbing at me, dirt spilling into my eyes and mouth. I screamed.

Douglas's face appeared in the hole above my head. I yelled at him to get me out, but he just shook his head.

"Not until you hand it over."

I didn't know what he meant, so I just kept screaming. Well, I kept screaming until Pello whacked me with a soda bottle and I jerked up in my seat. Sweaty and shaking, I rolled down the window and gulped at the fresh air.

"You okay?" Ramon asked. Nick stared at me, concerned. I leaned my head against the side of the car, letting the breeze cool me down. I closed my eyes and grabbed the pouch around my neck. The beads bit into my hand—it felt strangely reassuring.

"Yeah," I said. "Just a bad dream."

"If you say so," Ramon said, his voice tinged with worry. I didn't respond, but kept my eyes closed, allowing the breeze to push the last of my dream away.

I'd become pretty used to nightmares the last few months.

You don't survive getting kidnapped, thrown in a cage, tortured, and then killing a man without experiencing a few restless nights. Unless you're a sociopath, I guess. But I wasn't, or at least I was pretty sure I wasn't, and the dreams had been pretty regular. My mom had a natural sleep aid that she made, and I'd taken to putting a few drops of it in some water before I went to bed every night. It helped me sleep heavily, and I tended to remember my dreams less. It also helped for those times when I didn't want to spend the whole night chatting with restless spirits.

But the last few nightmares felt different, and I couldn't quite figure out what it was. Something tucked away somewhere in the folds of my brain was nagging me, and I tried to coax it out, but no deal. I put my medicine bag back under my shirt.

"You want to talk about it?" Nick asked softly.

"No, and with you, double no."

"Okay, but the guys have been filling me in with what's been happening in town, and it seems like it might be a good idea—"

"I really don't want to talk about it right now." My brain was still fuzzy with sleep, and I was having a hard time dislodging the nightmare from it.

Nick wearily rubbed his face with his hand. "Look, Murray got me a temporary pass so I could help him out for a few weeks, but I came up here to apply to the Council for a permanent stay."

"Is that so?" I said softly.

His shoulders slumped slightly in a defeated fashion. "I

know you need time to process, but I'm not sure we have that time. So for now, while things are the way they are, do you think we could call a truce? You can hate me all you want, but you might need me."

"You're about twenty years too late for that," I said. "Forced exodus or no." And that's when I felt the hurt that had been squatting underneath my anger. And that hurt was telling me that if Nick had just stayed around, even though being that close to Douglas would have been a danger, I could have been trained earlier, properly, and not half-assed. That my situation would be different and I wouldn't be mired down the way I was now.

"I know," he said, and I could hear the pain in his voice. Damn it. I was starting to feel sorry for him. The thing was, I knew it wasn't really his fault. Not really. And he'd done his best, but I could feel the anger boiling inside me where it had been stashed so that I wouldn't keep letting it out all over my mom. The binding, while well-intentioned, had led to my kidnapping, Ramon's "life change," and Brooke's death. I know there was no way they could have predicted this outcome, but it was still the consequence of their actions. I hadn't wanted to stay mad at my mom, though, so I'd buried it. Nick was a good, safe outlet. Which meant I wasn't being fair to him. Double damn it. Sometimes I wished I was more of an asshole. It would make my life so much simpler.

I stuck my hand out at him. "Fine. Truce," I mumbled.

He grabbed my hand quickly, and I could tell he was trying to get it before I changed my mind, which made me feel worse.

"I'm still mad," I said.

"I know."

"Well, as long as we're clear on that," I said. We were quiet the rest of the drive, but the tension was gone for now.

I made Nick wait in the car while I ran in and said hi to my mom. I found her in the kitchen, pouring some kind of infused oil into a jar.

"You look very sweaty," she said.

"Yes, well, I've been hiking." I opened the cookie jar on the counter and looked inside. Peanut butter. Sweet.

"There's a container in the pantry—better take them all, or Ramon will get pouty."

Best. Mom. Ever. "Okay, cool." I grabbed them and set them on the counter, chewing my cookie and trying to decide how to approach our conversation.

My mom glanced out the window. "Speaking of which, why is Ramon still in the car?"

"Ah, well, that's kinda what I wanted to talk to you about. Uncle Nick is in the back seat."

She put her pot back on the stove and wiped her hands on her apron. "Oh?"

"That's it? 'Oh?'!?"

"What did you expect, dear?" She smiled at me as she put the lid on the jar and twisted.

"I don't know," I said honestly. "Something. Anyway, I think he wants to stay here for a while."

My mom swiped at the jar with a towel, even though I didn't see any of the oil on the outside. Probably habit. "That might be best, actually."

I bit into another cookie. "And how might that be best?"

My mom leaned against the counter, finally giving me her full attention. "What with . . . the incident." She waved a hand in the direction of Haley's door so I'd know which particular incident she was referring to. "It might be best to have more people around."

"I'll come stay," I said without thinking.

She smiled and leaned over, swiping some cookie crumbs away from my mouth with her towel. "You've got your own house to look after now. I appreciate it, but I think your dance card is quite full."

I sighed. "Fine. What did James say about the house?"

"He recommended that I redo my wards, especially the one in the chimney, since that was done ages ago."

"That's all? Did he say how he thought they got in?"

She shook her head. "No, but he did suggest that making them simply repel those who wished harm was not enough."

"Oh?" I said, eyebrows raised. "Whom are they supposed to keep out now?"

"Everyone."

After we dropped off my uncle and Pello, we headed back to the house. A lot of things were whirling around in my head as we drove, and Ramon was kind enough to stay quiet while I tried to figure things out. What I needed was to speak to someone who knew what she was talking about. I pulled out my cell phone and hit June Walker's listing. I had her on speed dial. As the only other necromancer I actually knew, she definitely warranted it. She answered on the third ring, and before she could finish her hello, I'd unloaded everything on her. I was able to gloss over some of it, thanks to Ashley and Dessa. Apparently, between the two of them, they'd been keeping June abreast of things.

"What do you really want to ask me, Sam?" she asked once I'd finished babbling.

"Is there any chance he could have survived?" Between the dreams and all the weird crap, well, it just kept coming back to Douglas.

I heard the click of her lighter as she lit a cigarette. "I don't think so. With your power boost, the ritual he tried to inflict on you was obviously completed. That couldn't be unless he was dead." She paused to take a drag. "But—"

"Why is there always a but?"

She laughed. "Because it's Douglas. He complicates things. My suggestion? If you're worried, seek out evidence. Make your *pukis* show you where he took the body."

It took some fast talking and a lot of unpleasant wheedling to get James to comply. Finally he agreed to meet us there, and I gave Ramon new directions. We found James standing in front of the crypt, leaning against the side nonchalantly, like it was no big deal—like he hung out in cemeteries every day. Of course, working for Douglas, he probably had.

The inside was cooler than the outside in terms of temperature, but not in terms of aesthetics. Or smell. Even with the door propped open for light, the crypt was quite obviously home to a rotting corpse. Without a word, James escorted me over to the marble slab where what was left of Douglas was waiting for me. Ramon decided to stay outside—something about the smell and sensitive noses.

My necromancer status aside, I hadn't actually seen a lot of decomposing bodies. They're just not something you run across a lot of unless you work in a field specifically built around handling rotting flesh. Sure, I've been to a few funerals, Haden's for one, but those bodies had been embalmed.

Douglas had not. I was trying not to let my mind see all of it at once, but my stubborn brain kept thinking words like *maggots* and *goo*, and when I saw a beetle crawl through his empty eye socket, I have to say I backed up a step. Basically, my enemy had been reduced to a sloppy, bug-ridden mess. I choked on the smell and tried to cover my nose with the back of my arm.

James just stood there. Unaffected, merely curious, coolly assessing the cadaver like it was something else—a place setting, maybe, or my dress attire.

"I'm sorry I made you do this," I said.

James had leaned over the corpse, hands clasped behind his back, his gaze following another beetle as it climbed out of Douglas's suit jacket. "Why? Didn't it set you at ease?"

"What? No. I mean, yes, of course." I gestured with the hand not held under my nose. "I was just apologizing for making you see, um, him . . . like that."

James shrugged, eyes still following the beetle as it perched on the edge of Douglas's shiny black shoe. For a second, I really thought he was going to paw at it like a cat. "No apologies necessary," he said. "This is only a shell. He's not in here."

"That's an enlightened way to look at it."

James looked at me, silver eyes blinking in the dim light. "I suppose so, yes."

It was dark when we finally got home, and, despite the nap, I was still tired. There was a tranquility to the house, with everyone ensconced in individual activities. I headed to my room with a wave to James. I needed some quiet time to think.

Which was totally not going to happen, because I found Brid curled up asleep in the middle of my bed. It hadn't been long since James had ordered my new bed, but every time I walked into my room, I was hoping it would be there. Especially now. Brid shouldn't be curled up on a mattress and a box spring on the floor. Even with the hurt of what was going on, I wanted something better for her than that. She looked pale, and there were bruised patches under her eyes, probably because she wasn't sleeping, which wasn't too surprising. People handled grief one of two ways; they either cocooned themselves in blankets and slept too much, or sat hollow-eyed in their living rooms, sleeping too little. I'd learned that when Haden died.

I slid slowly onto the mattress, doing my best not to wake her. Of course, what I should have done was tiptoe out and shut the door so that she could grab some of that much-needed sleep, but I couldn't quite get over my own selfish need to hold her. Especially since I knew there might not be a next time.

My fingers snagged on the belt loops of her jeans as I slipped an arm around her waist. I curled up closer to her, resting my head behind hers. Her hair tickled my nose, but it was nice to be next to her. She smelled of sweat and the outside, a hint of her orange and sandalwood shampoo under that. There's something about being close to Brid that makes everything inside me go quiet. It's a restless feeling I don't notice until it stops, until I'm with her. She's my peaceful place.

"You are quite possibly the least smooth guy I know," she mumbled. "You can't even put your arm around me without tripping up."

"Isn't it amazing how adorable awkwardness can be? I'm actually very suave, but I do these things just to please you."

She squeezed my arm closer to her in response. We stayed like that for a while, pulling quiet and comfort from each other, knowing full well that it wouldn't last.

She rolled over and kissed my chin. "What's that smell?"

I looked down at her as she settled against my chest. "What is it with you and telling me I smell funny?" Some of her first words to me when we met were about how strange I smelled.

"You pick up some very odd aromas sometimes, and they cover up the *you* smell, which I happen to like. So what have you been up to this time?"

"What you're smelling," I said, "is the scent of the outdoors. Of rugged manliness. That is the stench of Bigfoot."

"Seriously?"

"Seriously."

"Was he sick? Because you also smell like rotting things."

"Oh, right. What I meant to say was that's the smell of rugged manliness and Douglas's putrefying corpse."

"Gross."

"Indeed."

"You realize you're getting dirt all over your sheets, right?" She plucked at my shirt with her fingers.

"It's my bed," I said defensively.

"Just making sure you're aware. Your sheets, your call."

I rolled off the bed with a heavy sigh. I'd left my shoes at the door so that I didn't violate James's house rule about no shoes past the entryway, but my socks were stiff with sweat and dirt, and the rest of me wasn't much better. I threw my socks in the hamper, followed by my shirt. Brid catcalled me when I took off my shorts. I threw them at her in response before grabbing a pair of clean jeans to slip into. She tossed them back. I made a show of adding them to the hamper before I jumped back into bed. She giggled, and it was a good sound to hear. I just wished it had lasted longer.

"I've missed you," I said when she'd stopped giggling.

"I know." She crawled back into my arms. "I don't know what to do."

"Me either," I said. "I feel like I've been chasing my tail. Tracking down each little clue or lead. How the hell do detectives do this? It feels like I've made zero progress." I buried my fingers in her hair, pulling it gently until the curls wound over the backs of my nails.

"My dad made everything look so easy."

I pressed my lips to the top of her head, turning only slightly when I needed to talk. "Yeah, he did. But he'd also been at it a long time."

"What if I screw up?" It hurt to hear her sound so scared

and broken. The Brid I knew was brash and fierce. This side didn't pop up too often. As I tried to think of a properly reassuring thing to say, I realized that Brid probably didn't get to let this part of her out on a regular basis. You had to look confident and assured, or people started to lose faith in you.

"People screw up," I said. "Just try your hardest and fix mistakes as best you can when they happen."

"Most people would have simply replied 'you'll do fine.'"

"I'm not most people." I hugged her tight and then pulled back so I could look into her eyes. "And you will do fine, but you know that deep down, I'm sure. You've had a bad shock, and you're hurt, and that would shake anyone's faith. But your dad picked you, Brid. If you can't dig up faith for yourself, at least trust in his abilities. He knew you could do it."

She cried then, and I held her while she sobbed. I knew that hurt, and it's a terrible thing to lose someone who is such a fixture in your life. I'd been having a shit year, but Brid's was worse. She'd had all my bad days pushed into a few months. The loss of her father, the sudden thrust into a position of power she wasn't expecting, being kidnapped and tortured by a psycho. It was a lot to take, even for someone as strong as her.

I held her tight to my chest. "I know it's hard," I said. "In fact, if there's anyone who knows, it's me. That kind of loss and then, right after it, before you can even take a breath, you get sucker punched with your new position."

Brid shifted so she could look me in the eyes. Hers were puffy, and her face was red and splotchy. I brushed her hair out of her face, running my thumb along her chin. "All those people watching you, waiting for you to screw up. Not helping, just judging and piling more things on you while they do." I felt my own frustration well up. "But you know, as much as I'd like to complain, I look at you and think, 'Well, shit, Brid's had all that at an accelerated pace and she's not bitching and moaning, is she?'"

"I am a little," she said with a sniff.

I gave her a bit of a grin. "You're not wallowing, though. And you know what? Screw those other people. I think you're doing great."

"And you're all that matters?" A hint of a smile played on her lips.

"Why, yes, I think I am." I put her in a headlock and kissed her forehead again.

"I'm so tired of crying," she said.

"I know." I wiped an errant tear away. "If you need a break, I can cry for you for a bit. We can take turns."

She smiled a little and nudged me. "I just bet you would, sissy."

"Hey," I said, pretending to be insulted. "That is one of the advantages of dating a sensitive Beta male. We cry for you, we remember anniversaries, and we might even hold your hair while you vomit. Classy with a capital *C*."

"I've never vomited around you, but I seem to remember helping you while *you* puked."

I gave her a quick kiss. "Hey, why you got to bring up old shit all the time?"

She laughed and kissed me back. "Thanks, Sam," she said.

Then she kissed me again. This time she didn't pull back as fast. When she got up to lock my door, I didn't stop her.

Brid dozed in my arms. I traced aimless patterns on her bare back while I thought. Though I felt pretty worn out myself, I was kind of afraid to go to sleep again. More nightmares were not what I needed right now. In fact, I felt like I had exactly what I did need at the moment, and I wanted to enjoy that.

My window was open, and the warm evening air blew in, bringing the smells of sea and summer with it. I could hear the gnomes yelling something in the distance, and I grinned.

Brid adjusted her position with a grumble and threw an arm over my chest. Her forearm sat awkwardly on my medicine pouch and I had to yank it out from under her, the lump of the egg I'd stashed in there was digging painfully into my chest. Slowly, I reached around the sleeping girl so I could use both hands to pull the jade egg out.

I tossed the medicine bag onto my nightstand and held the egg up so I could see it better. The carving really was exquisite, and even though it had been sitting in the pouch, close to my skin, it was still cold. That was weird, but it made some sense after Ashley saying it had some sort of death magic mixed up in it. I held it in my hand for a minute, fingers tightly closed. The chill remained. Was everything in this house weird? Maybe I was starting to get paranoid. Pretty soon I might accuse the coffeemaker of talking to me or think that the old recliner was the reincarnation of Winston Churchill.

But the house did have some strange things in it. I mean, wasn't that why I had to take the property in the first place? My lawyer had said something about how normal people couldn't move in because who knew what Douglas had left behind.

Cautiously, I traced the edges of the egg, looking for hidden latches or something. It seemed too small to hide anything in, but what the hell did I know? Finally, I closed my eyes to try and look at it with my mysterious magicky bits. There was probably a proper name for what I was doing like "using my sight" or my "third eye" or something, but again, what did I know? Very little, and it felt like the more I learned, the more my ignorance increased.

But whatever you wanted to call it, I looked at it and the damn egg lit up like a small moon. A blue, swirling moon. Crap. I recognized that particular nauseating swirl. Whatever kind of magic was involved, Douglas had done it, but was that really a surprise? His house, his egg, his magic. Duh. Still, he was dead. Shouldn't the magic have deactivated or something? Of course, I had no idea.

My phone rang. I rolled Brid over and jumped out of bed. She woke with a start. "Where's the fire?"

I ignored her while I pulled my shorts out of the hamper, digging my phone out of one of the pockets. Of course, I missed the call and had to hit a few buttons and call the number back—it wasn't one I recognized.

"Hi," the gruff voice said on the other end. "This Sam LaCroix?"

"That depends entirely on who is calling."

"You realize that by saying that, you've basically admitted that you are?"

"No, I implied that I might be, which is not the same thing at all."

"Fair enough. This is Gary—Murray's cousin?"

"Oh, right, Sexy . . . um." I sat on the edge of the bed. "This is Sam. What's going on?"

"Right, I'm the sexy one." And then he made a *rawr* noise into the phone.

Okay. I guess I'd asked for that.

"Murray told you I've been seeing some weird stuff out here, right?"

"Yeah, but I didn't get the impression that things were urgent. Has something changed?" Brid pulled the sheet up around herself and stared at me, attempting to follow the conversation. I mouthed that I would fill her in later.

"Well, I found a scent that was pretty unnatural and started to close in and, well, I found something. I know it's getting late, but I think you should see this now. Things being as they are, I think it's best if I get it out of the woods and bring it to you."

I hesitated, knowing I needed to ask, but for some reason fearing I already knew the answer. "Is it something that applies to me because I'm Council or because I'm, you know, me?"

"Both, but mostly because you're you."

I got up to get a clean shirt before making sure Gary had my address. "How long until you can get here?"

"I'm out toward Cougar Mountain, and I have to gather a few things . . . maybe forty-five minutes?"

I told him okay and hung up. I stared at my phone for a

minute, thinking about what I should do. To trust or not to trust, that was the question. I dialed my mom and asked for Uncle Nick. I didn't think he had anything to do with it, really, though I wanted to keep open to the possibility, and I figured if he was involved, including him would be the fastest way to find out. After Nick agreed to come over, I got up and finished getting dressed.

Brid pointed at my bureau, where the jeans hung haphazardly, and hopping on one foot, I tried to get them on. I filled Brid in, and about halfway through, she got up and started to get dressed as well.

I leaned in and kissed her quickly on the mouth. She smiled and pulled me in for another kiss. Then I ran for the door. I was halfway out before I remembered something else I was supposed to ask. "Does your pack have a patron saint, deity, creature, or some other thing that I don't know about?"

Brid nodded, puzzled. "Patron goddess—Bridget. She's the goddess of hearth, home, and, oddly enough, blacksmithing. I'm named after her—*Bridin* is a derivative of her name. All the firstborn girls in my line are. It's tradition. Why do you ask?" She finished pulling on her shirt and made to follow me.

"Just wondering."

After I tripped and almost fell down the stairs, I slowed down. I had no idea why I was in such a damn rush. Nick wouldn't get here for at least twenty minutes, and Sexy Gary was going to take longer than that. Though it was getting on the later side, just about everyone was still up. I could hear them making a ruckus outside. I peeked out the window and saw Ramon tearing up our new half-pipe. Frank and Sean were seated in the grass, some very awestruck gnomes scattered around them.

James padded up on his little cat feet. He hopped up onto the windowsill. "Just making my rounds. Everything seems fine. What are you doing up?"

His tone told me that he would prefer that I be back in bed getting my sleep.

"Got a call from Murray's cousin—he's bringing something over for me to look at. Nick's coming too."

"Yes, Ramon mentioned that your uncle was back in town."

I frowned down at James's little kitty form. "Why a cat?"

"Pardon?" His ears pricked forward and whiskers twitched.

"Generally, when I see you outside your room, unless you have to be human for something, you're in kitty form. Why?"

His tail twitched in irritation, and I saw him trying to decide how he should answer me. "This form is good for sneaking. People don't look down much." He stared through the glass, and I watched as his pupils dilated while he followed Ramon's spinning form. "I suppose I'm used to it. It's comfortable."

"Okay," I said.

"Okay?" He seemed confused by my response.

"Yes, okay, as in I'll stop forcing you to go human except when I actually need you in that form. I didn't realize that you weren't as comfortable that way."

He turned his silver eyes on me and stared, pupils narrowing as he contemplated what I'd said. "Thank you?" He drew it out like a question, and I wasn't sure if it was because he thought what I said was odd or if it was because he didn't quite believe me yet.

The temptation to give his little kitty head a scratch was kind of overwhelming for a moment, but I didn't think he'd appreciate it. Sure, I'd petted him once before, but I didn't know he was a person then.

"Look, James, it's pretty obvious I don't know what I'm doing most of the time. I'm winging it and hoping I do okay, but I just wanted you to know that I appreciate all the help you've given me and, well, I . . . I hope you like it here." I wanted to tell him that I hoped we'd be friends someday, but I stumbled over it for some reason. I guess I wasn't sure if we were friends now or not. Either way, he just scrutinized me for a good long time, then went back to staring out the window. I turned away quietly and headed to the bathroom to check on Taco, a creature I knew I could pet without getting my hand bitten off. You know, as long as he'd been fed first.

Taco was happy to see me, crawling quickly out of his nest, up my pant leg and onto my shoulder. This might have been a bad habit to let him get into because, once he'd gained his weight back, he might be kind of heavy, but on the other hand, he had very sharp claws and teeth, and it might have been an equally bad idea to refuse him.

By the time Nick got there, I was sitting on the porch watching the guys and Taco, who was chasing after a tennis ball and playing his new favorite game of "fetch the ball and chew on it instead of giving it back." To my surprise, Nick wasn't alone. Haley waved at me as she got out from behind the wheel.

"What are you doing here?" I asked.

She cocked her head to the side in amusement. "You really think Nick could sneak out of the house without me knowing?"

Nick flopped down next to me on the porch. "I tried to talk her out of it, I really did, but she had the car keys."

Taco jumped out of my lap and went to sniff Haley. "Trust me, I of all people know how impossible it is to talk Haley out of anything."

Haley put her palm out for Taco to sniff. "So what's the haps?"

I filled them in, which took all of a second because I didn't know anything.

A van pulled up a short time later, its green sides sporting the logo of the parks department on it.

It was obvious to me, if not to the rest of the crew, that Gary was wearing his purchased glamour when he got out of the car. How did I know that? Because he just looked like a really big handsome dude and not a huge shag carpet, that's why.

I introduced him and had Frank order the gnomes to stand down while Gary and I shook hands.

"Why don't you come in, and we'll take a look at what you've got."

Gary nodded, a genial smile on his face. He walked around to the back of the van and wrenched the doors open. Then, to my surprise, he pulled the body of a man, bound and gagged, out of the back. The man didn't struggle as Gary flung him over his shoulder.

"C'mon, you're going to need some light for this, and I wouldn't say no to a beer if you have any." And with that, he walked into the house.

SAN DIMAS HIGH SCHOOL
FOOTBALL RULES

As we sat in my kitchen, I'm pretty sure we were all thinking about the same two things. One, that Sexy Gary, at least whilst under the glamour, was indeed worthy of his moniker. He was all thick-corded muscle, auburn hair, and dimples. I could easily imagine him in a hot firemen calendar or a sexy lumberjack photo shoot. Not that I spend a lot of time imagining those things.

My sister and Brid were eyeing him pretty openly, as was Sean, but in Sean's case, it appeared speculative, like "should I start beefing up on the weights?" After about five seconds, I think he reverted back to his status quo of believing that he was already perfect. There was no reverting with Brid and Haley—they just kept right on looking.

I don't consider myself a jealous man, but I grabbed Brid's belt loop and pulled her closer to me. She smiled at me in understanding, because I am nothing if not transparent. I was a little worried about Haley until James stalked into the room, fully human and a little angry looking, and planted himself right between my sister and Brawny the Lumberjack. For an irrational moment, I wanted to shout, "All the women have been claimed!" in a dramatic fashion, but thankfully the moment passed. The girls would have beat me bloody if I'd even inferred it.

Haley raised an eyebrow at James, but he refused to look at her, his eyes firmly on the second surprise in my kitchen. I relaxed, knowing that James would keep Haley from fainting like some lovesick teen at the feet of Gary the Bigfoot. I may not always understand James, but he seemed fairly protective of Haley.

The second thing we were all thinking about was the guy tied to my kitchen chair. The air in the kitchen was still and quiet while we all stared at him.

Ramon spoke first. "Strange things are afoot at the Circle K."

I let my breath out in a whoosh. "Okay, so it's not just me then?"

Ramon shook his head and leaned forward to poke him. "Weird, completely weird."

I looked up at Sexy Gary, who seemed really pleased with himself as he grabbed another of Sean's beers.

"Gary, can you please tell me why you've kidnapped Ted and brought him into my kitchen?"

The Bigfoot gestured at him with his beer hand. "Yeah, so, here's the thing. Says his name is Minion, but it's not, right? I mean, it's totally him, or have I wandered into padded-room territory?"

"You're not crazy."

Gary looked relieved. "Good. So I was tracking, trying to find what was setting all the forest critters off, and I find this cabin. Now, it's been empty for a few years, but it's suddenly showing signs of life, and I see this one crawling around the bushes, making a huge racket."

I peered closer at our kidnap victim. The resemblance was uncanny. Maybe it wasn't him, though. Maybe it was an impersonator?

"So you brought him here?" Sean asked. "Why? Is it a crime to rent a cabin or something?"

"Cabin's not rented to him. I checked. And he doesn't smell right. He smells wrong—he smells like whatever I was tracking."

Nick sidled up to me. "Sam, I think I know where he's going with this. Have you looked at our new friend here? I mean, really looked?"

I did what he asked me to, even though I already knew what I was going to find. It was easier now, switching my vision over to my gift. Practice makes perfect, I guess. Sure enough, the man in front of us wasn't alive. I was pretty sure I recognized the swirling mass of sickening blue inside of him, but just to make sure, I pulled the egg out of my pouch and held it up.

They matched. Shit.

I flipped back into regular sight and opened my eyes. "Okay, someone needs to tell me what the hell is going on around here."

"What do you mean?" Ramon asked.

I held the egg up for him to see, realizing as I did that it wouldn't mean a whole lot to him. "This," I said. "This matches him." I jerked a finger toward the zombie. "Only it can't, because that's impossible. Because I saw his dead body. And dead bodies can't raise other dead bodies. That's just crazy."

Ramon grabbed me by the shoulders and shook me. "Slow down and explain to us plebeians. If you have to, use sock puppets." Taco scuttled up my leg onto my shoulder and hissed a warning at Ramon, who stared patiently at the little guy. "I'm not hurting him."

"Douglas," I said, holding up the egg so it was about an inch from Ramon's eye.

Frank cleared his throat. "Why don't we just ask him?"

We all turned to stare at Frank, and I think we were all feeling a little stupid right then. I know I was, at any rate. Ramon let go of me, and I turned around and pulled the gag off our houseguest.

"What's your name?" I asked.

"Minion." He blinked at me slowly, considering. "Did I take the red pill or the blue pill?"

I smiled at him. "Let's not get distracted, okay? Minion, who do you work for?"

"I work for Master!" He said this excitedly, like he'd done something right and deserved a treat.

"Ooookay." I glanced at Nick.

"Minion, who is Master?" Nick enunciated slowly, as if to a child.

"Master is my friend. He is good. I like Master."

"This is getting us nowhere," I mumbled.

Nick kept his eyes on Minion. "Patience is a virtue." He rested a hand on the zombie's shoulder. "Why did Master call you, Minion? Do you know?"

The creature looked at us, confused, like we weren't getting something. "Aren't you friends of Master? You must be." He nodded to himself, though the rope impeded some of the movement. "Otherwise, why would you have Master's egg? Master told me all about it." He had Ramon dig out a torn piece of paper, which showed a sketch of the jade egg. "See? Yes, you must know Master. You have the egg. And him. Hi, James." He looked behind me and frowned. "Where did he go?" He tilted his head closer to Nick and me. "Did Master call him?" he whispered.

Nick and I looked at each other, then looked behind us. Everyone looked back, except for James, who was nowhere to be seen. I grabbed Haley's shoulder, dragging her eyes off Gary and back onto me. "Haley, where is he? Where did James go?"

"Huh?" She stared at me stupidly.

Gary cursed and pulled a chain out of his pocket, slipping it over his head. "Sorry, forgot the other one." He walked past us and levered the kitchen window open. "Blasted pheromones."

Haley shook her head, her eyes clearing a little. "James? He was right here."

I looked at Ramon. "Well, he's not here now." And I was betting he wasn't anywhere in the house. "Just how stupid should I feel right now?"

"Let's not make any judgment calls on that until all the facts are in." Ramon pulled a knife out of the drawer and started slicing the ropes around Minion.

"Do you think that's wise?" Frank asked.

"I really don't think he's a danger. And besides, he's going to want to help us, aren't you, Minion?" Ramon asked as he cut the zombie's hands free.

"I am?" The zombie looked confused. Of course, he kind of always did, so that didn't tell me much.

"Yeah," I said, catching on to Ramon's thought process a little. "Because your master wants this, right?" I held up the egg. Minion's eyes zeroed in on it.

"Yes," Minion said. It was quite obvious that his master did want it. How badly? Had he come looking for it? And when he didn't find it, I wondered if he thought I had it. Knowing what I did of Douglas's style, he might think it would be totally logical to threaten Haley in order to set me off guard or distract me from what he was up to. But that didn't make sense either. If Douglas had made it that far, he'd have stabbed Haley, not her door. The past had told me he had no problem killing with little or no provocation. James had told my mom that she had to change her wards—they'd been set to only let in people who meant no harm. Douglas certainly lacked pure intentions, so he couldn't have done it. Maybe he'd sent Minion. I didn't think he had enough going on upstairs to actively mean harm to anyone.

"Then we're going to take it to him, aren't we?"

"We most certainly are," Ramon said, kneeling to cut the rope around Minion's feet.

Nick cleared his throat. "Are you sure about this, Sam?"

I adjusted Taco on my shoulder. He'd been moving around excitedly, probably picking up on all the tension. "I don't think we have a choice. I'm stuck between a pack and a hard place." I grabbed Brid's hand. "We need permission to enter your territory."

Her brow knitted, and she stuck her lower lip out in thought. "Why?"

"If Douglas is back somehow, we need to know. I think we can use the egg or even Minion here to call him out, but I don't want to give him home-field advantage." And I certainly didn't want to see his corpse again. I tucked the egg back into my pouch so I wouldn't lose it. "I think James has already gone back to him, and my hold here is too tenuous to expect everything else to choose me over him. And I'm certainly not going into some unknown wood to track him down." I squeezed her hand. "And the pack needs to see this."

She still had the "why?" look on her face. I could tell I hadn't quite gotten through. "They need to see justice. We've been looking for a necromancer, remember? If we can show them that Douglas has returned . . . They have to witness that it was Douglas, not me, or they will never trust me again."

Brid's eyes squinted in thought. She glanced over at Sean, who merely gave her a one-shoulder shrug. "Couldn't make things any worse," he said.

She squeezed my hand back. "Okay."

"You can get up now, Minion. We're going to go for a ride."

"Can I drive?" he asked hopefully. "I won't go under fifty."

"No," Ramon said, patting him on the back. "I don't think that would be a good idea."

"Yeah," I said, "and Ramon would make a terrible Sandra Bullock."

24

I'M A SOUL MAN

The coin was off, and he was drifting again.

This time he was thinking of his mother. He could only remember a few fuzzy details about her. Remembrances of his father were almost totally gone, wiped out by time and the fact that there hadn't been much to begin with. His dad had worked a great deal, so it had mostly been his mother around.

Douglas remembered her apron. Tiny blue flowers on a white background. She'd made it herself out of a leftover flour bag, that much he remembered. It was old and worn, but she'd loved it, he was certain of that. He could tell by the way she smiled at it when she folded it back up. She would often bake, and no matter what the state of the kitchen, his mother had always been clean. Only the apron had ever shown the telltale signs of a day spent cooking, the streaks of flour covering those small blue buds. Sometimes, in the summer, the smear of an overripe raspberry or peach would end up on there as well. He would hug her, always when she wasn't expecting it, and she'd be forced to wipe the light dusting of flour off his face. And she'd laugh then, a beautiful, wonderful sound.

Luckily his aunt had never made him hug her, and he was glad. It wouldn't have been the same. Auntie had never smelled of fresh bread and summer fruits. She smelled of perfume and powder, a cold smell he'd never grown accustomed to. And hugging her would have been about as satisfying as putting his arms around a museum statue.

On an impulse, when he was packing his bag for Auntie Lynn's, he'd grabbed his pillowcase. His mother had made it out of another old flour bag, one covered with a similar pattern. He'd tucked it into the corner of his luggage, hidden between his underwear and socks. Later, on bad days, he'd take it out and hold it close to his cheek. At first it held on to the smell of his home, that warm kitchen smell. But that had faded eventually, and it began to smell dusty and old, like Auntie Lynn's. The day that fact had sunk in, he realized that he was never going home.

He'd sniffled a bit; then, wiping his eyes on the tattered pillowcase, he walked over to his chest of drawers. Carefully, he folded it until the fabric became a square the size of his hand. Then he pulled open his drawer and placed it in the back, where it would stay until he left that house.

The ringing of a phone jolted him out of his daze. He'd purchased one of those cheap over-the-counter prepaid cell phones so he could get ahold of James. This was the first time he'd received a call on it.

He slipped the coin over his neck and answered the phone. A whispering James was on the other end.

"He found it."

25

STAND BY YOUR MAN

Brid held on to Sean, leaning with him as his motorcycle took the turn. The pack wasn't going to like Sam coming back onto their land, but they didn't have to. They just had to do it.

Sean slowed down as the bike moved onto the gravel road that led to the Den. She hopped off once they'd come to a stop, removing her helmet and tossing it to Sean.

"I thought you broke up with him," he said, catching the helmet one-handed.

"And I thought you disagreed." She folded her arms, even though it was a warm night. It was more for comfort.

"I do—I think you're being stupid," Sean said as he started to the house.

"Gee, Sean, tell me how you really feel."

"I can pretty up the words if you want, but it boils down to the same thing."

She sighed out into the warm night air. "I told you why."

"Yes, and good, logical reasons all of them. They're also wrong."

"Says the guy without a girlfriend."

"What's that got to do with anything?" He walked up to the front door, hanging the helmets on wooden pegs lining the outer wall. "You could do worse. He's a nice guy. Plus, you know, he's loaded."

She nudged him with her shoulder. "It has nothing to do with how nice he is or how much money he has."

"No," Sean said. "But your reasons are almost as bad. He can't help what he is." He shook his head. "I almost always back you up, you know that, and I will support you in this, but you can't get me to tell you I think it's right, because it isn't."

"I know," she said.

"But you're going to do it anyway?" It was rare to hear her brother angry. Of course, things had been far from normal lately.

"I can't see any other way right now." She looked away, trying not to cry. She hated crying, and in public she hated it more.

Sean looped an arm around her and pulled her into a hug, kissing the top of her head. "It's okay, Brid. It'll work out." After a minute, he added, "I just think you should fight for it a little bit more."

"I know," she said, sniffling. "But I can only fight for so many things at a time, and right now I need to fight for me."

"I can't argue with that," Sean said. They stared at the closed door of the Den, preparing themselves before they had to go in, before Brid had to put her professional face on. She hadn't yet picked up her dad's ability to walk into a room and dominate it immediately. Brid stiffened her spine. Maybe not yet, but she would. She just had to last long enough to get the chance.

Sean let out a breath. "But maybe I'll fight for Sam, since you can't. Someone has to, I think."

After a moment, Brid answered, "I'd like that. Thank you."

Sean glanced at his sister. "You ready?"

She squared her shoulders. "Open the door."

26

I HEAR YOU KNOCKIN', BUT YOU CAN'T COME IN

By the fifth ring, I was afraid Dunaway wouldn't pick up, but he did, greeting me with a wary hello.

"Dunaway, hey. Look, I need you to look up something for me if you can."

"Depends on what it is."

"Douglas Montgomery . . ." I stared out the window at the blur of lights as they sped by. Ramon was driving, and I was in the passenger seat, with Haley and Uncle Nick behind us. I'd tried to leave Taco at home, but he'd refused, and every time I returned him to the house, he showed up in the car again. After he chewed through the pet carrier, I gave up. Hopefully, he could hold his own. I watched the swirl of lights and did not want to finish my question, because once I had the answer, an answer I feared I already knew, then there was no going back. Of course, there was no going back anyway, and it was foolish to think otherwise, but knowing somehow made it official. "Has there been anything on him lately?"

"Like what?" I could hear the clicking of a keyboard in the background as he worked.

"I don't know. Movement on his bank accounts, arrests. . . . You're the cop, help me out a little here."

"Well, I found a death notice, but I think you already know that."

"Yeah," I said, putting my head against the window, "I inherited his estate, which I'm sure you found."

"There is that, yes, but as for anything since, as you might have guessed, no. Dead men don't usually get around much."

"I think this one is." I rubbed my hand over my face. "He's too smart to leave tracks, though." I thought, hard. I needed something. "What about property?"

"Wouldn't you know about that more than me? Don't you own it now?"

"No," I said, shaking my head even though he couldn't see it. "I think he has a cabin stashed up by Issaquah. Cougar Mountain territory."

I heard more clicking. "Not that I can see."

I hated to ask the next question even more, because it was going to confirm some things that I didn't want confirmed. "What about something in that area under the name of James Montgomery?"

"Give me a minute—I'll call you back."

My phone rang a short time later. "I found it. You were right. Do you need the address?"

"No," I said, my gut sinking. Had everything with James been a lie? I felt stupid and blind—what if my trusting nature got us killed? "Thanks, though, Dunaway. For everything."

"Are you okay, Sam?" Even over the phone, I could tell he was concerned.

"Not really," I said, "but I'm getting used to that."

"You'll get ahold of me soon, yeah? Let me know how this whole thing's panning out?"

"As soon as I can."

The line went silent for a second before Dunaway added, "I better not be called in officially on anything, Sam." Then he signed off. I couldn't blame him.

We parked and piled out onto the gravel parking lot. The night was warm, but I felt an apprehensive chill as I considered the evening before me. I grabbed Nick's arm, pulling him back from Haley and Ramon. "What do you need to undo a binding?" I asked.

Nick looked away, embarrassed. "Mine?"

"Yes, yours. Mom already removed hers. I have some juice due to that and . . . that thing with Douglas." That "thing" being the ritual Douglas tried to perform where he killed me and took my ability to wrangle the dead. It had backfired when I shoved his dagger into his throat and accidentally took his power instead. Not one of my more pleasant experiences, but it beat being murdered.

"Shouldn't take much, I'd think." Nick stopped, his brow furrowed. "Wait, Sam, if Douglas is alive like you think he is, how can you have his power? The ritual was based on death, correct? Namely, his?"

I stopped next to him, staring at the Den. Haley and Ramon, finally noticing that we weren't with them, turned back to see what the holdup was. Ramon raised an eyebrow at the look on my face, which I think was a mix of surprise and horror.

I pushed out my hands in a stopping motion. "Hold the

phone," I said. "The ritual had to have worked; my power base went way up afterward. Explain that, buddy."

Nick lifted up my chin and looked into my eyes. "Did you have your bindings checked after?"

"Well . . . no." I hadn't thought of it, to be honest.

Nick rested his hands on my shoulders, his eyelids closing at the same time. We were still standing like that as Sexy Gary pulled up with Minion, Frank, and a handful of battle-ready gnomes. I guess where Frank went, they went too.

Gary eyed us both. "You guys having a moment? Should we get back in the van? Give you some time alone?"

"No," I said. "We're cool. I think he's about done." I stared at Nick uncomfortably when he opened his eyes and let his hands drop. I had felt the cool brush of his power as it had sifted through me. It hadn't been what I would call enjoyable.

He was shaking his head. "I don't know whether to laugh or cry."

"Why choose?" I told him. "You can always do both."

"Your binding," he said. "It's gone."

"How is that possible?" I'd assumed—well, I think we'd all assumed—that my recent upgrade had been due to my usurping of Douglas's power. But if that wasn't the case, if he was still alive, and my binding was gone . . .

"So this whole time?" I asked quietly.

He nodded sympathetically. "Just you, kiddo. It probably snapped during the ritual."

"People always list laugh or cry—why isn't there ever a vomit option?" I felt slightly sick to my stomach at the news. I wasn't quite sure why. I had planned to get my binding removed eventually, of course, but for some reason, it had been nice to lean on the idea that most of my gift wasn't actually me. It felt better to say it was all a freak accident, that I'd really been normal before that, just a victim of circumstance.

But that wasn't true. This was me, all me. I felt my world spin and twist, and more than anything, I wanted to sit down. But of course, I didn't have the time. Taco, who was draped over my shoulders again, leaned in and licked my face in sympathy.

"You need a second?" Nick asked gently.

I shook my head. "No. We've got stuff to do." I looked up at the group. "Let's get out to the clearing."

The gnomes, war paint smeared on their faces, hats jauntily placed on their heads, yelled their war cry in agreement.

The pack was already in the clearing. Not all of them, at least I didn't think it was all of them, but it was still a lot. Some of the weres looked curious, but most of them gave only the impression of waiting to see what I was going to do. About a third of them still appeared openly hostile. I ignored them, the pack parting as we walked into the great circle they'd created with their bodies. Nothing like being encircled by a group of people who wanted to shred you into ribbons and knowing that they could do it to boost the ol' self-confidence.

I took off my shoes. I wasn't sure if it would make a difference, but I didn't want anything between me and the ground. The grass felt cold between my toes as I closed my eyes and summoned Brooke and Ashley.

Brooke leaned in to give me a hug. "What are you up to, Sam?" she whispered in my ear.

"I'm pretty sure they can hear you," I whispered back.

Ashley was staring at the crowd, face pinched. "Sam, more than anything else, you seem to have a real knack for putting yourself in a bind."

"I sure do. Now, stand back, ladies, and jump in if you see me screwing up."

Brooke put her hands on her hips and smiled. "You sure you want us to wait? Maybe we should jump in now."

I flipped her off and got to work. I made a big circle in the clearing. Since I didn't want the pack to kill me for destroying the grass, I didn't use salt. Instead, I used colored sand. You can get it pretty easily, since people use it for art projects and, for reasons I didn't quite understand, for weddings, but I bet the lady I bought mine from wouldn't have been able to guess what I was going to use it for. This sand was a particularly virulent orange color that would stand out nicely in the grass.

I made the circle big enough to fit a boxing ring into, then planted myself at one end of it. Once again, Taco had refused to stay where I put him, and he was curled up next to me contentedly, but keeping one wary eye out on the crowd. I sat cross-legged and tried to clear my mind and meditate, which wasn't easy, since I had an audience.

Time passed as I listened to the night sounds of croaking tree frogs and conversation.

"Are you going to do anything, LaCroix?" Ashley whispered fiercely. "The natives are getting restless."

"Fret not, dear one. At least, not yet. You might need to fret later. I've got an idea, but you two are going to need to get out of the circle."

A worried little frown appeared on her face. "What do you have in mind?"

I shook my head at her. "Nothing you need to worry about."

"Huh-uh," she said. "Whatever harebrained scheme you have rattling around in that little cantaloupe of yours needs to be shared with your adviser—namely, me."

"Trust me," I said.

"Trust you? Please. I'm dead, not stupid." Brooke stood behind her, hands on hips, an identical look of mule-headedness on her face.

I couldn't argue with both of their powers combined. "Fine. I'm going to summon Douglas," I said. "Happy?"

"No," Ashley said. "I'm not."

Brooke looked thoughtful. "How are you going to do that? I mean, can't he just ignore you?"

I held the egg up in the moonlight for them to see. "I don't think he'll be able to resist this. At least, I hope he won't."

Once I had finally shoved the both of them out of the circle, I closed it. Ashley was really unhappy with that, since she wouldn't be able to bust in and help me if things went wrong, and being Ashley, she felt it necessary to point out the fact that with me things often went wrong.

And it would have felt nice to have Ashley in there—someone to save my ass if things went awry. But all my power wouldn't mean a damn thing if it wasn't me pulling the strings. More than just fixing things, the pack needed to see me—not Ashley—kicking ass. They needed to know that I wasn't a screwup. That I didn't get onto the Council because of some fluke, which it turned out was true. The power that had landed me that seat was mine and had always been. Not inherited from Douglas, but 100 percent Sam.

Of course, none of this would matter if I fucked it all up again.

I winked at Ashley's furious little face. "I'll try not to screw up too bad," I said. "I need you guys to keep an eye on the outside, okay? Please?" I could feel the crowd turning, even from inside the circle. The angry weres were getting restless and agitated, arguing with some of the others around them. I could see Eric getting into Ramon's face and Ramon, arms crossed, telling him to back down.

Not entirely mollified, Ashley nodded anyway and didn't bring up any other arguments.

I'd become pretty proficient at closing a circle. I used a little blood because I wanted this one to be as sturdy as possible. Once I'd bandaged the cut on my arm, I took my place at one end.

I closed my eyes and let my head droop. I blocked out the sounds and the smells, concentrating on the cold jade egg in my left hand and the solid athame in my right.

The air was still warm and full of summer. I pulled it into my lungs, holding it before letting it go. I was a little worried about what I was going to do, and I needed to shove that fear down, to push it deep, where it wouldn't distract me. In some ways, calling up Douglas seemed stupid. I'd survived our last confrontation only because I'd been lucky. I knew that. I wasn't in his league. That being said, what else could I do? Let him run around, even though I was pretty sure he'd killed Brannoc? Wait for someone else to take care of the problem?

Ha. I may not have been qualified, but I was the closest thing to it. There was no cavalry, no badass to come and save the day for me. I was going to have to be the badass.

I tightened my grip on the egg. "Douglas Montgomery, I summon thee to get thy ass over here right now." Usually when I summoned someone—or something—I let the call go out into the ether and waited. This time, I sent it into the egg. If I was right, that was my connection to Douglas. That was the call he couldn't ignore.

Squeezing the egg even tighter, I whispered, "Olly, olly, oxen free."

I felt him appear. The temperature in the circle dropped about ten degrees. I looked out with my sight and found what I had expected, the electric blue dome of my circle stretching overhead, and the swirling, nauseating mass that was Douglas.

I opened my eyes.

He didn't look any different, despite his death. Immaculate and cool in his dove gray suit, cuff links twinkling in an errant shaft of moonlight, his body bore no mark of our fight—no scarring around the throat, nothing. Necromancers have a few neat tricks, but self-healing wasn't one of them, which made me wonder how, exactly, he'd pulled it off. The body I'd seen earlier was his—I was positive.

He still scared the crap out of me.

Douglas stayed at his end of the circle, head tilted slightly up, regarding me with faint curiosity. I held up the egg. "I've got something of yours." I wasn't sure what kind of reaction I'd been expecting, but I had expected something. He just kept staring.

"What do you want?" he asked.

That was a fine question. What did I want? I looked down at the egg, making sure to keep Douglas in my line of sight. "I want this all to be over. I'm sick of losing people—of you taking them from me."

The bastard smiled. "Life is about loss, Sam. You can't change that."

The image of the egg blurred as my eyes teared up. I was so angry, so frustrated, I wanted to scream.

"What are you going to do?" Douglas asked. "Destroy the egg? Try and kill me? Banish me? Subject me to more of your inane chatter?" That preacher's voice of his sounded amused, but there was an undercurrent of intense hatred underneath it. "And now that I'm here, what's to stop me from taking it?"

I kept looking at the egg. I hadn't really planned on what to do after this point. To be honest, I hadn't really thought the summoning would work. There was movement at the edge of my vision, and I realized that a few people had ignored the frosty stares of the pack and were now at the edge of my circle. They couldn't come any closer than that. I scanned the faces surrounding us. Haley, her countenance grim, stood next to Nick. He looked a shade pale, but had his feet firmly planted. Ashley looked determined, Brid and her brothers were angry, Frank looked worried, and James . . . James looked scared.

Wait. James?

He had his hands pressed against the dome, his eyes on Douglas. "You weren't at the cabin," James said. I don't think I'd ever seen such naked emotion on his face.

Douglas tapped the dome, looking at its construction, even

now studying me above all other things. No fear, just faint curiosity. "I was busy," he said. "And then I was summoned here." He cocked his head, finally tearing his gaze away from the dome and looking at James. "Did you know about this?" His voice held a hint of accusation.

James twitched his head, a small movement of denial. "When I couldn't find you at the cabin, I called the house. The Minotaur told me where everyone had gone." James's hands fisted against the barrier. "Please, don't do this." Was he talking to me or to Douglas?

Douglas gave him a faint smile in return. "It will be all right, James." He turned back toward me. He didn't say anything else. He just waited, his arms in front of him, holding his wrist with one hand, the very picture of patience.

My hand tightened on the knife. "All this stupid misery and pain—caused by *you*," I said. "It's gotta stop." I advanced on him now, unthinking. I heard the shouts of Brid and a few others outside, but I ignored them, my only thought focused on hurting the person who'd hurt me and the people I cared about.

I slashed at him with my athame and . . . nothing happened. I mean, the dagger passed through, but I couldn't see any damage. Douglas just laughed and then backhanded me so hard that I hit the ground. I'd been hit by Douglas before, and it was never fun. His being dead hadn't changed that.

He held up something that glinted in the moonlight. "You can't hurt me, sonny boy, not while I have this." He kicked me then, hard in the ribs. "But I can most certainly hurt you." He punctuated this with another kick, this time catching me in my stomach. Breath whooshed out of me, but I swung my hand clumsily, trying to catch him. He danced out of my reach easily.

He moved toward me again, and I rolled to my feet, backing away from him. The sight of me retreating made him laugh. "Don't you find it the slightest bit amusing that we keep fighting over power, power that I want, but you don't? That you'd give away if you had the chance?"

I saw Brooke leaning against the circle, her face scrunched and angry and afraid. "No," I said. "Not really. To be honest, I just think you're kind of an asshole."

He ran at me again, and I barely saw him. But I felt his fist as it hit my face, and I was once again lying on the grass. I tasted blood. The sudden image of me during training only a few days ago, my feet against a tree, a squirrel chattering at me, sprang to mind. I'd been so tired of getting my ass handed to me then. Looked like I hadn't learned a whole lot since.

I started to get up, and Douglas went for my ribs again, kicking me in the already bruised area. He did it again. And again. I couldn't breathe now, and I kept wishing that I'd at least landed one punch. Of course, if my athame hadn't caused any damage, my fist certainly wouldn't, but I thought I'd have felt better anyway. Outside the dome I could hear raised voices and commotion, but I couldn't lift my head to see what was going on.

Another blow, this time to my stomach. I looked back down at the egg. So much pain and hate brought on by one little soul—I was convinced that was what it was. More than most people on this planet, Douglas knew that death could be sudden and, I'm sure in his mind, inconvenient. So he had hidden a part of himself in this tiny jade egg. I didn't really care how he managed it, the simple truth was that I wanted Douglas gone and buried. I wanted it all to be over. But I was also tired of people dying. And I realized I knew what I wanted to do.

Of course knowing what you want to do and knowing how to do it are two separate things. I studied the egg. I had no idea what spell Douglas had used to hide himself in it, and I wasn't sure if there was a proper way to break it. So I did the only thing I really knew how to do—I called the soul out.

Necromancers have power over the dead. That's our main gig. But what does that mean, exactly? Is it the flesh we control, or the spirit? When I bring someone back, I'm not just putting the physical being back together—I mean, I could probably do that, but what would be the point? We aren't the shell that binds us, but that little intangible speck that hides within. As all the guidance counselors tell you growing up, it's what's on the inside that counts.

I stumbled to my feet, and Douglas let me. Why not? It wasn't like I'd been putting on a good show up until now. I opened up my hand so the egg could roll into my palm. I held it up at eye level so I could see it better and so Douglas knew what I was doing.

I grinned at him, tasting the blood on my teeth as I did so. "Come out, come out, wherever you are," I whispered, but the sound carried. Douglas watched, face unreadable, while I cast all my power into that egg.

Nothing happened. I frowned, knowing full well that

Douglas was staring at me in an amused fashion. Okay, so my first try didn't work. Maybe I could just smash it? I started to cast around, looking for a rock, but I seemed to have picked the one piece of land that was totally rock free.

"You can't smash it, can you? The spell is strong, and you have nothing to break it. You don't even have a *rock*." His voice took on a scathing tone. "You're lacking something even primitive primates consider a tool. I can't believe you got the best of me, even once. Brought down by something lower than an ape." He shook his head in disgust.

He was right. I didn't have a rock. But I was going to smash the egg anyway. I could use the pommel of my knife. I just needed to find something hard to sandwich it with. My palms started to sweat, the moisture making the cold, slippery surface of the egg hard to hold on to. It shot out of my hand and onto the ground. Taco, who'd been hiding quietly in the grass, spun out after it like it was a tennis ball.

"No!" I shouted. He ignored me as he went for the egg. "Taco! Be a good boy and give it back." Sure, he'd never brought anything back before, but there was always a first time.

Douglas peered at us. "What is *that*?"

I could tell when he figured out what Taco was, because his cold arrogance was replaced with a look of panic. Now, why would a tiny little thing like Taco cause that reaction?

Then Taco, apparently not caring one iota that his new ball was made out of stone, bit right into it, and I remembered why Douglas had forbidden chupacabras from entering his homestead. Taco's jaws tore right through Douglas's spell and cracked the egg open. It might as well have been made of paper.

Again, I'm not sure what I was envisioning. Maybe a glowing spark coming out of carved stone and floating over to Douglas, or perhaps some mystical smoke weaving its way into his body. You know, some peaceful magical crap.

But what I got was a sonic boom. The sound was deafening, and as I was thrown backward, I caught a glimpse of Douglas being similarly knocked down. Outside the dome, I could see a flurry of movement. Chaos appeared to be ensuing, but inside my magic bubble, and except for a persistent whine in my blast-deadened ears, things were nice and calm as I slipped into unconsciousness.

27

LOVE IS A BATTLEFIELD

Bridin Blackthorn had spent most of her life surrounded by Alpha males. She was used to the swaggering. The posturing. The jockeying for position. But that didn't mean she always had patience for it. So when Eric grabbed her shoulder and turned her away from the dome, away from her view of Sam—who had just now been blown back against the edge of the circle—she didn't even think. She reacted, smacking his hand and pushing him back.

"You don't touch me ever." She growled the words, advancing on Eric, who was now looking a lot less sure of himself.

He backed up, moving closer to the members of the pack who supported him. "But." Then he rallied. "Look, it's obvious what's going to happen. We need to get ready. When Douglas leaves that circle, we need to be here to take him down." He sneered at Sam's crumpled form. "He's not going to do it."

Brid didn't respond at first. She just stared at Eric, then the crowd behind him. It amazed her that, were Sam in Eric's place, he would have backed away at this moment. He knew how to read her in a way that Eric, whom she'd been around her entire life, didn't. Because Sam would have seen her silence for what it was—that quiet moment before the storm broke. But Eric, stupid Eric, was relaxing.

She smiled and got close to him, almost touching his chest. "I'm sorry, did you just try to order me around?" Her voice came out saccharine, which the boy in front of her again misinterpreted.

He rested his hands on her shoulders. "Look, you've been confused. We get that. Fell in with the wrong guy." He squeezed her gently. "But it's not too late. I'm here now."

She stared at his hands. His words rang in her head before bouncing down into her, knocking around inside, waking up all the emotions she'd lulled to sleep. The hurt. The worry. The overwhelming anger. She'd been lucky to get them to sleep in the first place. They weren't going to be quiet again.

Brid grabbed Eric's hand so fast he didn't have time to react. His wrist was broken before he'd even cried out in surprise. Before any of his cronies could say a word, Eric was on the ground, bleeding and moaning. Brid had no sympathy for him. He'd heal, after all.

"I said don't touch me." She looked at the rest of his group. "Well?" She felt the rest of the pack closing in around them, circling. The weres looked nervous, but didn't back away from where Eric lay.

Bran appeared at her side. "May I offer you my services, *taoiseach*?" The rest of her brothers joined her.

Brid pulled out her swords, making them appear from nowhere like always. They were her birthright, just like the bow Bran had inherited from their father. She hadn't used them in battle since the last time they'd fought Douglas. She hadn't needed to. "You guys take the ones to the sides. I'm going up the middle. Someone needs to teach them a lesson. Try not to do anything permanent."

She didn't hear her brothers agree. She was already following her own orders.

28

YOUR TURQUOISE AND SILVER
WON'T WEAKEN THIS OLD HEART

My skull was being pecked in. That was what it felt like. I opened my eyes to see the big freaking crow I'd left an offering to, and the pecking feeling had been because, well, he was pecking me. Hard.

"Please stop," I said politely—he was that big. One should always mind one's manners around big things. "Or you'll reach my brain soon, and I kind of need that."

Why? the crow said. *You certainly haven't been using it.* He pecked me once more for good measure. *You gonna get up, Meat, or do I need to do that again?*

"I'm up, I'm up." I sat up and realized immediately that I wasn't where I had been a minute ago. Well, I was in the clearing, but not at the same time, if that makes any sense. And guess who was sitting by a campfire?

The crow gave me one more solid peck on the knee before he took flight, perching on a rock next to the fire. I ambled over and joined them.

"You know this is, like, the worst time for you to come a-calling, don't you? I appreciate the visit and all the interest you've taken in me lately, but being unconscious and in some crazy vision kind of leaves me open for attack."

The goddess Bridget smiled at me and winked. "You're perfectly fine. He's in no state to be doing anything to you right now."

"What about everyone else?" I asked, thinking of what had happened the last time I was here. Had a bunch of zombies sprouted up and started attacking everyone now that I was unconscious?

"They're fine. Nick is holding the circle up."

"Really?" I sat down next to the fire.

"Really."

"Why am I here?" I asked. "I didn't try to raise Brannoc this time, so while I'm delighted to see you, I'm also a little confused."

The flower behind her ear came into full bloom as she considered me. "You have done a fine job, Sam." She smiled when I gave her a skeptical look. "Believe it or not, you have. The blast you just suffered, however, could have tipped the scales rather poorly, and so I chose to interfere a little. I suppose we all cheat when it comes to our champions."

"What, are you going to give me some amazing power to help me defeat Douglas? Like maybe the ability to shoot lightning from my fingers or something?"

The crow pecked me hard for my insolence, but Bridget was holding her sides as peals of laughter escaped from her.

"Oh," she said, wiping her eyes, "I do enjoy you, Samhain. No, I can't give you any special gift, and it would hurt a great deal to shoot anything from your fingers."

I squelched the desire to shake her and ask her why she bothered to bring me here, then. It isn't nice to assault a goddess. My mom brought me up better than that. Say please, thank you, and be nice to all deities. Can't say my mother didn't want us to be prepared.

"What I can give you is a quiet place to think, if only for a moment, where you aren't distracted by the impending possible destruction of yourself or others."

"Um, thanks?"

"Never underestimate the power of a quiet moment. They are few and far between, these days." Bridget, who had picked up a stick to poke the fire, dropped it and took my hands in hers. Later, I might freak out about this fact, as it wasn't every day I got to hold hands with a deity, but in the pocket of night we found ourselves in, I felt nothing but calm and reassurance.

"You need to think about how this is going to end, Sam."

"Douglas will most likely gut me and turn my carcass into a new double-breasted suit," I said. "And then he'll probably destroy everyone I love." My chest seized up at the thought. "I hope he doesn't make us all into suits, because then he'll need to get a bigger closet."

She gave my hands a little shake. "Is that what you want to happen?"

I blinked at her. "Are you kidding? Who on earth would want that to happen besides Douglas? Of course I don't want to be made into fashion wear, but I got lucky the first time, and we all know it. I don't think he's going to give me that chance again. This is Douglas's game, and he's going to win it." I stared up at the sky in frustration. "I'm just going to keep losing people." The stars looked weird, wherever we were. They kept spinning wildly, like someone was speeding up the universe. "All this death . . . it's exhausting and I'm tired of it. And yes, I am fully aware of the irony in that statement."

I tore my eyes from the whirling heavens and looked back down at my hands. They were dirty and bloodstained, with bits of orange sand sticking here and there. Hers were pale, the fingers long, with thin half-moons in her nails.

She let go of my hands and pushed my chin up with one fingertip, like it was a bird set to perch. There was a sad understanding in her eyes. She leaned in and kissed me, right between the eyes. By the time she leaned back, she looked happier. "You are what you are, Sam. But that doesn't mean you have to play the same as Douglas. If you don't like the game, change the rules." She searched my face. "Do you understand?"

"I'm not sure," I said.

Despite my answer, she seemed satisfied. Bridget turned toward the giant bird. "Thank you, Crow. I would appreciate it if you would help him back. He seems to have problems when I do it."

"Wait." I grabbed her hand. "Am I going to get sick like last time?"

"No," she said, placing her other hand on top of mine. "That was my error. I was treating you like your father's son, and forgetting you're also your mother's. Big mistake, that. If I'd been thinking, I would never have put my mantle on you." A little pat from her hand on mine and then, "Crow?"

The crow let out a caw and grabbed the back of my T-shirt with his beak. He yanked hard and—

𝕀 found myself in the circle. I was on my back, where I had apparently landed after the blast. From the feel of it and the way I was lying, I had bounced off the circle and was now crumpled on the ground. The crow was with me, and he was jabbing me quite painfully with his beak again.

Get up, Meat.

"You could at least be polite," I croaked.

Fine. Get up, Meat, please.

He hopped to the side as I pushed myself into a sitting position. I must have been out for a few minutes, because the scene had devolved. Ashley was pounding on the side of the protective circle. The pack was a roiling mess. Ramon was wrestling with a big were, both of them starting to shift as they hit the ground. Brid had her back to the circle, and her swords were out. She held them at her sides and screamed at her pack, trying to keep them at bay, trying to restore order. Bran stood next to her, smacking down a few of the pups who weren't listening.

Nick stood with them, his face toward me, his eyes closed. He was struggling to keep the circle up. All that magic inside, all those things trying to break in. Couldn't have been easy. The gnomes, Haley, and Frank were surrounding him, protecting him. Frank looked like he was about to wet his pants.

Brooke stood with Frank, a determined expression on her face. Only Taco, who was now chewing happily on the remnants of the jade egg, looked pleased.

The pack was a mess. It was like a bar brawl without the bar. Some were changing in the grass, others were shouting or trying desperately not to change. Fists were flying, and as I watched, someone was thrown into the side of the dome.

Then James's face caught my eye. Mostly because you usually had no idea what he was feeling. He was master of the blank face. Not this time. His hands were clenching and unclenching like he wanted to do something, but couldn't, and his face was completely conflicted. He looked like a lost little boy.

I hadn't known James for long, but in that time, I'd never seen him at a loss. He always knew what to do. His pained face swiveled back and forth between Douglas and me, and for the first time, I understood exactly what was going on in James's head.

When Haley and I were kids, we'd done some dogsitting for one of my mom's friends. The dog, an amiable golden retriever named Wallaby, had caused some friction between my sister and me because we were both convinced that we were Wallaby's favorite. After arguing off and on for days, we'd both gone to opposite sides of the room and called the dog to see who he'd go to. We needed an answer. That was my first lesson in the folly of making someone—whether animal or human—choose between you and somebody else. It never seems to play out the way you hoped. After a few minutes of us calling and offering treats, Wallaby hadn't budged. His head swiveled between us, unsure what was going on, but enjoying the attention. Finally he got tired of the game and went bounding off after a squirrel that happened to scuttle past. The squirrel hadn't been playing, but he'd won the game.

That's what happens when you force someone to choose. Maybe they pick option A, maybe they pick option B, but most will go for a third option that isn't asking them to pick favorites in the first place.

James reminded me of Wallaby just then. Torn between two sides of his life. I might hate Douglas with a fiery passion, but James . . . well, an image of that serious child by Douglas's side came to mind. I didn't really know where James was before, but he'd been pretty young when Douglas got ahold of him, of that I was certain. And when you're little, parents are almost godlike. Even if you end up with a mom, dad, or guardian straight out of a dysfunctional pantheon, you'll stick by them, because they are your whole world. They're all you know, and the idea of having empty space where they used to be, of having that horrible vacuum in your life, is unthinkable. Like it or not, for James, Douglas was family.

I looked over at Douglas, who was on his knees at the other side of the circle. He was sweating profusely and obviously out of it. I was pretty sure I could end it now. He certainly looked corporeal now—the beads of sweat and dazed look gave evidence of that—but then again, he'd appeared corporeal before. Still, in his state, he probably wouldn't even know what hit him. A few steps and a jab from my athame, and maybe this would all be over. Except for the nightmares and the self-recrimination I'd gain from killing someone who couldn't fight back.

I glanced at James, and I could see he understood. The panicked look of fear might have been comical if it hadn't been so damn sad. He said something then, and though I couldn't hear him, I knew exactly what it was. *Sam, please. Please.*

Not Master. Sam. Come to think of it, he'd been dropping the "Master" a lot lately. Maybe that was because he felt his real master was Douglas, but I didn't think so. And maybe I was a fool, but I wanted to believe—I needed to believe—that James had started to see us all as friends. As family.

Family. I knew then, with a strange certainty, that it was James who'd threatened Haley. James had put that knife in Haley's door. Douglas would've killed her, but James wouldn't. I remembered what he'd said to my mom about the wards— that they'd been set for someone who wanted to do harm. Whatever his orders had been, he hadn't wanted to hurt Haley. When I'd sent him to check their security, he'd mentioned the fireplace—easy access for a schnauzer-sized dragon—and had my mom change them so even he couldn't get in again. Maybe he'd been lying to everyone, and perhaps his alliances weren't set, but despite everything that had happened, I was absolutely dead certain that I hadn't been wrong about James. I hadn't made a mistake.

I thought about what Bridget had said to me. *Change the rules.*

I waggled the athame at James, then stabbed it into the ground all the way up to the hilt. The look on his face now was priceless. I winked at him. Then I walked over to Douglas.

Ashley was screaming now, shouting something, probably what on earth was I doing, but I ignored her. Minutes passed. The yelling and pounding continued, I'm sure, but I stopped hearing it. And slowly, Douglas came back to himself.

He looked up at me. I'd never seen Douglas look bewildered. Strike that—I'd never seen him look even vaguely human. But as he glanced around, quickly assessing everything, that's how he appeared. Confused and very, very human. Especially when his eyes, those cold, creepy brown eyes, settled on me.

He moved like a viper, and suddenly, I was held up against the side of the dome, Douglas's hand around my throat, the sweat on his forehead visible while I felt him slowly squeeze.

"I don't understand," he said, slamming me against the dome. "I don't like things I don't understand." He threw me onto the ground, disgusted.

"Few people do," I choked.

"You could have killed me."

It was a statement, not a question, but I answered it anyway. "Yes."

He digested that. It simply did not compute for him. "I don't understand," he said again.

"I don't want to play. You want to try and kill me? Fine. Go ahead. But I refuse to make murder my first answer for things. I'm tired of watching people die. You want to rumble, we'll rumble, but I'm not going to slit the throat of an unconscious man. Especially not in front of the only family he has."

Douglas looked surprised, and I'm not sure what astounded him more, my desire to not stab things or my reference to family.

"Look at James, Douglas. Really look at him. That is the only soul on earth who gives a rat's ass whether you die or not. He's the only one who cares about you. I want you to see what you're doing to him." I wasn't counting Minion in the list of people who'd care. He was sitting happily munching the grass outside the dome, completely unaware of what was going on.

He could have been at a soccer match or on the moon, and it wouldn't have made any difference.

Douglas grew angry then, his face contorting under the weight of his rage. "Don't you dare try to act like you understand what we've been through together or what James might think. You couldn't possibly fathom it. He's been with me longer than you've been alive."

I looked at the sad state he was in, still furious, even now. "There's a lot of shit going on that I don't get, but family I understand." Douglas continued his fuming, not grasping what I was saying. "And I think James also understands it—or is beginning to. You didn't order him to scare Haley, did you? Doesn't seem your style. No, she was going to be another one of your 'messages' to me. Why didn't he follow through, Douglas? Did you ask him?"

He swayed on his feet, his sweat dripping, and I felt pity. I couldn't help it. It was who I was, and I refused to let Douglas change that about me. And I felt it even more for James. I thought about what I'd said before, how I'd been between a pack and a hard place, but James had been trying to serve two very different masters. I wasn't happy he'd threatened Haley, and we'd talk about that if I managed to live, but he'd also managed to warn me that something was wrong, that my family was in trouble . . . and to strengthen the security around them. In a weird, messed-up way, he'd kept them safe.

"I'm not as smart as some of the people I know. But you know what? Neither are you."

He grabbed me again and lifted me to my feet, his hand grasping the front of my shirt right by my throat. I put my

hands on his and pushed my will into him. Douglas was probably going to kill me, but before that happened, I was going to
make that bastard remember what it was like to be human.

"Fucking look at him, Douglas!"

A sneer on his face, Douglas complied. The sneer dissolved
as he stood there, face-to-face with James. Because his friend,
his only friend, was a pathetic sight to see. Even from here, I
could see James quaking in place, terrified and unsure, still
looking like that lost little boy. Tears cutting down his cheeks.
Sparks of emotions came to life somewhere deep in Douglas,
and I reached for them, grabbed them, made them thrive. I
made Douglas remember. I took my memory of the old faded
photograph by James's bed and I shoved it at him, suddenly
realizing from my connection to Douglas how old that picture was. For a split second, I wondered how old each of them
was. This wasn't the first time my enemy had cheated death.

That's when Nick lost control of the circle. But we didn't
move. Outside of where James stood, the pack still fought, but
in the epicenter of things, there was only stillness.

"How long have you had him?" I whispered.

"We stopped counting after sixty, I think," Douglas
answered with a voice I'd never heard from him. Soft. Gentle.
"His kind mature at a different rate, you know. He's no more
than a teenager, really."

Then a strange thing, or perhaps I should say a stranger
thing, happened, and Frank—still looking like he was going to
piss himself—started it. My mousy little friend walked up to
James, staring at Douglas the whole time, and put his hand on
James's shoulder. I wasn't sure who was more surprised—James

or Douglas or Frank. My other friends, all except a fully changed Ramon, who was now laying a bear-style smackdown on Eric and a few other wolves, followed suit. Brooke slipped an arm around James's waist and glared defiantly at Douglas as Ashley slipped into the space between James and Frank. Sean and Brid stood behind him, arms crossed and eyes fierce, the only members of the pack caught up in our moment. Haley stepped in front of James, putting herself between him and Douglas, a look of stubborn determination on her face. She glared at Douglas. "He's part of our family now. You had your chance, and you fucked it up. You gave him to us." She crossed her arms. "No backsies."

James blinked in surprise. I don't think he would have been more shocked if a unicorn had come up and smacked him in the eye. "Haley, no. You don't understand—I threatened you. That's not . . . we're not . . ." He gave up on whatever argument he was trying to put forth. "I put that knife in your door."

Haley shrugged, not taking her gaze off Douglas. "We all make mistakes. Family means you get past them. And you buy them new doors."

Douglas pulled his hand back. Not the one holding me by the throat, of course. He hadn't changed that much.

"James?" Douglas's voice was steady, but something in the tone sounded uncertain. I was still connected to Douglas, and I could feel his confusion that James hadn't moved. The circle was broken, but James remained on the outside. He hadn't rushed immediately to Douglas's side. Instead he was staring at the huddled group around him, a perplexed look on his face. It was the look of someone who, on a dare, had asked a cheerleader out and was shocked when she said yes.

Something inside Douglas broke. If I were being melodramatic, I'd say it was his heart, but then, I don't believe Douglas had one of those.

"You're beginning to get it, I think." I spoke softly but pitched my voice so he could hear me. "You are like a rabid dog. A sick thing that needs to be put down. But there's hope for him. There's family for him." Douglas continued to stare at James. "I think you did your best. For James, I believe you tried."

"I keep underestimating you," Douglas said. He loosened his tie, a bemused look on his face, dropping it before turning toward me. "Pure sloppiness on my part." He let out a tired sigh. "I don't get you, Samhain, and I don't think I ever will."

It's hard to understand compassion when you haven't any, the crow said as he hopped up onto my shoulder. *Or love.*

"I don't want to kill you, Douglas. Not because you don't deserve it, but because I'm tired of killing. You probably don't understand what that feels like."

Douglas smiled then, and it was the closest I'd ever seen to a real smile on his face. He reached up and pulled a long silver chain with something shiny hanging from it over his head. He dropped it in the grass.

I didn't know what it was, but the reaction in James was instantaneous. He went wild, screaming and tugging against the hands that were now restraining him.

Douglas ignored him. He let go of me and walked over to where I'd stabbed the athame into the dirt. When he came back, it took everything I had not to turn and run the other way. There was nowhere to run to anyway. So I held my ground and tried to appear as badass as possible.

He came within reach of me and stopped. "I think you know what you have to do."

"I did that already," I said. "And nothing happened."

"Why don't you try again?"

Do you understand? I asked the crow.

I'm pretty sure he's mortal now.

You're pretty *sure?!?*

Only one way to find out, Meat.

I nodded at Douglas. I did know what I had to do. That didn't mean I wanted to do it. James screamed again and tried to buck the hands holding him back, but there were too many.

Douglas handed the athame to me, hilt first, a small, broken smile on his face. "It would have been kinder if you had killed me while I was still out of it."

"Not to James," I said. "And I can't let you break another person. I just can't."

He tilted his head and, for an instant, a fleeting, too-short instant, I saw what Douglas could have been. It hurt to see.

Then he grabbed my hand and used it to stab the dagger right into his chest. He choked and collapsed to the ground, dragging me with him. There was no blood, but Douglas gagged anyway, like his lungs were filling with it. With his hands on mine, I felt everything. The pain. The fear of dying. And above all that, his whole reason for sacrifice. His love for James, the closest thing to family he had.

And for the second time, I sat there and watched him die.

Only this time it was worse, because I was fully aware of exactly what was happening. Yes, he deserved to die many times over for what he had done. That didn't mean I had to like it.

His last breath rattled out, and power hit me, the end of the ritual Douglas had started in his basement so many weeks ago finally coming home to roost. At the end of the ritual, when I'd been flooded with power I thought was Douglas's but had really been my own, I'd been overwhelmed, an explosion of energy inside me begging to be used, needing to be used. This time, it was different. Douglas's gift slithered into me like an enormous snake, and it settled in until I was full, its tail spun tight around my neck, choking me. Like I'd held my breath until I was about to pass out, my head swimming and my heart fit to explode.

I swallowed it slowly, that too-big bite, and it hurt going down, but eventually I managed.

When it was finished, I closed Douglas's eyes and called to Ed. A torn portal gaped and then Ed towered over me, his jackal face solemn.

"I have need of your services," I said.

Ed nodded. *It is time for him to be judged.*

I wiped my hand on the grass, even though there was nothing on it. The crow, oddly enough, pulled on my ear gently with his beak. I think he was trying to comfort me. Taco ignored him, still chewing on the remnants of his egg. Somehow he knew that the crow wasn't food.

You feel sorry for his passing, despite all he has done? Ed's ears pitched forward out of curiosity.

"Yeah," I said.

Why?

I struggled to find an answer. Why did I feel so bad? Douglas was a terrible person, and he had caused untold hurt and pain to so many people. But I grieved for him anyway. "Someone died today," I said. "That should be mourned. And respected." I looked over at James, who had collapsed to his knees, anguish clear on his face. "My sorrow is for those he leaves behind and what he could have been."

I tilted back so I could look at Ed. "Is that wrong?"

It is not wrong, he said, *to have a good heart.* He reached down then and picked Douglas up gently. *I don't know if that will be enough to balance his scales, but know that Ma'at and Thoth are fair. Maybe he can avoid Ammut's jaws.*

Ed was saying that more to put a damper on my pity and guilt than from any real belief, I think. We all knew Douglas was not going to do well in his final judgment.

29

TAKE ME HOME TONIGHT

Ed opened up a vortex and took Douglas's body away. The crow on my shoulder gave me another soft bite on the ear, then he flew over to the grass, picking up whatever shiny silver thing Douglas had dropped. He flew after Ed, and with a nod toward me, Ashley joined them, her manner unusually solemn.

You'd think, after all that hubbub, that it would be eerily quiet, but that wasn't true. Frogs still croaked, wolves howled, trees rustled. The world kept moving, no matter what we had going on.

Most of the pack was gone, running through the woods, I hope comforted by the knowledge that Brannoc's killer was gone. The howls and yips sounded joyful at any rate. Only Brid and her brothers remained alongside my friends, family, and Sexy Gary. Oh, and Minion was chewing on the greenery. Mustn't forget dear, sweet Minion.

James sat, unmovable, in the grass. No one could get him to speak or even look up. I understood what he was going through. Sometimes, you just want to be left alone. I trudged over to where Ramon had been. Well, I guess Ramon was still there, technically, just not in Ramon shape. Brid was with him, absently patting his back.

"Okay to approach?"

"Yeah," she said. "He's got pretty good control generally, but I think the stress of what was going on . . ." She shrugged. "It's hard to take it easy when your friend is in trouble."

I stepped closer, but I can admit I held back a little. You try getting all close and friendly with a grizzly bear. Those suckers are huge. Ramon grunted at me in an amused fashion and sat down with a thump.

"Sorry, buddy," I said, hands dug into my pockets. "That seemed painful."

"It is," Brid said, hand still on Ramon's back. "But it's worth it."

Haley ran to my side and squeezed me so tight it was hard to talk, which did a number on my bruised ribs.

"Ease up there. I need those ribs."

She smacked my shoulder. "You had me worried."

I wiped my hand on her shirt, leaving a dusting of orange sand. The blood was too dry to rub off. "I have been rather busy today, haven't I?"

She looked around, taking in Ramon in bear form, me, the busted circle, and the people standing awkwardly around the broken-down James. She scratched Ramon's ears. I'll tell you one thing: my sister is pretty unflappable. As soon as she felt Ramon and I were okay, she nodded, turned on her heel, and walked over to James.

I couldn't see his face. His head was hanging down from a drooping neck and shoulders. Haley walked over and stood in front of him. That's all she did. James stared at her shoes for a few seconds. When he looked up, it was heartbreaking. I haven't seen such anguish since Haley and I lost our father. And, sure, our dad was nice and Douglas was a psychopathic killer, but to James he was more. He was family, and that family was gone.

Haley stared down at James. Then, very gently, she sat next to him and brushed his hair back from his face. And even though everyone else had been trying to comfort him, it was only Haley that James would allow. He collapsed into her arms and sobbed. Haley held him, shooing everyone else away with one hand.

We left them on the grass. There was nothing more the rest of us could do.

30

PAPA DON'T PREACH

Brid gave me a ride home on Sean's motorcycle. I'd left the car with Haley so she could bring James back to the house whenever he was ready, and I'd made the rest of the crew follow in Gary's van.

Once I got home, I went straight to the fridge. I chugged a soda without closing the fridge door, something my mom would have berated me for. But it was my damn house, and I could do whatever I wanted. So I leaned in and enjoyed the cold.

Brid came up behind me and slid her arms around my chest. I hugged them to me one-handed and grabbed another soda with the other. I shut the fridge with my foot while shuffling over to the counter to set down my drink. Then I turned and gave Brid a proper hug. If she hadn't pulled away, I don't think I ever would have let her go.

"You look terrible," she said.

"It's good to look like one feels. I think it's more honest that way."

She grinned. "I need to get back."

"Hm."

"We're going to keep Ramon for the night. I don't think

he'll want to change right back, so I figure we'll let him run." I nodded and held her, but all too soon, she walked out the door.

After she left, I slogged my way up to the bathroom. I didn't have the energy for it, but I took a shower anyway. I needed to wash off the sand and blood. It felt good, but I still didn't feel clean. Bringing about someone's death will do that to you. Doing it a second time only amplifies the feeling.

My fingers were pruney by the time I got out. I don't really remember drying off or pulling on pajama pants, but I must have, because when I found myself standing in the middle of my room, staring absently off into space, I was dry and pajamaed. Absently, I noted that I was probably in shock. I also noted that I didn't care. Crawling into bed, I vowed never to leave.

My window was still open, and the breeze had started to chill enough that I pulled the blanket up to my chin. The fresh air felt nice, though, so I didn't close it. I couldn't sleep. I was bone tired and emotionally exhausted, yes, but my brain was spinning like a hamster wheel.

So much had happened lately, I just didn't know how to sort it. I missed Brannoc. At least with him I knew it was something big—death and a protective, nosy deity—keeping him away. It made the things keeping Brid and me apart seem tiny and insignificant, but I missed her just as much. She couldn't keep sneaking into my bed, not if she wanted to convince the pack to believe that she'd given me up. On top of that, I was worried about James. I felt bad about Douglas. A thousand other thoughts and uncertainties swirled and wouldn't stop. I threw off the covers with a growl of frustration.

"Not easy being all grown up, is it?"

I yelped in surprise. Brannoc was leaning against my wall. My hand went involuntarily to my neck, but my medicine bag wasn't there because I'd taken it off to shower and in my daze had forgotten to replace it.

Brannoc chuckled as I tried to regain composure. Someday I'd be used to ghosts popping up out of nowhere, right? He came over and sat on my bed.

"I think," I said after I'd calmed down, "that I could handle either growing up or being a necromancer on its own, but the combo is a bit problematic."

"I hear you."

I sat on the edge of my bed, my fingers picking at the blanket. "I'm sorry. You know, about everything."

"Don't be. I hear you found my killer. That's enough comfort for me. I'm sure it wasn't easy."

"Bridget sure didn't make it simple."

Brannoc grimaced. "Don't blame the goddess. It's bad form. Besides, it was mostly my fault." He looked away.

I examined the uncomfortable expression on his face. "You asked her to intervene so I couldn't bring you back." As I said it, I knew it was true, whether he admitted to it or not. "Why the hell would you do that?" I was too tired to get angry, really angry, and it was hard to attach that kind of emotion to Brannoc anyway. He'd always been such a good guy to me. But then again, I'd been mad at a lot of good people lately.

"Tough love," he murmured.

I let that sink in. "You had to see if we could function. If the pack could do it on their own."

He nodded. "Hardest thing to do, with kids, doesn't matter if they're yours or someone else's. At some point, the training wheels have to come off."

"And if I'd raised you—"

"They'd never have made their own way. My kids, the pack, they would have kept coming back to me every time they hit a hard spot. Never would have learned to trust their own judgment."

"You didn't want to drag it out. So you did it quick," I said. "Like a Band-Aid." He didn't answer me, but he didn't need to. "I wouldn't have kept bringing you back, you know. Sometimes it's just not right. I learned that with Ling Tsu."

After Douglas had kind-of-sort-of-not-really-died that first time, I'd broken into the zoo and laid to rest the zombie panda that he had raised. Ling Tsu had died at a rather inconvenient time, so the zoo had paid handsomely for Douglas to fix the problem. Now, I could have left Ling Tsu. He wasn't hurting anybody. But he wasn't happy, and it wasn't right, keeping him alive like that. Sometimes what I do is good, but sometimes it's toeing a little too close to the line. Ling Tsu was quickly becoming my barometer for what was okay and what wasn't.

"So, how'd we do? You know, with the being all responsible business," I asked.

He patted my shoulder, just like the last time I'd seen him at the Den. When he was still alive. I looked at my feet, my throat suddenly feeling thick and painful.

"You did good," he said.

"If I did so good, why do I feel so shitty?"

Brannoc patted my shoulder again, in sympathy this time.

"It's called growing pains, kid. You've had a lot going on the past few months. Some good, some bad, but all change. When you hit a spot like that, it hurts while you try to catch up to it. Give yourself some time to grow."

"I'd love to," I grumbled. "But it seems life isn't giving me much time to adjust."

He laughed. "It most certainly isn't, is it? What's that curse? 'May you live in interesting times'?"

I pulled my knees to my chest. "I got interesting in spades."

"Yeah, you did, and I can't promise that's going to end anytime soon. And I hate to add to the pile, but I have a favor to ask you, O mighty champion of the Blackthorn pack." He grinned while he said the last part.

"Name it."

"Keep an eye on my kids, will you? I know they're all grown up and everything, but it's never easy to lose someone, no matter how old you are."

"Of course," I said. Then I grimaced. "If they let me. There's been some tension between the pack and me lately."

He nodded. "Yeah, I know, but do your best. I know you will." He got up to leave.

"Hey, Brannoc?"

"Yeah?"

"Thanks, you know, for everything."

"You're welcome." He started to fade, then reversed it, slamming back into existence. "Oh, and Sam? If my daughter ever decides she wants to keep you around on a more permanent basis, let her know that she has my—and Bridget's—blessing."

He grinned widely when he saw how beet red my face got. He gave me a farewell wave, then disappeared.

It was easier sleeping after his visit.

Breakfast in the morning was a little awkward. James was subdued, but no longer appeared to be a broken man. My sister had crashed in one of the guest rooms and was kind enough to cook breakfast before she drove home. It was nice to have her there, and I told her she could claim a guest room as her own for whenever she needed to stay.

Things were tense with me, James, and Haley in the kitchen. I was trying to be normal and lighthearted, but there were several elephants in the room—my guilt over Douglas's death and James's guilt over threatening Haley being the two biggest metaphorical pachyderms in the bunch. I wasn't sure how to resolve it. Do I apologize to him? Does he apologize to me?

Then Haley put silverware in front of us and made us set the table. As she placed a big pile of butter knives in the center of the table she fixed me with a gimlet eye. "Try to not kill anyone while you're setting the table." Then she poked James. "And I don't want to find these in any doors. Knives next to spoons, boys. Not in people or furniture—once is a slipup. Twice is impolite. Three times is downright rude." She turned and went back to cooking breakfast.

For a long, drawn-out breath, no one said anything. The only sound was the snap of butter on a hot skillet. Then James picked up a handful of knives and placed one carefully by a spoon. He nudged it with one finger until it sat perfect and straight. He stepped back and examined his handiwork, leaning so Haley could see.

She nodded, pleased. "Very good. Baby steps. Keep this up, and I'll tell you where I hid the steak knives."

I couldn't help it then—I collapsed into a chair, laughing. James didn't laugh—but I could see the beginnings of a smile twisting at the edges of his lips. Haley was right. Baby steps. Leave it to my little sister to settle a complicated issue with place settings.

Ashley and Ed transported in while we were eating and Ashley accepted Haley's French toast in lieu of the usual waffle payment. Haley makes killer French toast. Ed took a cup of coffee, but only after he explained to me, in full detail, how much American coffee was lacking in comparison to the kind they brewed in his homeland. After I was done eating, he asked to speak to me privately.

Once we were alone, he handed me what appeared to be a coin on a chain. "What is this?"

It's what was keeping Douglas in his state of half life. A Stygian coin.

The coin felt cold in my palm. I flipped it over. Both sides were worn down with use. It wasn't a quarter, but that was about all I could deduce.

"A Stygian coin? As in the River Styx?"

He nodded. *Yes. People used to be buried with silver coins over their eyes in order to pay Charon. The coins are difficult to obtain, since you have to go to the other side to get them, and many mortals, if they have the proper combination of bravery and stupidity needed to undertake the journey in the first place, don't make it back.*

"That's really nifty and all, but why are you giving it to me?"

After much discussion, we have decided that you have earned such a reward.

I held up the coin. "Well, it's shiny, I'll grant you that. What do I do with it?"

With an amused expression, Ed took it out of my hands and put it around my neck. I immediately felt the same curious feeling I got when I summoned a circle or offered up blood in sacrifice. "Whoa."

Ed's ears flicked. *Ashley has told me that certain aspects of being a necromancer trouble you—namely the sacrificial part?*

I mumbled an agreement while I picked up the coin off my chest so I could look at it more closely.

This coin pays the sacrifice for you.

I looked up at him. "Really? I don't have to kill things or slice up my arm anymore?"

No. But you might need to feed it once in a while. Do I smell bacon?

Haley had made bacon for the carnivores, and unless they'd been complete gluttons, there should have been some left. Ed returned to the kitchen before I could stop and ask him what he meant by "feeding" the coin. I didn't like the sound of that.

I tucked the coin in my pocket for now. There would be time for questions later.

31

WE ARE FAMILY

Ramon came back a few days later. Things had settled down a bit by that time. I was lazing about on the front porch steps, drinking my coffee, petting Taco, and watching the gnomes train Frank in some of their fighting techniques. It was pretty hilarious.

Ramon grabbed a cup of coffee and joined me. "Why is that gnome wearing a cowboy hat?"

"That would be Chuck the Norriser. He's convinced that, since Chuck Norris wears one in *Walker, Texas Ranger*, he must do so in real life. It's caused quite a hullabaloo in the gnome community. They think the break from tradition might be a slippery slope and that soon all the gnomes might turn away from their customary garb. It got pretty ugly there for a while."

"Wow."

"Yeah, but then Frank said he was giving Chuck a special sanction because of his namesake, but the hat will still have to be red. So we've ordered a tiny red cowboy hat to be made, and everyone's happy."

"That is truly bizarre."

I shrugged and sipped my coffee. "To outsiders, everyone's home life is weird. Mine just happens to be extra weird."

Ramon glanced at me. "So you've finally accepted this as your home, huh? No more 'I'm going to bulldoze this place and burn the rubble' talk?"

I thought about that for a minute and looked around. Frank and the gnomes were now going through a set of what looked like Tai Chi. The Minotaur was playing Frisbee with the nymphs. (The nymphs were winning.) One of the big stone lions was basking in the sun, its tail flicking slowly. The gladiators were trimming the shrubs, and James, in cat form, was ruthlessly stalking a butterfly. My sister, in a ridiculously floppy sun hat, was tending the garden. I yelled at her to keep an eye on the hedges that had been snaking forward to snatch her hat. The scene was almost idyllic, and I realized that at some point, somewhere deep down inside, I'd decided that this was home. Ramon was right.

I took another sip of my coffee. "No, no bulldozing or rubble-burning."

"Good," Ramon said. "I like it here."

"Me too."

Taco got up, stretched, then flopped out into as much sun as he could manage.

"What about your uncle?" Ramon asked.

"We are in a delicate state of truce. That's enough for now, I think." I stared into my half-empty cup. "Are you . . . okay?"

Ramon was also having a staring contest with his coffee. "It really bothers you, doesn't it? What I am?"

"What? No. I don't care if you start turning into a purple-spotted giraffe hell-bent on world domination—you're still my best friend."

He set down his mug and turned to me. "Then what *is* bothering you?"

"I guess I feel, I don't know, responsible."

"For what?"

I waved my hand out toward Frank. "It's like Frank. I mean, yeah, he's pretty happy right now, and the gnomes have started calling him Frank the Fearless, but what trouble is my association with him going to bring? You were leading a perfectly happy and normal life, and now presto-chango, it's become complicated, and it's all because of me."

Ramon started to laugh. Really loudly, too. It was one of those gut busters where you can't stop until it's all run out. I let him go, a frown on my face. Here I was in deep emotional turmoil, and he was having a giggling fit, the bastard.

I was able to go get a fresh cup of coffee while he contained himself.

"That's what's been bothering you?"

"What the hell did you think was bothering me?" I was feeling a little grouchy over the fact that Ramon wasn't taking this very seriously.

He shrugged. "I don't know, I thought maybe me turning into a giant bear was kind of weirding you out for some reason."

"You thought I was having adjustment issues because of that? Dude, half my friends turn into wolves, one of my roommates turns into a dragon, and Frank is training with *gnomes*.

That is not the problem." I socked him in the arm. "I felt bad that you were going through all this because of me."

Ramon hit me back, harder. "*Dude*," he mimicked, "it's as much my fault as yours. You didn't ask to get kidnapped. I chose to come after you, knowing full well I might get hurt. I honestly don't think any of us could have anticipated this outcome." He leaned back on his elbows. "Anyway, it's done. And you know what? I don't mind."

I set down my mug and hunched forward, resting on my elbows. "You're not just saying that so I'll stop festering in my guilt?"

"Do what you gotta do, man. All I'm saying is, it's not that bad. Sure, there are downsides—I'm still having control issues, and it hurts like a son of a bitch, but there are upsides too."

"Like what?"

"Like getting to be a big-ass bear. You can't tell me that's not fierce. Look at it this way, with all of your new crazy powers, doesn't it reassure you to know that you can use them to help your friends?"

"Yeah."

"It's just like that." We watched as Frank tripped over his own feet, landing facedown in the grass. "Someone has to take care of you guys. It will be a little easier to do that as a were-bear, you know?"

"I have this vision of your room covered in Care Bear paraphernalia, right down to the grumpy bear sheets."

"If you start asking to see my were-bear stare, I'm going to eat you."

"Aw, don't be grumpy there, sunshine bear."

He shoved me.

I held up my hands in mock surrender. "I will say this—I was surprised you turned into a grizzly."

"What, are you saying that because I'm Mexican? You don't think a man of my heritage can handle a grizzly bear?"

"I was just going to say because you're so short."

It went downhill after that.

32

I NEVER PROMISED YOU
A ROSE GARDEN

A few weeks later, I was back in Olympic Park, hiking with new escorts. Ramon was spending some much-needed time with his family. He'd been easing into visits with them since his accident. When I told him I felt bad that he'd had to miss out on family time because of me, he'd shrugged and reminded me that it could have been much worse. A few misplaced punches in the basement brawl could have resulted in him not seeing his family again ever, unless you counted his funeral.

I didn't really want to know what Pello was up to. With him, less information tends to be better. So I found myself hiking with Ariana and Ione from the Council. Ione was there for very practical reasons. She was going to be helping with the rune work and whatnot for the charms Murray requested. The ones the Bigfoot needed were a little complicated, or so I was told, since the illusion had to fool the eye and the nose. Not everyone could bang these kinds of charms out—they were fairly labor-intensive, and you needed someone skilled to produce a charm that was anywhere near decent.

Ione was skilled, or she wouldn't have been on the Council. The witch was so quiet during the meetings that I'd had a hard time getting to know her. But out in her element, she was markedly different. Her hair was pulled back so you could see her face, and she was smiling. Though by no means a chatterbox, she was actually talking.

Ariana still scared me, but I think that was healthy and normal, since she was one of those people who could kill you eighteen different ways with a relish fork.

"You are sad?" Ione said. We had taken a break to enjoy the view and drink some water. At least that's what they were doing. I was trying to look less sweaty than I was and sitting on a rock. Ione only glanced my way when she spoke, still shy of me. I think it had taken her some courage to ask me the question in the first place.

"Yes," I said. "I am." There was no reason to lie. The only time I'd seen Brid in the last few weeks was at the Council meeting we'd held about the Bigfoots (Bigfeets?) and their request. Gary had shown up to the meeting as the local representative. It was nice to see him again, even though he tried to convince me to bring Minion back—he could have used some help, apparently. But Minion had been gone from Hollywood too long already, so I'd returned him as soon as I was able. There was really no reason to keep him. I didn't have anything for him to do, so he'd spent most of his time sitting around, looking sad and eating sandwiches. I think he missed Douglas. Besides, he required an around-the-clock babysitter, and nobody deserved that duty. I explained that to Gary and tried my best to not even glance at Brid. It was too hard to look at her.

When you break up with someone, and I'm not talking casual breakups here, it's hard to take the sudden absence of such an important person in your life. It reminded me of when I'd stopped going to school and the weird uneasy feeling I'd gotten afterward, like I was forgetting to do something. My life until that point had pivoted around some form of education, and all of a sudden, it was gone. Homework, classes, running around, and then—*bam*—nothing but a life of work stretching out before you. No one prepares you for that feeling or even mentions it. You just suddenly have a gap and have to decide how to fill it.

A breakup is like that gap, only much, much more painful. One day the person you talked to constantly or did stuff with is just absent. Gone. *Poof.* And even though I'm not one of those people who has to be in a relationship all the time, I was feeling at a loss.

Later, one of the many times I went over the breakup in my head, I realized I probably could convince Brid to take me back. The pack didn't love me yet, but Brannoc and Bridget had given me their blessing. Surely they would overrule the rest? But I couldn't do it. Oh, I totally wanted to, don't get me wrong, but if I did, then I'd always wonder why Brid had changed her mind. Was it because she loved me, or was it because Brannoc thought it was a good idea? No, she'd have to choose on her own, and I'd have to be patient.

I sucked at patient.

But that wasn't the only reason I was sad. I'd had to kill someone. Again. I didn't really want that to become routine. Killing people in general, not Douglas specifically. Now that I'd seen Ed take him off, I knew he was dead for good. Still, I didn't want to make murder a habit. They don't make a patch for it, like they do for smoking.

Ione drank from her canteen and stared out over the vista. The sun was out, birds were chirping—all in all, it was beautiful. Nature kept banging on my head, trying to remind me that the world was still a stunning, wonderful, mystical place, but I was having a hard time understanding the language anymore.

Ariana gave me an awkward pat on the shoulder. I think she was only used to touching people when she was assaulting them. "It'll work out," she said.

I cocked my head at her. "What will work out?"

She twisted the cap shut on her water bottle and gave a little one-shouldered shrug. "I don't know. That's just what people always say when something is bothering someone. Then the other person accepts it and says thank you." She eyed me. "That's what polite people do, anyway."

"Thank you, Ariana."

Ione smiled at me and winked when Ariana wasn't looking. A kind of she-means-well expression.

We started walking again, and I tried to not get mired down in soul-sucking depression. Ione walked with me in companionable silence. I found myself liking the quiet witch. There was something soothing about her presence.

"It will get better," she said. "Ariana might not know that, but I do."

"I hope it does," I said.

We started talking a little then, Ione asking me about my family—she was very interested in my sister and mother, and I promised to introduce her to them. She was laughing and telling me about some spell she'd tried that had backfired when we met up with Murray.

He greeted us warmly and escorted us back to the same glade we'd eaten in before. I think it was one of his favorite spots. During lunch, I told Murray that we were going to do our best to support his people. We were bringing only a few charms this time—Ione needed more time and supplies to get going—but it was a start. I was providing a lot of the money myself, but I didn't tell him that. Grants take time, even with our little local government, and I desperately needed to see some good happening.

He kept hugging me, he was so overjoyed. Let me tell you, you haven't been hugged until you've been hugged by a Bigfoot.

"You've made my people very happy," he said, setting me back down on my feet.

"Just keep up the good work," I said, taking a few deep breaths to expand my aching ribs back out to their normal place. We cut the meeting short after that. Murray was eager to get the charms back to his people, so we said our good-byes and headed out. I was thinking the day through, happy that things had gone well, when Ione tapped my shoulder and cleared her throat.

"That plant seems to know you," Ariana said. She looked pretty unfazed by the whole scene, which involved my shocked face, Ione's interested one, and a friendly but huge devil's club plant.

The plant was dipping and swaying happily in a nonexistent breeze and looking a bit like a puppy. I put my hand out, palm up, a little hesitantly. One of the bigger leaves arched down and slid softly along my palm so that none of the barbs pierced my skin. Which was a tricky maneuver to do and not entirely successful, but I pretended it was. "Nice to see you again, boy."

Ione studied the plant and me. "This happen to you a lot?"

I shook my head, still staring at the devil's club. "As far as I know, it's just this one. I sort of bled on it." I gave her a quick sketch of what had happened before.

Ione listened, thoughtful. Ariana quickly grew bored and started playing with her knives. She has a lot of them hidden in strange places all over her body.

"Have you trained with a witch at all?"

"Nope." I didn't remind her that I'd just recently started training as a necromancer. My ignorance didn't really need to be bandied about any more than necessary. "Never really occurred to me."

"Well, you should," she said. "You've got a little talent in that area, I think."

I said good-bye to the jaunty plant, earning myself a few more barbs in the process, and we headed out. "I'll make a note to do so," I told her. It would be nice to do something that didn't involve death once in a while. I might end up having only a spark of what my sister or my mother had, but I didn't think any talent should be wasted.

That night Haley joined us for a little party. When she arrived, I was standing next to the half-pipe, winded from only a few passes, my ribs hurting like all get-out. She pulled up dressed to the nines and started unloading a few grocery bags from her car, things the caterers weren't bringing. I went to help her, taking the bigger sacks so she only had to manage a smaller one. Which of course made my rib cage scream, but I ignored it.

"You look beautiful," I said.

"Thank you," she said, eyeing me carefully. "Everything okay, big bro?"

"Remember a few months ago when I was kidnapped and beaten and almost died?"

"Uh, yeah."

"After the last few weeks, I officially feel worse."

"Well, then, let's go set up for this party, and you can tell me all about it while I try and hide the cutlery from you."

"What cutlery? You still won't tell us where the steak knives are."

She snorted. "You're a vegetarian—what the hell do you need steak knives for anyway?" She adjusted the small bag in her arms. "I told you. I'll give them back when you've earned it."

I nudged her with my elbow. "I love you."

"I know."

"I take that back. You're a jerk."

"Too late, you already admitted it," she said with a wink.

James appeared and took the bag from Haley. "Children, don't make me separate you two."

Haley stuck out her tongue at him.

"C'mon," I said. "I think it's time we got our wake on."

𝕿he wake we held that night was for Douglas. I know that sounds weird. I mean, who holds a wake for an enemy, right?

I do, that's who. Okay, maybe it seems a little unorthodox, but it wasn't always so. I had to read *The Iliad* in high school, and there's this big hubbub at the end when Achilles kills Hector and then drags his body around behind his chariot. Everyone is really upset because that's just not what you did—no matter what beef you held in life, you treated the body of a fallen warrior with respect. Mistreating the corpse of Hector didn't make Achilles look powerful and mighty. It made him look like an asshole.

I didn't want to be like Achilles. I'd already taken Douglas's life; no need to prance around about it. During that short span in Douglas's basement when he'd tried to train me, I'd seen how he'd treated the dead, and it sickened me. It had also formed some ideas in my head and showed me that there were lines I didn't want to cross.

Besides, I wanted to do it for James. He deserved some closure and a chance to say good-bye. I'd given him a few weeks to pull his act together and give the rest of us a break, and then we held a ceremony for my fallen enemy, and we did it Irish-wake style.

So it was a summer-warm Friday when we found ourselves in our Sunday best seated around several rented tables. Lanterns were strung and lit, food was laid out, and flowers were everywhere. I sat at the head of the gathering, which was a motley crew of friends and creatures, with James to my right. He was still a little quiet and withdrawn, but I think he was pleased to be there.

I topped off his wineglass with whatever he'd picked out—I

was somewhat amazed by the fact that he'd let us buy actual wine for once—and raised my glass for a toast.

"Some of you have wondered why we are here tonight and why I, of all people, am throwing a wake for Douglas." There was a murmur of assent. "And I get it, it's weird. But wakes aren't really for the dead—they're for grievers, the loved ones. Family. And I look out at this table, and I understand that even though Douglas may not have been the best person in the world, he most certainly left some great people behind." I looked out at the crowd, at the gnomes already singing merrily over their cups, at the nymph adjusting the crooked flower in the Minotaur's lapel, and at James, who couldn't quite look up from his wine.

"So I'm raising my glass to the person who brought all of us together." I lifted my wineglass and the others followed suit. "To Douglas! A bad man with good friends. May we all be as lucky."

There were a lot of hear-hears and general revelry, and I think everyone finally grasped why we'd gathered. We weren't celebrating Douglas's life, not really. We were celebrating the beginning of our family.

Dinner was served, food was eaten, and a lot of wine was drunk. James and the others told a few of the less disturbing stories they'd collected featuring Douglas, and we laughed and talked until several of us couldn't stand very well.

At the end of it, when cleanup had begun and a few people were sleeping on the grass, James came up to me. He looked like he was trying to say something, but couldn't quite figure it out. Finally he gave up and picked me up in a giant bear hug instead. I think I would have been less surprised if he'd hit me over the head with a wine bottle.

"Thank you," he said, and then he was gone before I could reply.

I stood there, surprised and a little bewildered in the midst of all the drunken revelry, and wondered at how interesting my life had become.

𝕴 stayed up long after everyone else had gone to bed. The night was clear, and the stars were shining as best they could with all those city lights running interference. I sat in the grass trying to sort out my warring emotions. I felt lonely and sad, because I missed Brid something fierce, but I also felt full and happy and loved from the evening's festivities. Sometimes life offers you up that kind of dichotomy, that soul-shearing rift of two very different things happening at once. My mom refers to them as life's growing pains, a phrase Brannoc had unknowingly echoed the last time I saw him, and they aren't pleasant.

I whistled and Stanley came tromping out of the woods. I needed a little company. I patted his velvet nose, and he told me how happy he was to see me. Then he chewed on some grass, out of habit more than anything.

I felt something land on my shoulder.

How you holding up, Meat?

"Okay, I guess. I don't know. I think I'm still trying to decide how I feel about things."

Humans. What does it matter how you feel about something? Is that going to change what happened? If you decide you don't like it, will history do some song and dance and change around to make you feel better?

"I guess not."

Then why bother? You're not a hatchling anymore. You know the world isn't always sunshine and roses.

"Maybe not," I said. "But it's human nature to try and understand our part in it."

No wonder you guys never get anything done.

A week later, I got my first tattoo. I'm not much of an artist, so I didn't bother trying to sketch anything out. I was a little nervous, but committed, and grateful that the tattooist didn't blink when I told her what I wanted. I guess they hear all kinds of strange requests in their line of work.

"How big you want it?" she asked, pulling out some sketch paper. We figured out the details, and I came back later to get it done. And yes, it hurts. Tiny needles are jabbing into your skin—that's not a pleasant feeling, people.

She smiled when she was finished and sat back, satisfied with her handiwork. "I've done a lot of good-and-evil chest pieces," she said. "You know, an angel on one side, a devil on the other. Sometimes it's swallows, or some other animal, but this is the first time I've done one with pandas."

I got up and looked in the mirror. On the right side of my chest, a happy bust-style portrait of Ling Tsu the panda with a background of bamboo. On the left side, the same image, but zombified. Of course I knew it was exaggerated—Ling Tsu hadn't been rotting, his eyes red, his mouth snarling, and his ear falling off.

"I like pandas," I said, poking at the tattoo with my finger.

She slapped my hand. "Don't do that." She rattled off the aftercare, smearing ointment on my chest before wrapping me in Saran Wrap. After she was done, she cocked her head. "Usually, people want the good side over their heart, you know."

It was kind of hard to explain why I'd chosen to place it where I had. I guess because the zombie Ling Tsu wasn't a representation of evil in my mind. He was a reminder to do good, of what was right and what was wrong and how fuzzy that line might become if I let it.

I shrugged at her and put on my shirt. "I've got a thing for zombies."

She snapped off her gloves. "Who doesn't?" she said, and grinned.

Acknowledgments

I can't believe I made it to book two. Seriously. For a little while there, I had doubts. But some excellent people helped me, so I feel they should be thanked here. To my family and friends—you are amazing. The amount of support I get is unbelievable, and I can't get over how lucky I am to have you all. There would be no silly books without you. And I think it goes without saying (but I'm going to say it, just in case) that every book is dedicated to my mother, even if her name isn't listed there. She got me through college and the stress of the first book, people.

Thanks to Team Parkview and my writer friends, especially Jen Violi, Sonja Livingston, Casey Lefante, Jason Buch, Léna Roy, Danny "Bee-swallower" Goodman, Abby Murray, and Jeni Stewart. Hugs and *bebidas*, friends. To Brent McKnight (and occasionally Melissa) for showing up and helping me make time to write. Special thanks to all my gnome-namers—Matt Peters, Leeandra Nolting, Rory McMahon, Mark Babin, Bill Loehfelm, Nick Mainieri, and Jesse Manley, just to name a few. I can't remember who suggested what, so if I forgot you, just pencil your name in here: _____. To Erika and Eric at Imaginary Trends for making such amazing T-shirts for me, and for J'romy Armstrong for helping keep that particular dream alive. Of course, great love and thanks to Devon "Porkchop" Fiene, for lots of reasons, but mostly for telling me to write faster. Tiny and Erica Crane—you know why. I have the best friends on the planet.

A special shout out to *The Normal School* and her fine staff—specifically Kirsten Sanft, Matt "Manbraska" Roberts, and Steven "Mansas" Church. Keep up the good work, and thanks for being part of my street team. Bradley Bleeker and Aaron Carlton should get mentioned for great webpage shenanigans. I owe you so many waffles and chickens.

To the bestest agent in the world, Jason Anthony, who only

complains a little about my freakish typos, mistakes, and the occasional use of made-up words like *bestest*. Maria Massie for tackling fancy foreign markets for me, and of course to the rest of the Lippincott Massie McQuilkin team for your continued support. Sylvie Rabineau, Jill Gillet, Valerie Mayhew, and the RWSG agency team—thanks for all your hard work.

To everyone at Holt—thanks for making this such an amazing year. A girl couldn't ask for a better publishing experience. My editors, Reka Simonsen and Noa Wheeler, are fantastic. They send me cookies and oranges and silly e-mails and remind me to breathe, and I can't imagine two more helpful and wonderful people to work with. You two should get some sort of award for dealing with me. Lastly, from team Holt, I want to send my appreciation to Rich Deas for creating such awesome cover art for me. If I ever meet you, I will hug you, and it might be a little awkward, but you're just going to have to accept it.

Finally, I'd like to thank all the readers, bloggers, booksellers, and librarians out there—thanks for putting my books in people's hands, and thanks for all those years of putting books in mine. Awkward hugs all around.

2/13, 9/13, 11/14, 9/15, 4/17, 12/17